PANGEA ONLINE 3

Vials and Tribulations

S.L. ROWLAND

ALSO BY S.L. ROWLAND

Tales of Aedrea

Cursed Cocktails

Sword & Thistle

Pangea Online

Pangea Online: Death and Axes

Pangea Online 2: Magic and Mayhem

Pangea Online 3: Vials and Tribulations

Sentenced to Troll

Sentenced to Troll

Sentenced to Troll 2

Sentenced to Troll 3

Sentenced to Troll 4

Sentenced to Troll 5

Path to Villainy: An NPC Kobold's Tale

Collected Editions

Pangea Online: The Complete Trilogy

Sentenced to Troll Compendium: Books 1-3

For Tim K, who has waited quite a while for this one.

PREVIOUSLY IN PANGEA ONLINE

Previously in Pangea Online:

After winning the first ever Pangea Online Developer's Tournament, Esil uses his prize money to pay for treatment for Buzz's mom, Maria. With his identity as the son of deceased developer Howard Allen confirmed, Esil moves into Pangea Online Headquarters, where he is offered the opportunity of a lifetime: to test out their full-immersion gaming technology.

The new technology is controlled completely by an AI that evolves and responds as the player base grows. The experience is more real than Esil ever imagined. The NPCs he meets in The Broken Lands feel and act like real people, and he finds himself on a quest to bring magic back to the world.

Esil eventually learns that there is more to the testing than just deeper immersion in gaming. The technology is designed to rewire the brain, to open new pathways with the potential to end degenerative diseases like dementia and Alzheimer's.

As the world continues to expand and evolve in The

Broken Lands, the small town of Carolton finds itself under attack by a goblin army, and Esil is forced to defend the town from their onslaught. With his new Enchanter class, and the help of friends old and new, the goblins are defeated, but at a great cost.

One year after the events of *Magic and Mayhem*.

A flaming arrow whizzes by my ear. There's a warm pulse as my haptic suit attempts to mimic the sensation of the imbued arrow Aleesia just fired. The arrow lodges in the eye socket of the orc before me, cutting off his battle-cry mid-grunt as he falls forward and his HP drops to zero.

"Nice shot!" I tell Aleesia as I bury my axe into the skull of the nearest orc.

The broad-jawed, green-skinned barbarian's eyes stay wide, even in death, as I pull my weapon free and kick the body to the ground. Another arrow sails by me. This one explodes upon impact and bolts of lightning arc from one orc to another, stunning four of them in place.

I take a step back and equip Staff of the Water Ancients, which boosts all my magical abilities. I cast Haunted Earth, and roots rip through the ground, rooting the stunned orcs in place for even longer. Next, I use Binding Thorns. Leaves and vines sprout from the roots, entangling the orcs further. Aleesia continues to barrage the orcs that funnel down the narrow pass with arrows imbued with fire and ice. The vines cinch tighter as thorns erupt, ripping into orc flesh and dropping their HP in chunks.

Using my last bit of mana, I cast Sunbeam, and a wave of light engulfs the orcs. They scream as they struggle against the vines, trying to escape the burning light.

"Finish them off!" I yell as I work my way up the pass, switching to my mace and smashing orcs off the narrow, snow-covered pass into the depths below.

Aleesia's red eyes flare with intensity as she nocks her next arrow. Her dark, charcoal-colored fingers wrap around the bow string, and she pulls it back. Purple energy pulses through her ornately-carved ivory bow, working its way down the string and onto the arrow itself. The tip of the arrow glows purple, then black, and dark energy coils around the shaft.

She releases the arrow, and it soars toward the orcs as Sunbeam's last ray fades away. The orcs turn to run, each one with only a sliver of health remaining. The arrow morphs into pure dark energy and separates into four smaller arrows. They track down the fleeing orcs like homing missiles.

Each arrow hits, and dark tendrils wrap around the orcs, sucking the last of their HP away. Tiny orbs of darkness fly back to Aleesia, dissipating into her body and healing her for the small amount of damage she took earlier. With her dark skin and purple cloak, she stands out prominently against the snowy landscape.

She tucks a strand of black hair behind her elven ears and winks at me. "Bring us home, Esil."

The last of the orcs trudge down the pass carrying massive shields formed out of crude iron. The jagged edges function as bludgeoning weapons. Three orcs walk side by side, their shields pressed firmly together in a barricade.

I only have a few moments to make a decision. With their current formation, my mace is practically useless. I cycle through all my weapons, but none of them can pierce the shield wall. With my mana depleted, magical abilities are a no-go as well. I need to get behind them somehow.

"Aleesia, sweetheart, can you shoot a Gravity Arrow overhead." There's no shame in relying on my partner to finish the job.

"Sweetheart? Really, Esil? Are we that couple now?" She laughs, and the arrow clicks slightly as she nocks it.

There's a thrum as she releases. The air shimmers slightly around the arrow as it soars overhead. An unlucky bird gets caught in its gravitational pull and is sucked in. It squawks as the arrow's magical properties keep it pressed against the shaft at an awkward angle.

I equip Grappler, one of my most unique weapons that I bought on my first day in Steamworld. It has served me well over the years.

Item: The Grappler. Raygun. +7 strength. Ability: Grapple, fires a grappling hook and attaches to the first object it hits. 30 second cooldown. *"You'll not get away that easy, Bucko."*

It's a beautiful weapon with a rotating barrel. One barrel shoots ray beams and the other fires a grappling hook. A small tube on the top swirls with lime green smoke.

The ray gun doesn't work here in a fantasy world, but the grappling hook does. I fire the hook and it wraps around Aleesia's arrow. The arrow's properties mean that my weight doesn't pull the arrow off course. Instead, it jerks me forward. I activate the grappling ability, and the chord retracts, launching me into the air and over the three orcs.

I let go of Grappler and land with a thud in the packed snow behind the orcs. The orcs attempt to turn, but their shields are lodged together. Before they have a chance to disengage, I equip my Elvish Battle Spear. I have just enough mana to use Rapid Strike, allowing me to place three attacks in quick succession at the base of their necks. The critical strikes are enough to one-shot the three orcs.

They collapse underneath the weight of their shields, and I toss the bodies over the edge of the pass along with the shields. Nowadays, I don't keep loot unless it's particularly valuable or something I can use.

I don't spend as much time in Pangea as I used to. I've leveled up nicely over the past year, but I don't grind. I still honor my streaming contract, entertaining my fans several times a week. My partnership with VR Haptix is the only reason I was able to get out of The Boxes in the first place, so I feel I owe it to them even though I could buy my way out of the contract if I wanted.

I spend most of my time beta testing full-immersion in The Broken Lands with Buzz and Grayson, but this is where I get quality gaming time with Aleesia. Her busy schedule with school and her internship doesn't leave her a lot of free time, but we come back to the Mortican Mountains when we can, back to where it all started.

My haptic suit is top of the line. It mimics smells, textures, and the weight of holding a weapon, but it's nothing compared to full-immersion.

"Not bad, handsome." Aleesia flashes me a smile.

I kiss her on the cheek. "Couldn't have done it without you."

She laughs, and then rolls her eyes. "Oh, come on! You're Esil Allen, the kid from The Boxes who won the Developer's Tournament. I'm sure you would have figured something out." The sarcasm drips from her voice. She walks past me up the pass to where the orcs came from, and I follow.

The view from atop the pass is spectacular. Forests, rivers, and towns pepper the landscape in every direction. The town square where the main portal empties players into this world is nothing more than a tiny dot from our position.

Aleesia pulls a fur blanket from her satchel and spreads it on the snow. She takes a seat and uncorks a bottle filled with red liquid.

Substance: Fire Whiskey. Buff: +2% attack for the next hour.

She pours some in a cup and hands it to me before pouring herself one. She raises her glass. "To us."

I clink my glass against hers. "To us," I echo. I drink the fire whiskey and my haptic suit goes warm around my throat and slowly trails down to my stomach.

It's more of a symbolic gesture than anything. We don't need the two percent attack buff since we out-level most of the enemies in this part of the map, but it's a reminder of our first adventure together, when she took a chance on me and we raided a dungeon.

"Are you excited about your trip?" She puts the fire whiskey away back into her bag and moves closer.

"I am." I take her hand in mine. "But if I'm being honest, I'm also a bit nervous. This will be the first time

I've been back to The Boxes since the Developer's Tournament."

"Yeah, but it will mean so much to them. To see that someone just like them made something of themselves."

I'm supposed to give a talk to the kids at the orphanage where I grew up. I'll also be making a donation to help with their schooling. There's a lot of pressure in going back, mostly from myself. I want to tell these kids that they can do anything, to do my best to inspire them, but the truth is that I don't feel like I made it out on my own.

"It's not quite the same though. I had luck, and then I had you and Buzz and Grayson, and in the end, I had my dad. Without all of that, I wouldn't have stood a chance."

She squeezes my hand, and her fiery red eyes burn with passion. "That doesn't make it any less special. Buzz and Grayson, you met them in the mines. That Developer's Chest, you found it in the mines. Yes, your dad helped you in the end, but you had already made it out of The Boxes and were living in Civic City by the time that happened."

I shake my head, but I can't fight back the smile. "You're right. You always are."

We enjoy the view for a while longer, watching the sun set over the surrounding mountain peaks. It's easy to see why people love Pangea Online so much. There's so much more to it than just fighting and leveling.

Where else can you watch a watercolor sky this beautiful? Maybe at Pangea Headquarters, but there aren't a lot of places in the real world with a view like this.

Aleesia's eyes glaze over for a moment as she checks her notifications.

"Time to go. I have a bit of work to finish before bed tonight." She gives my hand a gentle squeeze.

We gather our items and teleport back to the town square.

I should get some rest, too. Tomorrow is a big day in The Broken Lands, and then there's my talk at the orphanage the next day. It's going to be a busy week.

CHAPTER TWO

As I approach Carolton, I can't help but appreciate how much has changed in a year. Smoke wafts over the city walls at dawn, and two guardsmen wave at me from the guard tower.

Chains crank as the drawbridge slowly descends. Several farmers wait beside me, their wagons filled with produce and meats that they'll sell at the market. The sweet aroma of freshly-picked peaches has me salivating. The guards stand sentry on the parapet above the bridge with their crossbows pointed to the side. Thorny vines run along the walls' edges, a beautiful yet threatening warning to anyone foolish enough to try and sneak in.

All across The Broken Lands, society is evolving, and Carolton is at the forefront.

Over the past year, as more and more beta testers have entered the game, magic and technology have boomed in unison, creating new demands and ushering society into the next age. Adventurers sell their loot in the market. Stories and songs of great deeds and explorations travel from town to town. No longer do the townspeople talk about the drudgery of their jobs, but of the excitement that surrounds them.

With all the new adventurers and tourism, Carolton has been heavily populated. Many lives were lost in the great goblin battle, but the influx of new players has filled the void, and the town is now more prosperous than ever.

After I used my magic to explode the front wall of Carolton, the gate needed to be rebuilt. Grayson had the idea to expand the walls during the rebuild to prepare the town for the arrival of new players. That was such a wise decision. Not only have new players moved to Carolton, but new NPCs as well. There's an energy in the air, and everyone wants in on the action.

In the aftermath of the goblin battle, a massive moat was constructed around the town's edge. A large drawbridge now keeps intruders at bay and bars access to the town after sundown. The remainder of the old wooden wall was torn down and replaced with stone, further increasing our defenses. Several covered guard towers protect our scouts on each side. Storming these walls will be no easy task.

The guards nod to me as I pass, and I return the gesture as I cross the bridge into town. I was the first at the gate this morning, having bound my location to an outpost in the nearby forest before logging out last time. Several safe houses have been constructed throughout the kingdom so that adventurers can bind themselves in safe areas to store their belongings if need be before logging out.

Today's agenda includes dealing with an outbreak of Giant Weevils that have been decimating local farms around the Cursed Forest. The annoying insects are even able to infiltrate Carter's magical plants. We'll be gearing up to care of them before the problem has a chance to spread too far. I've pinpointed the source of the infestation and plan to take a group out to deal with them later today.

The sun is just beginning to rise as I enter Carolton, but the town is already alive. Smiling faces greet me as I walk through town, a far cry from my first day here.

People come from far and wide to visit Carolton. Once only a minor trade-post on the outskirts of the kingdom, it has become one of the most prosperous cities in The Broken Lands, due in large part to Carter and the botanical gardens he has created.

Once the defenses were set back in place, Carter found himself without a lot to do, so he began growing things. Odd little plants that have no real purpose in the world other than entertainment. They are truly a sight to behold. Fruit trees that juggle their fruit, dancing palm trees, an orchestra of flowers that put on a concert every night. It's a veritable circus at times, and people can't seem to get enough.

As part of my reward for completing the quest to save Carolton, I'm now a part of the town council that makes all decisions regarding Carolton's well-being.

The inn is always full, and the taverns and restaurants boom with laughter and music every evening. Peace and prosperity have spread across the kingdom.

And of course, tourism has opened many other avenues for money-making. Gertle opened a restaurant, The Squawking Hen, and Clarence, the moneylender, decided to strike out for himself and opened a pub, The Elixir. One of his bartenders is an alchemist with the ability to make enchanted cocktails. Needless to say, business is booming for him. The request for permits to build and sell inside of

Carolton overflows as soon as we make a dent in them. Everyone wants a piece of the action.

If the excitement of running a city isn't enough, there are now nearly one hundred adventurers, with dozens of branches of magic, running across The Broken Lands. A majority of them have settled in Carolton, but several have spread out to other towns and villages with a few being so bold as to move to the king's castle.

The kingdom has been at peace since the goblin attack, though many towns fear that an invasion is imminent. Elves have been spotted more frequently along the edge of the Endless Forest, and dark tidings drip down from Thunder Mountain. Word is that one of the new mages has aligned himself with the goblins and they are gathering more tribes together for another assault on the kingdom.

I hope this isn't the case, but if it is, they'd be wise to stay away from Carolton.

I spot Carter sitting beneath a large tree that shadows over the entire town. He wears a violet tunic with brown trousers. His bushy brown hair is as erratic as always. The trident I enchanted for him leans against the tree. I allow my gaze to drift upward along the trunk, following it to the heavens. It might be the largest tree I have ever seen.

"How is Florian this morning?" I ask, gesturing at the tree.

Carter pats the trunk firmly. "He grows stronger by the day. I miss having him follow me around everywhere I go, but the fact that I was able to save him is all that matters. Now, he watches over the town. He communes with trees miles and miles from here and will be able to warn us if we are ever in danger."

I still can't believe it worked. In the goblin battle,

Florian was burnt and chopped to pieces. The once-great walking tank of a tree was nothing more than a pile of charred wooden debris once the battle was over.

Carter refused to accept that his friend was gone forever. He took the remaining pieces of Florian and buried them in the ground in the town's center. For the next week, he poured all his mana into the earth with one goal in mind: pushing life into the broken timber. The town feared he had gone mad, but on the seventh day, a sprout shot up and has been growing ever since.

Florian is a tree unlike any I have ever seen. He towers above the town. Each branch contains dozens of needle-like leaves, almost like a pine, but instead of cones, beautiful white flowers blossom from its branches. A soft glow radiates from them at night. Occasionally, a branch shakes or the trunk rumbles, a gentle reminder of the life inside.

"What's on the docket for today?" he asks, standing and offering me his hand.

"A new batch of adventurers should be popping up across the kingdom today. That's a low priority for now, though. I'll be taking a team out to try and sort out this whole weevil nonsense before it begins to affect prices at the market. They've managed to eat through several of the crops you magically buffed, and the last thing we need are prices going through the roof."

Carter nods. "Let me know if I can be of assistance. I'm planning something special for tonight's show, but I can always make time to help. Speaking of which, I best be getting on my way. My morning relaxation is at its end." He turns to the behemoth tree and places his hand against the bark. "I'll see you later, Florian."

Several branches shake in response, and pine needles fall on our shoulders.

"We should be good, but I'll keep you posted."

I'm making my way towards the council room when Neil—a red-headed, freckled, young man—approaches me in the street.

"Esil, is it true? Are there more adventurers coming today?" he asks, excitement coating his voice.

Neil wears the blue tunic and gray pants of the city watch. He must be on his way to guard duty. Before the goblin attack, Neil was as green as they come, but he has become a formidable swordsman and one of our most vigilant watchmen.

"It certainly seems so. I don't imagine it will be long before some of them show up at our gates."

"I heard you are going out into the forest today. Do you mind if I come?" Neil asks, his eyes wide.

"Aren't you on duty?" As interested as he is, it wouldn't be right to take him from his post. Discipline is key for our defenses.

"I just finished my patrol actually. I was on night duty." His eyes bore into me with fierce desire.

Neil is always looking for adventure, but the thing he's truly after is magic. There's an awe in his eyes when he watches others use it. He's spoken to Kindra about it several times over the last few weeks. Questioning how she learned her own. But the system only provides the questline for magic to those it finds worthy and so far, Neil's name hasn't come up.

The kid has spunk, though. A night shift and still wants more, who am I to stop him?

"Alright then, gear up and meet me by the market in an hour. I'm going to meet with the council and then we'll be on our way."

Neil clenches his fists and takes off running. He disappears around the corner next to the blacksmith.

I find Kindra and Jacob in the council room deep in conversation, discussing adding members to the city watchmen in order to keep the peace during large events. When I'm logged out, they are the ones who make sure everything is in order. Jacob is the town governor, but being a wise man, he established the council under the idea that more heads would give sounder advice. Currently, the council consists of Jacob, Gertle, Clarence, Terence the town blacksmith, myself, and Kindra.

Kindra, Carter, and I were all asked to join the council after the goblin battle. Carter declined, choosing to focus his time on the botanical garden and his plant-based defenses.

"Is it true?" asks Jacob, running his fingers through his gray beard. "Are we getting more adventurers today?"

"It is. This should be the last group that comes through for a while. Any word on Priscilla?"

Kindra slides her chair back from the table. "There have been sightings of a woman in white all over the kingdom. She's never any place for too long, but it's usually around some new adventurer appearing or a magical occurrence. I don't know what she's playing at, but I feel like she's definitely involved in this somehow."

Over a year of game-time has passed since she up and left Carolton without so much as a note or a word. We still have no idea why. It all has to be connected, though. I'm still not sure what she is, but I know she is ancient and powerful. I have my suspicions that she and the AI are connected in some way.

She was the one who sent Carter and I on the initial quest to unlock our own magic. Over the course of that journey, magic returned to the world for the first time since the Age of Mages, thousands of years ago. Now, magic is everywhere.

Maybe her part has been played, and now she's content to watch from the background.

I lean forward against the table. "I'll be taking Neil and a couple of others out to try and deal with the weevils. Are you free to come, Kindra? Your abilities are always a welcome addition. You might be able to track down an adventurer or two while we are out."

Her mind magic is powerful, and she can often sense the presence of other people if they are within a certain radius, even if they are hidden.

"Are you good to handle things without me?" she asks Jacob.

He gives her a proud smile. "I think I can manage. Try to be back by sundown if you can. Carter has something special planned this evening."

Neil and Grayson wait for me in the market, along with two of the newer adventurers who have unlocked magic: Margarita and Titus. Neil wears a sword strapped to his side, and Grayson carries a wooden staff.

The tip of Grayson's staff holds a magnificent emerald. Since his body here resembles his real-life body and not the sexy, muscled pirate of Pangea, the staff fits with his aging wizard look. After moving out of The Boxes and into Pangea Headquarters, Grayson has let his beard go and it almost resembles the version I remember from the mines.

Margarita's olive skin and flaming red hair drapes down her back, accentuating her light blue dress that flows in the breeze. She has the magical ability to control the wind so wherever she walks, a gentle breeze always caresses her.

Titus, on the other hand, is perhaps the palest person I have ever seen. His eyes seem too large for his face. He has short black hair, and two teeth that jut down over his lips like a rat. There is nothing rat-like about his personality, though. In contrast, he is one of the kindest people I have ever met. Meek and unassuming, he has the ability to flash in and out of our plane of existence.

I'm actually pretty excited to go out with Grayson today. He's had magic for a while now but has yet to tell me what his affinity is. Maybe I'll finally see him put it to use.

Kindra shows up a few minutes later, her hair pulled into a messy bun. Her yellow tunic contrasts with her surly disposition.

"Alright, let's get his show on the road," she says, quickly bypassing us, not waiting for the go-ahead.

She's been like that for as long as I've known her. Defiant, stubborn, and hard to crack. On the few times I've broken down her walls, I've discovered there is actually a very caring and kind person underneath.

Before we start, I take a moment to draw runes on each of our boots with a quill, enchanting them and tripling our walking speed. A recent update by the AI changed how my own magic worked. Instead of channeling mana into my items, I carve runes and then push the mana into them. It's more limiting since I now have a list of runes to remember, but I can string multiple runes together for new effects.

My mana pool has grown a great deal over the past year as well, allowing me to have multiple enchantments running at the same time. While I push mana into enchantments I give to others, I'm able to power up some of my own enchantments by pushing more mana into them. It's been a while since I have run out of mana, but as my pool has grown, so has the power behind some of my attacking enchantments. If a big battle were to occur, I could still conceivably run out.

Tracking down new adventurers has been no easy task. For the most part, we let them find their own way. Most villagers around the kingdom will usually point them in the direction of Carolton, since we have the largest population of adventurers. Still, some choose to strike a path of their own. I double-check the pack I brought and make sure it's filled with both food and clothing in case we come upon any.

When new players spawn, they are as naked as the day they're born. The experience is a bit overwhelming, showing up in a new world, every sense on high alert and nothing but your own two hands to protect you. Or at least it was for me. I still remember the frying pan that clocked me in the shoulder for trespassing on someone's farm my first day in the game. When you expect your vision to flash red and instead feel shooting pain, it's a quick wake-up call.

Still, we do our best to find the new players when we can. Some of them find their own way or take us up on the offer of clothes and a warm meal before they go off on their own. Others have spawned so far away I've never met them.

Kindra stops long enough for us to catch up. "Alright, where the hell are these damn weevils? And what are we supposed to do when we find them?"

"Oh, my!" yells Neil. "Is that it?" He points to a nearby cornfield, where two large antennae and a snout protrude above the top of the corn stalks. A loud crunching can be heard from the depths.

"I don't know what else it would be," I say.

We follow the path through the cornstalks and find a

weevil grazing. Two long pincers chop the corn at the base while the long, tuberous snout shovels the stalks into its mouth.

Giant Weevil. *With a tough outer shell, weevils have a greater resistance to magical attacks than most beasts. Their hides often fetch high prices for their usage in armor.*

The creature moves slowly through the field, unaware or uncaring of our presence. It looks like a giant beetle with a luminescent green outer shell and black undershell. It continues to munch, leaving a steaming trail of dung in its wake. At the rate it's moving, a single weevil could destroy an entire field over the course of a few days.

"It's immune to magic, huh?" asks Margarita, hands on her hips. "How do you suppose we tackle this?"

"Like this!" yells Neil as he pulls his sword and takes off towards the weevil.

His sword clanks against the hide of the creature, dealing no damage. Neil attacks again, faring no better. The blade bounces off the tough exterior like it's made of plastic.

The weevil turns its head to look at Neil and knocks him to the ground with a thrash of its hindquarters. Without so much as a second thought, the weevil returns to its meal.

"With a tough shell like that, weapons aren't going to work either." Titus scratches his chin in thought. "Maybe we could try to guide them somewhere else?"

"That won't work." Grayson's gruff voice is commanding. "If there was only one, maybe, but from what we've heard, there are probably dozens of these creatures. I think we'd be best to find a way to dispose of them. They're pests, nothing more."

Titus frowns at Grayson but says nothing.

"Besides," says Margarita, "we can take their hides and make some pretty good armor. Even sell what we don't need."

I can't really argue with her logic, but that still leaves the question of how in the hell are we going to kill it.

"Kindra, can you get inside of its mind?" I ask.

She presses her fingers to her temples, channeling her magic. She winces, and then shakes her head. "It's not working. It actually hurts when I try to get inside of its mind."

Normally, the offending party would go slack, or a vacant look might run across its face. However, the weevil remains unaffected and continues chewing stalk after stalk. Another pile of steaming hot dung falls to the ground.

Substance. *Giant Weevil Dung. This substance has been used in many potions for increased magical defenses.*

Not a bad ingredient if you can get past the smell. I'm sure it would fetch a nice price at the market.

I pull my sword from its scabbard and focus my mana into the bottom-most rune along the blade. Maybe we just need a little more power.

Exploding Touch. *Your next attack will explode for 500 damage, damaging all within a five-foot radius.*

"Everyone, stand back."

Once the others are out of the way, I slash with all my might at the giant weevil. A violent explosion erupts when the blade hits its metallic shell, and flames run up my arm, singeing my tunic and burning the hair from my arm. My health drops, and a burning pain flares along my arms.

"Oh, that was such a bad idea." I gingerly press my finger to the burn that is radiating heat.

The weevil continues as if nothing happened. I take a

bite of some of Carter's enchanted fruit and step back as my health slowly recovers.

"Maybe we just need to think outside the box." Neil ponders for a moment. "Everything has a weakness. Even dragons have a soft underbelly."

"You know..." Margarita places her thumb and index finger on her chin. "I think I have an idea. Get your weapons ready."

Neil and I both pull our swords. Kindra nocks her bow. Grayson and Titus both stand back. Grayson's staff won't do much, and Titus prefers not to carry weapons.

Margarita steps beside us and holds out her hands, palms open, toward the weevil. Air rushes around the weevil, swaying the corn like a summer storm until a miniature tornado springs up from underneath the creature, flipping it on its back.

Underneath, between the head and the body, a space of unarmored flesh is exposed. Kindra fires an arrow into the soft underbelly, and the weevil's health drops. Neil follows up with several quick stabs while the creature rocks back and forth, attempting to right itself to no avail. The long, spindly legs reach out at the sky, but there is nothing for it to grab onto. A final strike of Exploding Touch drains the life from the creature, and we collect the loot.

Item. *Giant Weevil Shell X4. Can be used to create magical armor.*

The weevil's shell, along with the armor, makes this a pretty good trip already and no sooner have we gathered the loot than another weevil appears in the distance.

It takes a while to track them down without Kindra's psychic abilities to help locate the weevils, but over the next few hours, we eliminate twelve giant weevils until we are loaded down with so many weevil shells that we could outfit most of the city watch if we wanted.

Grayson and Titus mostly look on as Margarita flips the weevils, and Neil, Kindra, and I kill them. Grayson still doesn't show me his magic, so I'm guessing it may be something non-battle related.

Stacking the new set of weevil shells beside the rest, I'm pretty proud of the day's work.

"I think that's a good starting point for today. A few more days like this and the weevil population should be in check. What do you say we get back in time for Carter's big show?"

CHAPTER THREE

Florian's white flowers cast a glow against the night sky as I step out of the council room. The council has just finished discussing the new adventurers that arrived in town. Five new beta testers from The Boxes.

Jacob steps up beside me, his head tilted back as he looks up at Florian. His grey hair has a silver sheen in the moonlight. "It's something else, isn't it? In all my years, I've never seen anything like this." He turns toward me. "To be honest, I've seen a lot of things in the past year I never thought I'd see."

I pat him on the shoulder. I know exactly what he means. Florian's presence is both comforting and awe-inspiring. "I'm sure you'll see many more before it's over. Let's go watch the show."

The candles flicker inside the inns, but they are empty. Even the streets are barren. We are the last to arrive at the botanical garden located in the center of the town, where hundreds of people sit or stand around its edges. Carter's shows are one of the main attractions of Carolton.

The garden is shaped like a massive circle, with stone pathways running throughout the many species of plants. There's a stone stage in the middle. For the moment, all the plants are still. They look almost wilted as they collapse in on themselves, showcasing nothing of their magical power. It's all part of the show, though. One big spectacle. During the day, the plants are vibrant and alive with movement.

A murmur snakes through the crowd as people chat among themselves. Jacob and I join the other council members on the outskirts of the garden. Buzz waves at me from the other side. I return the gesture, and Grayson nods in my direction. I'll meet up with them after the show.

"Any idea what Carter has planned?" I ask Kindra.

She shrugs. "No idea. He's been very secretive about this one."

The crowd goes quiet as Carter takes the stage.

"Welcome!" He removes his straw hat and tips it to the crowd. His bushy brown hair dangles across his eyes. "I'm glad to have your company tonight. The plants are happy too. Isn't that right, Florian?"

The massive tree shakes, and the glowing flowers pulse slightly.

Carter leans against his trident. He has such an easy way about him, like everyone he is talking to is an old friend. "For those of you who have witnessed our performance before, this one is going to be a little different. Sit back and enjoy the show."

He lifts his trident in the air and a green aura surrounds the weapon. He slams the butt of the trident against the stage, and tendrils of green energy shoot out into the garden, dissipating into the plants. There's a rustle as all the plants suddenly move. Leaves and branches unfurl, and the show begins.

Bushes erupt with purple and pink flowers and a fragrant aroma fills the air. The flowers glow with magical energy, giving their movement an ethereal quality. The short fruit trees near the stage juggle lemons and limes. Every so often, one will toss a fruit out into the crowd to a round of applause.

This is cool and all, but nothing we haven't seen dozens of times before. I wonder what Carter has in store.

He kneels on the stage and presses a hand to the ground. His hand glows green and several dozen stems erupt from the earth in a circle surrounding the stage. The stems continue to grow until they're about four feet high, then leaves peel off from the stems and flowers bloom. Long yellow flowers shaped like horns.

Carter whistles and the fruit trees quit juggling. A moment of silence passes before one of the new plants shudders. A long bellowing note erupts from the horn-shaped flower. It sounds like a trumpet as the note pierces through the night. A second flower joins in, then another, until they are playing a jazz symphony. The flowers sway back and forth in time with the music.

I can't help but smile at how Carter has chosen to use his power. After the violent battle with the goblins, where he was forced to create plants capable of going to war, he has focused on entertainment and happiness. He finds joy in bringing happiness to others.

The Broken Lands is so much more than a game. The NPCs here are as real as anyone I've met in the real world, each one with their own hopes and dreams. If Carter wants a simple life without battle, he has every right to it.

The other plants join in, and the juggling resumes. The

flower bushes sway back and forth as if dancing to the rhythm of the music. Their flowers open and close. The fruit that the trees juggle suddenly pulses with light, turning the performance into a glow-filled rave like I've watched in some of the cyberpunk worlds in Pangea. Yellow and green citruses streak through the air in a blur.

For the next half-hour, we're entertained with music and light. The crowd oohs and ahhs as the lemon and lime trees interact with one another, juggling long distances but never losing a piece of fruit unless it's being tossed to the crowd.

Eventually, the music fades to a dull hum, and Carter takes the center stage again. "I hope you enjoyed the show tonight. I will leave you with this."

The trumpet flowers blow deep notes that resonate in my chest. Then, the flowers from the other plants detach and float into the air. One explodes above our heads like a firework, and streaks of pink light ignite the sky. Another explodes in purple light, another yellow, another blue. Each flower crackles as it explodes.

The townspeople watch with wonder, the light of the fireworks reflecting in their eyes. When the last one explodes in a burst of brilliant red, the music fades and we all stand in silence.

Jacob claps his hands together and the crowd roars in applause. I've gotta hand it to Carter, this was quite the show.

Carter takes a bow, and then disappears off the stage deeper into the garden.

Jacob beams, still clapping. "If the garden wasn't a tourist attraction already, wait until word of this gets out." He turns to the other council members. "We may even need a new inn to accommodate."

If Carolton continues to grow, it might be smarter to start building taller buildings. We can't exactly keep expanding outward with the new moat.

I excuse myself and make my way over to Buzz and Grayson. Buzz shakes his head, a massive grin on his face. "These just keep getting better and better."

I embrace Buzz and Grayson, clasping my hand around their forearms in turn. "I know, right? It's crazy how Carter thinks this stuff up. Especially since he's spent his entire life living on a farm. How are things with the new recruits?"

Buzz shrugs. "Not too bad, they have lots of promise. We'll have them whipped into shape in no time."

Buzz has taken to training new recruits for the city watch. The extensive knowledge of fighting he's learned in Pangea has made him a great teacher.

I squeeze Buzz's shoulder. "It was good seeing you, but I need to get out of here. I have a busy day tomorrow."

"Oh yeah!" Buzz presses his palm to his forehead. "I almost forgot it's your big day at the orphanage tomorrow. I've been so busy between training the new recruits here and setting up my tournament in Asgard that it slipped my mind." He scrunches his brow. "You're still coming to the tournament, right?"

I laugh. "Buzz's First Annual Chicken Cup Classic. I wouldn't miss it for the world."

His face returns to his normal cheery disposition. "Good, because I saved you a spot in the opening rounds."

I nod. Just one more thing to add to my plate, but if it makes Buzz happy, there's no way I could turn it down. "I'll be there."

CHAPTER FOUR

The buzzing of my alarm wakes me up. I wipe the sleep from my eyes as the dull drone continues to echo from the speakers hidden in the walls and ceiling of my apartment.

"Alarm, off," I tell my robot overlord as I sit up in bed.

"Good morning, Esil," a comforting female voice greets me. "You have one appointment today scheduled for two hours from now. A taxi pod will be arriving to pick you up at ten AM."

The apartments at Pangea Headquarters have the most advanced AI integrated with each living quarters. Mine handles my scheduling and appointments and can order a pod for me. I can even order a delivery drone from the cafeteria without having to move a muscle, though I try not to do that. Now that I'm no longer having to power up my Box, I have to stay active somehow.

After eating breakfast and taking a shower, I go for a walk around the headquarters' campus to clear my head. I don't know why, but I'm incredibly nervous about speaking at the orphanage. Maybe it's because these kids are just like I once was. Several of them were probably living at the orphanage at the same time as me, not that I made friends with them.

I know it's important for them to have hopes and dreams, but my story is one in a million, and I don't want to promise them something they will never have. More than anything, I don't want to give them false hope.

I stroll through one of the pathways without a destination in mind. The mirrored surfaces of the main building reflect the bright blue skies, but I turn away and walk deeper into the park.

Birds chirp and squirrels race from tree to tree. As I let my thoughts wander, I follow the path until it leads to the Zen garden. A wooden bench overlooks a small pond filled with koi fish. The orange-and-black fish zoom through the water beneath a gurgling fountain.

I take a seat and listen to the splash of the water, trying to let the calmness of nature wash over me. Before I know it, my watch vibrates and the screen tells me my taxi pod is here.

I find it waiting for me out front of the headquarters' entrance. Aleesia stands outside of the automatic doors to the building, her hands on her hips.

"Hurry up or you're going to be late." She smiles at me.

I give her a hug and the smell of her lavender shampoo enraptures me. "What are you doing here?"

"I wanted to wish you luck. I know this is important for you. You're going to make those kids' day." She kisses me on the cheek. "I have to get back to the lab. Knock their socks off, Esil. I'll see you later."

I watch her go back inside before taking a deep breath and approaching the pod. The door unhinges with a suction of air and slides up, allowing me to enter.

I climb inside the immaculate interior with white leather seats. A hologram with the destination and route floats above my head. Now that I think about it, I should have requested an older pod. I'm going to stick out like a sore thumb traveling through The Boxes in this thing.

"Welcome, Esil. Please equip your safety belt and we will be off shortly. Your route and destination are displayed on the hologram in front of you. The display can be changed to provide entertainment at your request." The strangely human, yet somehow still robotic voice tells me of the newest entertainment options, but I decline.

I want silence for the ride to gather my thoughts. The door closes and I strap on my seatbelt. For a moment, my stomach churns as the pod rises high into the sky. I glance out the window. The people on the ground are so small that they look like toy figures as they walk around.

"We have reached sufficient altitude. You are free to remove your safety belt," the digitized voice informs me.

I elect to keep it on. After what happened to my parents, I don't know if I will ever fully trust one of the pods, no matter how advanced they may be. Today's pods travel higher above the ground than the one that killed my parents, but that doesn't make me feel any safer. It just means I have further to fall if something malfunctions. My entire life is the result of one malfunction, and I have too many people counting on me to risk my safety.

A panel in the wall opens and a package wrapped in cellophane emerges.

"Due to the location of your destination, you will need to wear a hazmat suit upon exiting the vehicle. Privacy glass can be toggled on and off at your discretion."

I take the package and unwrap the plastic to find a gray suit and facemask. I haven't had to wear one of these since moving to headquarters but anytime someone steps out of their home in The Boxes, these are a requirement. The radiation is so toxic that those living on the streets suffer from a slew of deformities. Being homeless in The Boxes is a death sentence. Even though the pod will be docking directly with the orphanage, the precautions are still a requirement to move into the sanitation chamber.

We pass over my old neighborhood in Civic City. It isn't as bad as The Boxes. The residents there can wear normal clothing, but a filtering facemask and long sleeves are still required to avoid sickness while walking the streets.

Most of the kids I'm about to meet have probably never even left the orphanage since they moved in. Everything from food to clothing is delivered via drone. They go to school inside of Pangea and have access to a handful of beginner worlds thanks to Benjamin. But most of Pangea is still off limits to them.

They have it better than I did, though. Before I started beta testing, those in The Boxes only had access to the educational worlds and the internet. Or the mines if they were old enough.

I put the hazmat suit on over my clothes and strap myself back in. Thirty minutes later, the pod descends toward The Boxes. My chest grows tight as the wasteland of shipping containers comes into view.

Row after row of boxes, a sea of gray structures and blinking lights as drones navigate the toxic atmosphere. Even at this hour, the skies are dark and gray. After all these years, how are people still living here when there is so much empty space around Pangea Headquarters?

It's not fair for anyone to be born into this.

As the pod descends, I equip my mask and press the

button on the side. It suctions against my face and begins filtering my every breath. The pod docks with the entrance to the orphanage and the door opens with a hiss of air.

I step into the entryway and steam fills the room, sanitizing me before I can enter. When the steam fades, the door into the orphanage opens.

The orphanage is what I would call a mega box. Four or five boxes converted into one building capable of housing a multitude of parentless children.

Mr. Green waits for me with a smile. He has run the orphanage for years. His head is balding down the center, and two white clouds of hair surround both sides. I remember him as a stern man, but maybe that's just because I was a child. The man before me doesn't seem very threatening or harsh. He was always a stickler for the rules, and swift with justice to those who would break them.

"Welcome back, Esil. We're so excited to have you. If you want to follow me this way, the kids are waiting."

As he leads me through the orphanage, it's just as run down as ever. Some of the monitors have cracks in them, and cobwebs coat many of the corners. I remember the spiders here vividly. The way their glowing red eyes would stare out at me from the darkness as I lay in bed. They too sought protection from the radiation outside.

Nearly two dozen kids sit cross-legged on the floor of the entertainment room. They range in age from six or seven all the way to near adults. I recognize about half of them from my time here, though I don't recall many of their names. Back then, I was a loner. I kept to myself and found solace watching streams on the internet during my down time. A small redheaded girl holds an action figure with a missing arm. I think her name was Katy. A pair of teenagers in the back look as if their days at the orphanage are almost over. Then it'll be off to the mines for them.

Half of the kids wear their headsets, the optics covering their eyes as they play or learn in one of Pangea's game worlds. No haptic suits for any of them, though. The orphanage can't afford anything that nice.

Pangea provides the headsets. They promised no student would ever be denied access to knowledge, but that is the extent of their generosity. Until they turn eighteen and receive their very own Box and haptic suit so that they can live and die in the mines.

"Alright, kids." Mr. Green gathers their attention, and the children remove their headsets. "We have a very special guest today. He used to live and play in this very room. He won the first ever Developer's Tournament. Now he's working on some top-secret project at Pangea Headquarters. Here's the man of the hour, Esil Allen."

The kids look at me with astonishment. Several grin, a few have their mouths hanging open. I'm not sure if it's because of who I am or because they don't get visitors. Either way, they sit in silence.

I don't blame them. I would have done the same thing when I lived here.

"That's no way to treat our special guest. Show him a warm welcome." Mr. Green claps, and the children join in.

Now, I feel more awkward than ever. What are they even clapping for?

"Uh, thanks for having me. Like Mr. Green said, I grew up in these very rooms. I know what it's like to grow up with noth—" I catch myself before I finish. The last thing these kids need is a reminder of how little they have. "Are you all enjoying the new worlds you have access to?"

Several nods, but no one answers. I get it. Even though I used to live here, I'm just a stranger to them now. More of an urban legend than a real person.

"Did any of you watch last year's Developer's Tournament?"

They sit up straight at the mention of the tournament and I get more enthusiastic nods this time. One kid even speaks up. "I did."

I focus on the kid who spoke up. He's probably ten or eleven. "What did you think about it?"

His eyes light up with excitement. "It was so awesome. The zombies, and all the contestants, and the race, and the maze. And that crazy death knight! It was so cool!"

I grin at his enthusiasm. "Yeah, it was pretty awesome. What about the rest of you? Did you have any favorite parts?"

I go around the room, calling on children as they tell me all the things they loved about the tournament. Everyone has their turn to speak, everyone except for one of the older kids in the back. He sits with his arms crossed and a scowl on his face. Shaggy black hair nearly covers his eyes.

I nod to him. "What's your name?"

"Dean," he mumbles.

"Well, Dean, did you watch the tournament?" I ask.

"Yeah."

"And?"

"And what?" He leans back against the wall. This kid definitely has a chip on his shoulder.

"What did you think?"

He changes the subject. "I know why you're here."

That's funny, because I don't even know why I'm really here. "And why's that?"

He uncrosses his arms and leans forward. "You're here to tell us that the world isn't so bad. That if you can make it, then we all can. You're trying to give us hope that our lives won't be as monotonous and as dull as every other person who lives in The Boxes. You'll feel good about your good deed and then go back to your fancy life at Pangea Headquarters. And in a year, I'll be working at the mines."

The room sits in a shocked silence as their eyes dart between me and Dean.

Mr. Green finally breaks the silence. "Dean, that is enough. Go to your room."

Dean starts to stand, but I turn to Mr. Green. "No, it's okay. Let him stay."

Mr. Green gives me a questioning look, but he nods. "Okay."

I lock eyes with Dean. Fury and passion burns within him. More passion than I ever had living here.

"You're not completely wrong, Dean. But you're also not completely right either. I don't know why I came, other than the fact that Mr. Green asked me to. I spent the past week stressing over what I would say to you all. I have a lot of bad memories living in this place. I'm sure you all do. It's hard growing up without a family."

Dean sits back down. I start to pace, trying to find the words, and all eyes follow my every movement.

"I used to believe that it was luck that got me out of The Boxes. Luck that I found the Developer's Chest. Luck that I made it through each stage of the tournament. Luck that I finally found out who my parents were and the gift from my father that came from that knowledge." I stop pacing and stand before them, pausing for a moment before continuing. "Yeah, I was lucky. But it took a lot more than luck. It took grit and drive and desire to turn that luck into action. It took friendship, too. More than anything, it was my choices that got me to where I am. I doubt I could have won the tournament if I hadn't been from The Boxes."

Something Aleesia said long ago flashes across my mind. She said I can't help everyone, so I should focus on the ones that I can.

"So no, I didn't come here to give you hope. I came here to help you. To give you choices so that you can make your own future." I had no idea where I was going with this speech before I got here, but an idea finally comes to me. Now that I've acquired my family's stocks in Pangea, I have more money than I know what to do with. "I'll be buying you all haptic suits, so that you can fully experience what Pangea is really like. For those of you fifteen and over, you'll be given a Premium Worldpass. This is contingent on keeping your grades up each semester. Anything less than a B and you'll be stuck to the free worlds until the next semester. I can't promise you a great life, but I can give you the tools so that if you want to find a way out of The Boxes, the only thing stopping you is you."

Some of the younger kids whisper to one another. I'm sure they are wondering if this is some sort of trick.

"I'll also be hiring someone to come and clean this place. You'll finally be able to sleep at night without spiders keeping you company."

There are several hoots and clapping at that.

"That is very generous of you, Esil. You have no idea the difference this will make in their lives." Mr. Green turns to the kids. "What do you say we all say thank you to Esil."

"Thank you, Esil," they all say in unison.

The room seems more at ease now, so I spend the next

half hour answering questions about the tournament and my life outside of The Boxes.

"Alright, I've got time for one more question. What's it going to be?"

Several hands shoot up. For the first time since I started answering questions, Dean has his hand up.

"Dean."

He brushes the shaggy hair away from his eyes before speaking. There's less contempt in his voice this time. "Are you going to be entering the Pro-Am Tournament next month?"

I shake my head. "I'm not sure what it is, but I can safely say my tournament days are behind me. I'll place the order for your new suits and have the Worldpasses ready as soon as I—"

Dean cuts me off. "It's a new tournament Pangea is putting together, where a winner from a previous tournament has the opportunity to coach someone who has never competed. I was wondering if you had found someone to mentor yet."

"Like I said, my days of competing are over."

Dean nods, but I can see the disappointment on his face.

I have zero desire to be in the public eye again. Besides, what I do in the Broken Lands is more important. "Thanks for having me."

CHAPTER FIVE

The first thing I do upon arriving home is order the new haptic suits and Worldpasses for the orphanage. I pay extra for expedited shipping so that they will be delivered by drone before the day is over.

I don't know why I do it, but I check my messages and search for the Pro-Am Tournament Dean was talking about. Once I find the announcement, I notice it's been nearly a month since the contest was announced.

Greetings, Esil! As a winner of Pangea Online Developer's Tournament, you have been invited to become a mentor in our newest tournament designed to pair the great adventurers of the past with the promising talent of the future. In Pangea Online's Pro-Am Tournament, each contestant will be paired with a champion from a previous tournament. The winner will receive a full scholarship to the online college of their choosing, as well as the opportunity to intern at Pangea Online Headquarters. For previous champions, the winner will have a sizable donation made

*to their preferred charity in their honor. Please respond if you are
interested in being a mentor.*

*Thank you for everything you have brought to Pangea Online,
and as always, never stop leveling!*

-Pangea Online Developers

Interesting. It's for a good cause, and I already know
where I'd donate the money, but even if I wanted to, I'm
not sure I could fit in a full-time training regimen on top
of my responsibilities with testing the Broken Lands.
Truth be told, I have no desire to be a mentor. I still
remember the nasty messages and spotlight of attention
from the last tournament. I wouldn't wish that on anyone,
least of all myself—again.

I close out the message and head toward the headquarters. Maybe I can help Buzz and Grayson train the new
recruits in Carolton.

The door to Benjamin's office is open, so I step inside.
He stares at a tablet, deep in thought, and doesn't notice
me as I enter. The man radiates success with his immacu-
lately-tailored black suit and neatly-parted blond hair.
There's not a strand out of place. He shakes his head and
sighs before setting the tablet on his desk.

Something is up. I clear my throat and his eyes go wide
when he notices me standing in the door frame.

"Everything okay?" I ask.

His surprise turns into a frown. "Shut the door and
have a seat. There's something I want to tell you."

For some reason, my heart starts racing. Whatever he's
about to tell me, it can't be good.

I take a seat. "What's going on?"

Benjamin runs his hand through his hair, setting it askew. "They're shutting it down."

My heart jumps into my throat and for a moment, I can't speak. "Shutting what down?" I ask the question even though I already know the answer.

"Testing. The board thinks I'm too close because of my mom. They think I'm distracted and want me to focus on business." He leans back against the tall leather back of the chair. "It's a bunch of crock."

I look down and notice my hands are shaking. How could they do this? And what happens to the beta testers? All those people from The Boxes that I promised a job and a new life. What happens to Buzz and Grayson?

I take a deep breath and try to find my words. "So what does that mean?"

He intertwines his hands together and leans forward. "They're off-shooting the research to another lab. A less invasive form of full-immersion is going to be integrated into Pangea with The Broken Lands being the first world to offer this new technology. It offers the same experience as full immersion, but without the neurological effects on the brain. No time-dilation either. We'll slowly be pushing it across all of Pangea, but there is a lot of work on the back end."

"What does that mean for the beta testers?" It would be cruel to take this away from them.

Benjamin smiles briefly. "Don't worry, Esil. They'll be taken care of. I've already signed off on keeping them on to test the new tech. The research phase will be moving forward with patients who have suffered from degenerative diseases." He lets his hands rest on the desk. "I wish I could be a part of it, but I know my talents are better suited here. At least I can say I got the program up and running."

"What about the NPCs in the game? What happens to them?" I'm ashamed I didn't think of them to start with. Kindra and Carter have become real friends to me. They're more real than any NPC I have ever met in Pangea."

Benjamin chuckles. "They'll be fine. The programming for the NPCs is separate from the AI that is being offloaded. We'll spawn new characters for the medical testing."

That's a relief. It's crazy to think that their entire existence could vanish with a simple command.

"What now?" This is a lot to take in.

"For now, you all get a mini vacation while we switch over the AI and prepare the new full-immersion lab. We sent out an email to everyone. It'll take a few days to dismantle all of the equipment. You've put in a lot of work, so enjoy the rest while you can." He gives me a half-hearted smile. "I've got a lot of calls to make. Shut the door on your way out, please."

I really should be better about checking my emails. I missed the tournament announcement and this. Who knows what else I've missed.

I stand and head to the door, turning around before leaving. "You should be proud of getting this project off the ground. Even if you're not directly involved anymore, this will help a lot of people because of you."

I close the door and head toward the lab, not sure if Aleesia will be there or not. After scanning my retina to enter the hallway to the lab, I stop in front of a window overlooking the laboratory. Technicians scurry around the floor below disassembling the massive units that have been used for full-immersion for the past year.

The tanks have been drained of the blue gel filled with nanoreceptors. Drills zip as each screw is tediously removed and the glass casing placed on a dolly. There are close to a hundred units they'll have to take apart, so this process will definitely take a while.

I won't be going back to the Broken Lands anytime soon.

I shift my gaze over to the viewing deck and catch Aleesia just as she is leaving. The automatic door shuts behind her and she steps into the hallway.

"This is crazy, right?" I ask.

"Yeah, you would think we would have gotten more warning. It looks like I'll be working from home this week." She gestures to the laptop she's holding.

"Why? What is there to do if no one is logging in? Benjamin said we were all getting a vacation."

She laughs. "Maybe for you guys. But the programs are still running. The world of the Broken Lands still turns even if you aren't there to watch it. Somehow less work for you means more work for me, so I don't think I'll be making it into Pangea tonight."

"Hmm, maybe I'll see what Buzz and Grayson are up to."

Aleesia smiles. "There you go. Make the most of your free time. I really do have to get going though. Do you want to walk me out?"

I walk with Aleesia to the pod waiting to take her to her father's mansion located on a beautiful estate. I kiss her good-bye and head back to my apartment, messaging Buzz while I walk.

. . .

Yo Buzz,

It's been a while since we explored Pangea. What do you say we hit up some of the old haunts tonight? Maybe a game of steamball?

-Esil

By the time I reach my apartment, he's already responded.

Esil!

I wish I could. With my tournament coming up, I've got a lot of last-minute details to get ready. It's kind of a blessing that they are shutting down beta testing for a bit. You're welcome to stop by.

-Buzz

The scanner outside of my apartment reads my palm and I go inside. I flop down on the couch. For once, I have nothing to do. I reach out to Grayson. Maybe he's free.

Grayson,

Want to go listen to the mermaids sing tonight?

-Esil

While I wait for him to respond, I play a mindless game on my tablet where I match different colored fruits together in order to get them to explode. I make it to level twenty-five before a message from Grayson pops up.

·   ·   ·

Esil,

I'm enjoying my time out of VR for the night. Maria and I are cooking if you would like to join us.
-Grayson

I'll leave Grayson and Buzz's mom to their evening together. As I sit on the couch exploding fruit on my tablet, hours pass, and before I know it, I drift off to sleep.

When I wake up, it's dark out. I call out to the apartment AI to turn on the lights and a soft yellow glow fills the room. The clock on the wall says it's a little past midnight.

Well, there went my evening. I get up to go brush my teeth and get ready for bed when I notice I have a new message. I don't know how he got the number, but it's from Dean.

What could he possibly be messaging me about? I tap the screen on my tablet and the message expands.

Mr. Esil,

I wanted to apologize for giving you a tough time today. It's hard to believe that anyone would be looking out for us in The Boxes. Mr. Green does the best he can, but this is not exactly paradise. We never talked much when you lived here, but I remember you always rushing through your work so that you could sit alone in your room and watch streams. When we look at you, we don't see someone we can become. We see someone who got out and never came back.

Except you did come back. You've done more for us, and for those in The Boxes, than anyone else.

Mr. Green gave us our Worldpasses. The haptic suits will be here later tonight, but I couldn't wait. I put on my headset and gloves and went and explored Triassic World. I've always had a thing for dinosaurs, and it was an amazing experience. I can't wait to feel it with the haptic suit!

The real reason I'm messaging you is because I wanted to ask you a favor. I know you don't want to be involved in the tournament, but I was hoping to give it a shot. This is the only way someone like me would ever have the chance to intern at a place like Pangea Online. If you know any champions who are looking for someone to mentor, I would appreciate it if you told them about me. I don't have a lot of gaming experience, but I promise to work hard if given the chance.

Thanks for everything.

-Dean

I read the message over several times. He must have gone through a lot of effort to get that to me. I don't blame him for reaching out. This would be a big opportunity for anyone, but for someone from The Boxes, it could be life-changing.

Tomorrow, I'll reach out to Aleesia and see if she knows any former champs looking to take on an apprentice.

I hop in the shower and let the hot water wash over me. Steam quickly fills up the bathroom, making the glass and mirrors opaque. I try to clear my mind, but I keep coming back to Dean's message. There's something about him that reminds me of myself at that age. Maybe it's the dream of something greater. Or grasping at straws. Whatever it is, it has struck a chord.

After I get dressed, I send Dean a message.

Dean,

Meet me at my home portal tomorrow after your classes. I'm attaching the pass code.

-Esil

CHAPTER SIX

Fenrir rests his massive head in my lap as I wait for Dean to show up. I've already messaged Aleesia about finding him a mentor, but I don't know how willing someone will be to train a kid from The Boxes. There's still a certain stigma associated with living there. I remember the first time we took Buzz's mom to the hospital. Even the nurses treated us like we were contagious.

I scratch Fenrir behind the ears and he wags his giant tail, knocking the arcade machine I bought a few inches across the floor. It's a mindless game, one from the 1980's where you guide a hungry yellow circle as it tries to eat fruits and clear a maze of dots before being attacked by a gang of ghosts. I've sunk countless hours into its monotony.

Over the past year, I've spent a lot of gold bringing my home portal to life. It's filled with statues of great warriors, paintings depicting some of my favorite moments in Pangea, and plenty of knick-knacks to keep me entertained without ever having to step foot into a game world. I have a display with a livestream of the

Mortican Mountains town square on one wall. Sometimes I will just sit and watch the various heroes as they walk about for hours. It reminds me of all the people-watching I did when I lived in The Boxes.

A portrait of Merlin, my pet owl, hangs over the fireplace on the far wall. It's been more than a year since I lost him and sometimes, I still feel a pang in my chest when I look at it. The flames of the fire alternate colors every minute or so, cycling through every color of the rainbow.

Once upon a time, this would have been my paradise. Nowadays, I find just as much solace in my own apartment. I come here for Fenrir, to keep him company. Maybe I'm crazy for thinking he needs me around, but I've always treated Pangea as more than a game.

A loud ding announces a visitor outside of my portal. A moment later, a rift of energy opens and Dean steps through. Fenrir stands in a hurry and pounces on the poor kid. His face is stricken with panic until the wolf licks him, covering him in slobber.

"Fenrir, down." I pull the giant Asgardian wolf off Dean and offer him a hand. "Sorry about that. He doesn't get many visitors these days."

Dean wipes the slobber from his face and slings it to the floor. He wears dull gray pants, a white t-shirt, and a pair of plain white sneakers. Starter gear from the education worlds. We'll have to change that at some point.

His eyes are wide with wonder as he looks around my room. "All of this is yours?"

"It is." I'm sure this place is like a mansion to him. I take a few minutes to give him the tour. When we're done, I press a button on the wall and a portal opens. "Ready to get out of here?"

He scrunches his brow. "Where are we going?"

I grin. "Are you wearing your haptic suit?"

He nods.

"Good, let's go see some dinosaurs."

I step through the portal and focus on the destination for Triassic World. It's not a game world I'm familiar with, but if Dean likes it, I think it would be a real treat for him to experience it in his haptic suit. Who knows, if things go well then maybe one day, he can experience it in full-immersion.

Hundreds of portals surround us as we zoom toward Triassic World. The Mortican Mountains, Steamworld, The Haunted Forest, and hundreds of others are now open to Dean and the other teenagers.

Welcome to Triassic World. This is a non-magical and non-technological world. All levels and abilities have been reset while entering this world.

The portal empties us into a dense jungle. The stone structure that houses the portal is the only thing that shows we aren't actually millions of years in the past.

Giant ferns as tall as trees with drooping leaves the size of my body cast shade on where we are standing. Brightly-colored birds chirp, and dozens of lizard creatures the size of cats scurry across the jungle floor. One turns and hisses at us before darting into the underbrush.

Fenrir sniffs at the air. Next to him, Dean grimaces as he holds his hand over his stomach.

"Upset stomach?" I ask. "It happens to everyone the first time they use a portal wearing a haptic suit."

Dean stands up straight, looking around. "This is

amazing. It was cool in my old headset, but this is better than I imagined. I can smell the hot air." He reaches out and touches a dangling branch. "I can feel the weight of this against my palm."

I pat him on the shoulder. "One of the perks of a top-of-the-line suit. Just don't fall into a pile of dinosaur poop. So what is this world? Do you go on quests or what?"

He grins at me. "Not quite. You explore and you survive. You can unlock trophies for certain achievements. It's all based around the Triassic period, where dinosaurs first evolved. This is also when Pangea the supercontinent existed."

"So this is where Pangea Online got its inspiration?" We've come a long way since the age of dinosaurs.

Dean nods. "One giant world. No barriers. Survival of the fittest."

"How do you know all this?" I always knew about Pangea, that it was the basis for Pangea Online, but I never dug too deep into it.

Dean blushes. "I'm a bit of a history nerd. Dinosaurs always fascinated me."

As soon as he finishes the sentence, a giant red three flashes across my vision, then a two, then a one. I guess it's game on.

There's a rustling of movement behind us, and Dean steps behind me. I equip my elvish spear just as a skinny dinosaur with a long neck and even longer tail emerges. The dinosaur is as big as Fenrir, but not nearly as muscular. Its tan scales are speckled with brown dots, and a hawk-like face with dozens of sharp teeth stares at us as its long, whip-like tail swishes back and forth. It leans back and roars in our direction. Next to me, Fenrir growls, showing his teeth. The dinosaur stays at bay for the moment as I keep my spear extended. I focus on its stats.

Coelophysis. Length: 3 meters. Weight: 27kg. One of the first true dinosaurs of the Triassic Era, the coelophysis feeds on smaller reptiles and amphibians. Its sharp curved claws allow it to slash, making it capable of taking down larger opponents when necessary.

The bushes rattle again and two more surround us. I jab my spear in their direction, keeping a safe distance between us. They look at us with interest but don't attack.

"What's the plan, kid?" I ask.

"I don't know. This didn't happen last time."

One of the dinosaurs snaps at us, and I jab my spear again. "Do you have a weapon?"

"Nope."

Alright, it looks like this is up to me and Fenrir then. None of my abilities will work in this world, so I'll have to fight using only my skill. I try to calculate which dinosaur to attack first when a deafening roar echoes over my shoulder.

The trees shake violently and the earth trembles as the roar grows louder. The *coelophyses* turn and run, and I pull Dean behind a tree just as a massive dinosaur steps into range. Its dark green scales blend into the landscape, making it nearly invisible from a distance. Branches snap as it barrels through in pursuit of the smaller prey.

I catch its stats as it passes by.

Gojirasaurus. Length: 5.5 meters. Weight: 199kg. Gojirasaurus, also known as the Godzilla Lizard, is one of the largest meat-eating dinosaurs in the Triassic Era.

My heart pounds as the monstrous dinosaur disappears into the jungle. Dean grins at me excitedly.

"Close call. What do you say we get out of here before

they come back?" I pet Fenrir on the shoulder. His muscles are tense, and his eyes are still locked in the direction the dinosaurs went.

"Yeah, let's go. I know a pretty cool spot where we should be safe." He leads us in the opposite direction of our attackers.

"Hold up." I pull my battle-axe from my inventory and hand it to him. "We can make you a spear when we stop, but you should have this just in case."

I check the stats as I hand him the weapon.

Item: Meteoric Iron Axe. +10 strength. 10% armor penetration. *This double-edged axe was forged from the heart of a meteorite.*

He looks at the axe with wonder. "Wow. This is beautiful. You used this during the tournament, didn't you?"

"I did." That was the first weapon I ever bought in Pangea. "Keep it. It's yours now."

Dean gives the axe a few practice swings, grinning as it cuts through the air. He pauses for a moment and his eyes glaze over. "Here, I shared our destination on the map."

I focus on the map in the corner of my vision and the image expands. There's one giant landmass, with the word "Pangea" written in the center. A tiny purple dot marks where we are headed.

It's crazy to think that the world used to be like this. That the ground we walk on in the real world has shifted over time into seven different continents.

I zoom in on the dot and notice it's at a location called Triassic Falls. It must be some sort of waterfall. Most of the map is covered in jungle, except for a small area of plains. A red square on the map catches my eye. Next to it, it says "Shop."

"I see there's a shop here. What do they sell?" I ask.

Dean shrugs. "Mostly just survival gear. I don't have any gold so I never checked it out."

"Time to change that." I wink, adding my own destination marker to the shop. "We'll hit up the falls after."

I keep an eye out for stampeding carnivores as we make our way toward the shop, but all I see are small reptiles scurrying through the forest floor. The slate-colored creatures dart around like chickens from one area to the next.

We pass by a calm river, where a giant dinosaur plucks leaves from a tall tree while cooling its body in the water. It would be terrifying except for the fact that all its teeth are square. They grate against one another as it chews the leaf like a cow at pasture. The dinosaur has a thick tail and frame, and dull gray skin with black stripes that run along the crest of its spine. Its neck is long and skinny, with a tiny head.

Plateosaurus. Length: 10 meters. Weight: 4000kg. *A bipedal herbivore, the Plateosaurus usually travels in herds like modern elephants.*

Wow! This dinosaur weighs over four tons and only eats plants. It must eat all day long to get enough food.

Trees shake behind the massive creature, and I notice several more of the herd feasting further back. Fenrir watches them intently, but he doesn't seem threatened by their presence.

"Pretty cool, right? Can you believe these things actually existed?" Dean shakes his head in astonishment. "They're so huge."

"Yeah, they're pretty cool. I'm more partial to minotaurs, griffins, trolls, and things like that, but I can see why you like this place. So, where's the T-rex?" It's about the only dinosaur I actually know.

Dean laughs. "Wrong era. The T-rex came around in the Jurassic Period. That's when dinosaurs really took over the world. T-rex, triceratops, the giant brontosaurus. When most people think of dinosaurs, that's what they think of. Everything you're seeing here will go extinct long before they ever come around. And then there will be another extinction in many millions of years."

"And then in the far future, we'll nearly kill off ourselves and be forced to hide from radiation inside metal boxes." It turns out humans can be just as devastating as Mother Nature.

The shop is pretty underwhelming when we arrive. I don't know what I was expecting in a prehistoric world, but it's basically a wooden hut with items sitting on shelves. I glance over the contents, but there's not a whole lot I need.

Item. Rope. *For tying things.*

Item. Dino Treats (Carnivore). *Treats for luring meat-eating dinosaurs to your location.*

Item. Dino Treats (Herbivore). *Treats for luring plant-eating dinosaurs to your location.*

Item. Wooden Spear. *A basic weapon for protecting yourself across Pangea.*

There are more items, but nothing I'm interested in. Dean is the brains of this operation, so I defer to him.

"Do we need any of these items to help you get those trophies you're after?"

"Umm..." He frowns as he scans the items. "Definitely rope and treats. I can probably make my own spear with the axe you gave me."

"Pick out what you want and I'll pay for it." Most of this stuff is incredibly cheap compared to items in other game worlds.

Dean doesn't hesitate, picking up three strands of rope and several bags of Dino Treats. "Thanks! This will be fun, I promise."

While he gathers the goods, I can't help but wonder where the other players are. "Are we the only ones here? I haven't seen anybody else."

Dean tosses the rope over his shoulder and joins me and Fenrir outside the shop. "This isn't an MMO world. Each player gets a separate instance each time they come here."

"Interesting. Kind of like in the first stage of the Developer's Tournament. We all had our own version of the apocalyptic world where we had to rescue the girl." I much prefer worlds with other people in them.

Dean fits the rest of his items in his small satchel. "Exactly. There are no lasting effects in this world when players leave, but there are unlimited possibilities while you're here."

"What do you say we ride Fenrir to our next location so that we get there faster?"

Fenrir lays down so I can climb on his back. I extend a hand and help Dean climb on behind me. I sink my hands into Fenrir's fur and hold tight, and Dean wraps his arms around my midsection as Fenrir stands.

As we travel through the dense jungle. I catch glimpses of creatures soaring across the sky. They're like feathered pterodactyls, with long beaks and enormous wingspans, bigger than the pod that brought me to the orphanage.

Fenrir's paws dig into the dark soil as we climb a hilltop. The marker Dean placed is just on the other side of the hill. There's a roar coming from ahead of us, but it's not the roar of an animal.

We crest the hill, and a gust of wind hits me in the

face. Fenrir's fur whips in the breeze. A wide river plummets over a mighty waterfall that must be several hundred feet tall. The noise from this natural wonder is so loud that I can barely hear Dean when he speaks.

"Pretty cool, huh?" he shouts.

I nod and step closer to the river. The water is calm right up until it drops off the edge. Down below, mist sprays into the air for several dozen feet and choppy waters create a whirlpool in the clear blue water. Several dark splotches move in the river's depths.

Dean ties a rope to a nearby tree and tosses it over the cliff next to the waterfall.

"Are you afraid of heights?" He grins mischievously.

"No, why?" Though I already have an idea of what he has planned.

"Follow me." He doesn't wait for my response before running toward the river and leaping over the edge of the waterfall.

I rush behind him, reaching the edge just in time to see him plummet into the choppy waters. The kid is a bit of a daredevil. That will serve him well if he finds a mentor for the tournament.

I look at Fenrir and take a deep breath. "Wish me luck."

Stepping back, I gather speed and launch myself over the edge. My haptic suit clenches around me and releases, mimicking the effect of weightlessness as I soar toward the water below. As I fall, a notification flashes in the top corner of my vision.

Congratulations! You have unlocked the trophy "Swan Dive." Difficulty: Easy.

I plunge into the water, and a chill runs through my haptic suit. Underwater, several large fish swim away from me. Some reptile lays in wait on the bottom of the riverbed, undisturbed by our intrusion.

I kick toward the surface, and as I break above the water, Dean punches the air in celebration. He says something, but I can't hear him over the roaring water.

He waits by the dangling rope at the base of the waterfall. "Want to go again?" He takes the rope in his hand and starts scaling the cliff. "This is much quicker than walking around."

"Wait, I've got a better idea." I use my mental connection with Fenrir to urge him to grab the rope with his mouth.

Dean looks at me confused when I pick up the leftover rope behind him. He nearly falls when Fenrir jerks on the rope and we start moving upward.

"Work smarter, not harder," I yell above the water.

Slow and steady, Fenrir pulls us up the cliff. We toss the rope back down and go again. This is probably the most excitement Dean has had in a while. I watch him go several more times before he takes a seat next to me on the river's edge.

Across the river, a massive creature that looks like a cross between hog, a cow, and a turtle stands belly deep in the water.

Dean picks up a tree limb and starts whittling it into a spear with the axe I gave him.

I grab a pebble and skip it across the river. "So, how did you end up in the orphanage?"

He stops whittling for a moment and stares into the water. "My dad died a few years ago. I didn't have anywhere else to go."

"What about your mom?"

"She passed during childbirth." He sits the spear across

his lap. "I watched a lot of videos in my free time. About how things used to be before we screwed up the planet. Child mortality, cancer, disease, they were all on the decline. Nowadays, I doubt anyone knows someone who hasn't suffered. At least in The Boxes."

I reach out and pat him on the shoulder. "I'm sorry. I know it's rough."

"It's not your fault. It's funny how we lived in the same box for a couple of years, but never knew one another. I guess by the time I arrived at the orphanage, you were keeping mostly to yourself."

I shrug. "I guess I found more joy watching others play games than interacting with those around me. It was my escape."

He smiles at me. "Thanks to you, we all have that escape now."

I'm glad to know that I've been able to help them in some small way. "What now?"

"Want to try for some more trophies?" His eyes radiate excitement.

"Yeah, what do you do with the trophies once you have them?"

"Well, most people just put them on display in their home portals. But there are certain ones you can get that allow you to buy special costumes or items. And then there are collections to complete that offer actual prizes." He glances at Fenrir. "One is a special mount that you can use in the other worlds."

"Nice, what do you need to get them?" I still remember the teamwork that it took for me to get Fenrir.

Buzz, Aleesia, Grayson, Ordin, Klink, Glordin, and Tinker all helped me that day. I haven't seen any of the dwarves since the tournament ended. I don't think Aleesia has either. Since she started her internship, she doesn't stream much anymore, and most of her friendships have faded away.

Dean rubs his fingers against his chin. "There are two I would really like. One is to find a hidden egg. It's hidden in the burrows of one of the smaller dinosaurs. The trophy is awarded if you're able to dig it out. The other is to mount a *Liliensternus*."

"What's that?" Once again, my lack of knowledge is showing.

"It's only one of the biggest predators around." Dean grimaces. "Bigger than the *Gojirasaurus* we saw earlier, which is why I got so much rope."

I laugh. "Go big or go home. Lead the way."

"I think we have a better shot at finding the egg, so we'll start there first. The burrow isn't that far from here."

We climb on Fenrir, and Dean marks our next location on the map. The rushing water fades as we travel through dense jungle. Eventually, the jungle clears to an area filled with large ferns. The ground around the ferns is full of holes the size of a basketball.

A low hiss fills the air as soon as we enter the area. Small red eyes stare out at us from the depths of the tunnels.

"They're *Daemonosauri*." Dean scans the area. "They're a lot like wolves, following an alpha and working as a team to take down larger prey. We need to find a way to lure them out and distract them while we dig through the tunnels."

"What are you thinking?" I ask.

He shrugs. "Uhm, I thought we might use the dino treats to get them out, then we could take the dinosaurs out one at a time."

"Not a bad idea. That's a lot of fighting, though. And there's no guarantee they all won't rush in at once as soon as you pull out the treats. We don't need to kill them; we just need to buy us some time." I have an idea brewing, but it would benefit Dean more if he can figure it out himself.

Dean nods. "Right. Work smarter, not harder."

The dinosaurs continue to watch us as we sit atop Fenrir. Dean's brow furrows as he puts his mind to work.

"What if we made a trail of treats for them to follow?" He looks at me expectantly.

"If these are like any of the other dinosaurs, they're pretty fast, right?"

He nods. "Yeah, they'd snatch up the treats quicker than we could search. What we need is something that is constantly moving for them to chase." His eyes light up with recognition. "What if we tied the treats to Fenrir so that they could chase him?"

I pat him on the shoulder. "Now that is a plan I can get behind."

We dismount from Fenrir, and the hissing intensifies. One of the small dinosaurs pokes its head out from the burrow. A round skull covered in black feathers with a short, blunt snout and round red eyes snarls in our direction. Black feathers cover its entire body, except for patches of tan around its hands and feet. Each appendage is tipped with three sharp claws. Despite its long tail, the creature is no bigger than a small dog.

Dean uses the axe to cut off several pieces of rope to tie around Fenrir's midsection. Then he takes the bag of treats and secures it beneath the rope.

He looks at me. "Ready?"

"Ready."

"As soon as I cut the bag, Fenrir needs to run."

Dean slices the bag, spilling treats onto the ground. The jungle descends into madness as I send Fenrir bolting away. The hissing stops immediately and dozens of feet patter against the ground as the pack of tiny wolf-dinosaurs sets off in pursuit. They run like chickens of darkness, hell-bent on a mission, darting in the direction of Fenrir.

"Not bad. Let's get to digging."

Dean lifts his axe in one hand and his handcrafted spear in the other. "Uh, which one should I use?"

"I don't think either one of those will help you too much. I've got just the tool, though."

I pull up my inventory and find my oldest item hidden at the bottom.

Item: Basic Pickaxe. +2 attack. *A pickaxe is a miner's best friend.*

The wooden pickaxe is the first item I ever received in Pangea. Along with my miner's clothing and hat, this was all I had for most of my first year in the game. It still feels familiar in my hand, like I could swing it and watch a stream of data sprout from the earth.

"Whoa!" Dean's eyes are wide. "I'm surprised you still have that."

I take my first swing and the tip of the axe breaks through the top of the tunnel. "Let's talk while we work. I'm going to break the soil. Shovel it out behind me with your hands." I swing again, breaking up another chunk of earth. "Why are you surprised?"

Dean follows me, shoveling dirt through his legs like a dog at the beach. "I don't know. It seems like a pretty useless item. And one that would remind you of your time in the mines."

"Maybe that's why I've kept it. I don't hate my time in

the mines. It was boring work, yes, but I made some of my closest friends in those mines. I wouldn't be who I am without them. And so far as it being a useless item, I think it's coming in pretty handy right about now."

We continue digging, occasionally having to reroute as the burrow underneath takes a sharp turn. We have a bit of time. Fenrir can run for hours without needing to rest, especially without someone riding him.

On my next swing, I hit something hard and hear a slight crunch. "I think I found something."

Dean crawls in front of me and starts rummaging through the soil. He pulls up a shard of black shell covered in dirt and slime.

"Dang it! It's cracked." He digs in deeper until both arms are buried past the elbow and his face is nearly pressed to the ground. "Maybe…I just…ugh…just a little… there!"

He struggles against the earth, trying to free himself. His body wiggles like a snake as he heaves and fights to pull something out. After a struggle, the soil breaks around him, freeing his arms, and he falls on his back holding a dark black egg speckled with gold.

"Got it!" He cradles the egg against his chest.

I reach out a hand to help him to his feet. As our hands embrace, a loud howl sounds from behind us.

Fenrir.

I turn just in time to see him pouncing through the jungle, no signs of the rope or dino treats hanging from his side.

I jerk Dean up swiftly. "The treats must have fallen off. We need to get out of here quick!"

The patter of feet announces the arrival of the dino pack returning home. We quickly climb onto Fenrir. Dean rummages through his pack and pulls out another pack of treats. He rips the bag open and tosses it behind us.

"Run!" he shouts.

The *Daemonosauri* burst into the clearing, and their eyes are on us. They hiss loudly before noticing the treats on the ground and swarming to them.

We're already blazing through the jungle before they're done.

CHAPTER SEVEN

Fenrir's powerful legs propel us through the jungle, far away from the *Daemonosauri*. Dean clutches the egg to his chest with one hand and clings to my side for dear life with the other. Once we are safely away, I bring Fenrir to a halt.

"This is awesome!" Dean beams, admiring his new egg.

I check the clock in the top of my vision. We've already been in this world for several hours, and I don't want to keep Dean out too late. "It's getting late, but we can make a go for one more trophy if you want. You said there was a challenge for a special mount?"

He nods. "It's not special like Fenrir. It doesn't have any perks or special abilities, but it does look incredibly cool."

I stroke Fenrir behind the ear, and he leans into me. "A mount is a mount. The important thing is that it gets you from point A to point B. Lead the way."

Dean points into the distance. "They usually appear in the northern coast more than anywhere else, so that's where we should head."

A destination marker appears on my map. "Before we get going, you might want to put that egg away. Your inventory will keep it safer than you can."

Dean stuffs the egg in the small satchel around his waist. The basic bag only has eight slots for items, unlike my own which is almost limitless.

As we travel through the jungle, Dean taps me on the shoulder in quick succession, telling me to stop.

"What is it?" I grip Fenrir's fur as he slides to a halt.

"Over there" He points in the distance where a large dinosaur hunches over a massive boulder. "It's a *Liliensternus*, and it's feeding."

I squint and notice that the giant boulder is actually the corpse of an even bigger dinosaur. The *Liliensternus* rips off chunks of red flesh with its powerful jaws. The predator has bright green skin with stripes of faded blue running down its side. A brilliant red crest runs down the center of its head like a mohawk.

Liliensternus. *Length: 5.2 meters. Weight: 200kg. One of the largest predators of the Triassic Period, the Liliensternus is a fast and active hunter.*

"You want to mount one of those?" I don't want to ruin his excitement but it seems a bit dangerous for a low-level character.

"The version you unlock is a lot smaller. It's more like riding a horse. We just need to find a way to subdue it."

"I guess it's a good thing we have all this rope, because we're gonna—"

A familiar roar cuts me off as a second dinosaur emerges from the jungle. It lowers its head, and a deafening scream pours out as it challenges the *Liliensternus* for its meal.

I've seen this dinosaur before. The *Gojirasaurus*, the

Godzilla lizard, rivals the *Liliensternus* in size. If not for the crest running down the *Liliensternus's* head, it would be hard to tell them apart.

The *Liliensternus* turns from its meal and answers with a roar of its own.

"This is gonna be awesome!" Dean's eyes light up with excitement. "I've heard about these battles, but I've never seen one live."

I urge Fenrir forward so that we can get a better view.

The two dinosaurs square off, their tails whipping back and forth in agitation. The *Gojirasaurus* lunges at the *Liliensternus*, but the latter is much quicker and moves out of the way, leaving the *Gojirasaurus* snapping at air.

The *Liliensternus* uses the opening to launch an attack of its own. With a rapid strike, it sinks its teeth into the *Gojirasaurus's* neck. The *Gojirasaurus* pulls away, but not before losing a huge chunk of flesh.

The two dinosaurs descend on one another in a display of primal dominance. No battle plan, no tactics, just pure instinct. They bite and claw, painting one another with streaks of red.

"Can we get closer?" asks Dean.

I move Fenrir even closer. With the chaos unfolding before us, we are the least of their concerns. "Depending on how this all shakes out, we may have a much easier time getting you that mount."

"As long as the goji doesn't kill it."

The battle is a fairly even match so far. Though the *Liliensternus* is quicker and slightly bigger, it's not enough to give it a major advantage. Both dinosaurs are covered in blood. I wish this was an MMO so that we could see their health bars, because right now, it's impossible to tell who has the upper hand.

The *Liliensternus* lets out a roar of pain as the goji wraps its mouth around its neck. It falls to the ground, legs kicking as it tries to break free.

"We need to help it!" Dean yells as he jumps off Fenrir and sprints toward the battling dinosaurs. "If it dies, I don't get my mount."

This kid is going to get himself killed. I climb down from Fenrir and follow Dean. With this being a non-magical world, I don't have access to Fenrir's ability to fight for me, so it's best to leave him out of it.

Dean rushes in with his spear raised and stabs the *Gojirasaurus* in the leg. It roars in pain, releasing its death grip on the downed *Liliensternus*.

I equip my own spear and take position beside Dean. "Keep it at a distance or we are screwed."

The Godzilla lizard towers above us, blood and flesh dripping from its many sharp teeth. While it is focused on us, the *Liliensternus* crawls free. It moves much slower than before as it pounces on the *Gojirasaurus*, raking its claws down its opponent's side while simultaneously biting the goji on the neck.

The *Gojirasaurus* rolls over and the *Liliensternus* loses its grip. The two blood-soaked dinosaurs crawl to their feet and roar at one another.

Dean moves forward, taking charge. "We need to help kill the goji. Then we can tie up the other one."

He strafes to the left, attempting to gain positioning on the *Gojirasaurus*, but the dinosaur sees him and unleashes a warning roar in Dean's direction. It lunges for the *Liliensternus* again but misses.

Dean stabs the goji in the leg, and it snaps its head around with lightning speed, chomping his spear in half.

I rush to his aid, but I'm tackled to the ground. A

massive weight shoves my face into the earth. I roll over, and my vision is red at the edges. The *Liliensternus* has its mouth wrapped around my leg. Sharp teeth tear into my flesh. With a heave, it rips my appendage clean off. The effect is so real that my stomach goes queasy. I'm thankful now that this isn't full-immersion.

"Oh no," Dean gasps from behind me.

He rushes to my side, but just as he reaches me, the *Gojirasaurus* grabs him by the leg. It shakes its neck violently, slamming Dean's body into a tree. His body goes limp at the same time as my vision fades to black.

CHAPTER EIGHT

I respawn at the base of the portal we entered the world through. Dean grunts, rubbing his hands through his hair next to me.

"Are you okay?" I ask. That was probably his first in-game death, and it was a pretty brutal way to go.

"Yeah, are you? The way it ripped your leg off, I know I'm going to have nightmares about that one." He shakes his head. "It didn't hurt, but my haptic suit tightened around my leg hard enough for my brain to fill in the rest."

I pat him on the shoulder. "Sorry we weren't able to get you your mount."

I expect disappointment, but Dean just grins at me. "Are you kidding me? That was the most fun I've ever had. I can't wait to get home and tell the others."

"I'm glad you had a good time. This is just the beginning of your adventures in Pangea. As long as you keep your grades up," I add.

"I'll do whatever it takes to keep this up. Thanks again, Esil. You're a life-changer."

I don't know about that. I'm just trying to pay it forward where I can. "You're welcome."

I whistle for Fenrir and a few moments later, he comes prancing through the trees. That fight would have gone a lot differently had he been able to help.

Dean steps up to the portal and then turns back. "I hope we can do this again sometime."

I nod. "Before you go, I just wanted to let you know that I've reached out about finding you a sponsor for the Pro-Am Tournament. I can't make any promises, but I'm doing my best to find you a mentor."

His smile spreads even wider. "That would be awesome. Catch you later, Esil."

He steps to the portal to go back to the orphanage. A moment later, me and Fenrir are in my home portal.

Over the next few days, Dean and I explore some of the various worlds of Pangea. We battle orcs in the Mortican Mountains, ghouls in The Haunted Forest, and play a few games of steamball in Steamworld. Buzz is busy preparing for his tournament, but eventually, Grayson agrees to team up with us.

He and I wait for Dean in Wild Old West, more commonly known as WOW, a world based on the American frontier, playing cards in a saloon.

The saloon is elegant, yet rustic. Everything is either solid wood or leather. A long bar stretches along the back wall with dozens of bottles of spirits lining the shelves. Kerosene lanterns ignite the room in a rusty glow. A polished banister runs along the stairs and mezzanine to the rooms available upstairs. In one corner, a woman in a ruffled dress sings about heartache. There are various tables for poker and other games. Dartboards hang along the far wall. Men sit in the lounge area drinking or smoking. The heads of massive buffalo and caribou adorn the walls. The bulletin board underneath one lists all the open quests for the town.

Grayson and I sit around a wooden semi-circle table playing blackjack.

"No one wants to sponsor the kid?" Grayson looks up from the ace and three he has just been dealt.

He plays the role of the cowboy well, though it's not all that different from his normal pirate garb. With his long gray beard and mustache twirled at the ends, it fits well with his new outfit. He wears a white shirt with ornamental blue vines over each breast pocket. The topmost buttons hang free, revealing the bear tattoo underneath. A large belt buckle depicting a mermaid takes up the majority of his midsection, and a wide-brimmed tan cowboy hat hangs low over his eyes.

I went simple with my own clothing, donning a black bandana, black cowboy hat, and a red plaid shirt. My buckle is the same wolf buckle I purchased in the Mortician Mountains. It felt right to keep some of my old style.

I shake my head in response to his question. "Aleesia has asked everyone she has connections with. Either they already have someone, or they're not interested."

The dealer flips me a five and a four and then deals himself an eight face up and another card face down.

"Hit me." Grayson taps his fingers on the table and is dealt another three, bringing his total to seven or seventeen, depending on how he wants to play the ace. He returns his gaze to me. "It doesn't surprise me. You know how people feel about us."

He doesn't get into specifics, but I know exactly what

he means. A recommendation from someone as well-liked as Aleesia isn't enough to quell the disdain most people have for those from The Boxes.

"Hit me." I tap my fingers, and the dealer flips me a nine, bringing my total card value to eighteen. Not a bad hand to have, but it could be better. The goal is to have a higher hand than the dealer without going over twenty-one. The dealer builds their hand until they hit at least seventeen or bust. At eighteen, I'd need an ace, two, or three to improve my hand, so I'll stand next round.

The dealer nods toward Grayson.

"Hit me." He gets a king, bringing his total to seventeen and forcing his ace to be used as a one. He cocks an eyebrow at me. "You sure you don't want to sponsor the kid?"

I bring my hand over my cards in a slashing motion, telling the dealer I'll sit on my current hand. "No way. The last thing I need is the stress of another big tournament. I'm only agreeing to help out Buzz as a show of support for everything he has built. Besides, I'm excited to get back to the Broken Lands. Benjamin says they almost have the new units ready."

Grayson sits in silence as he ponders his next move. "What the hell, hit me."

The dealer flips a five, bringing Grayson's total to twenty-two and causing him to bust. He reaches across the table and adds Grayson's poker chips to his own.

Now it's just me versus the dealer. He flips his face-down card, a two, bringing his total to ten. He flips another card, a six. At sixteen, things are looking in my favor. He flips another card. A five. Blackjack. I lose.

He grabs my chips and clears the cards from the table.

Grayson stands up, tucking the rest of his chips into

his pocket. "No surprise, the house always wins. I'll take rolling dice with pirates any day."

I'm about to make a witty comment about the mermaids he loves so much when the saloon doors open and sunlight spills into the room. A dark figure stands in the doorway, their face hidden in shadow. The room goes quiet for a moment, all eyes on the interloper. The mystery person steps forward, and the doors swing back and forth on a hinge.

Light from the lanterns illuminates Dean's face, and the room returns to normal. His eyes dart around as he takes it all in. A busty waitress approaches, offering him a drink, and his mouth falls open.

I rush over to save him from his baser instincts. "Give him a minute to get settled in." I pat Dean on the back and step between him and the waitress.

He reminds me of Buzz the way he ogles at the waitress as she walks away. I usher him to the lounge area where Grayson sits with one leg crossed over his knee. His rattlesnake boots gleam in the dull light.

Grayson stands and extends a hand to Dean. "Nice to meet you, kid."

"Nice to meet you." He takes Grayson's hand in his own. "Esil tells me you helped him a lot during the tournament."

"I gave him a nudge here and there, but Esil has good instincts. I hear you have grand ambitions of your own."

Dean nods enthusiastically. "I'm just waiting for someone to take a chance on me."

We all take a seat in the oversized leather chairs of the lounge.

Dean's head turns like it's on a swivel. "What is this place?"

"This is the Rusty Nail Saloon. Grayson's choice. It's based on the American Wild West. No magic or out of world items. I'm guessing the fact that you have on starter rags is the only reason you're allowed to walk around wearing that, but we'll get you sorted out soon enough."

"Oh, man!" He points to a bullseye hanging on the wall. "They have darts. Want to play? I've always wanted to try."

I shrug. "Why not? Grayson, you in?"

We each take a handful of darts as we enter the throwing area. Aside from two mustachioed men playing one another on the far end, the other three dart boards are empty, so we each take our own lane.

I toss my darts one at a time, but my aim is off. Even though I aimed for the bullseye, two of my darts hit the outer ring, and one misses the target entirely.

"Nice throw, champ," Grayson taunts me. His throws weren't great, but he did manage to get inside the middle circle.

Dean stands next to his dartboard grinning. One dart is in the outer bullseye and the other two are just barely outside of it.

"You did that on your first try?" That's some beginner's luck.

He plucks the first dart from the board. "I've always had pretty good hand-eye coordination."

He walks back to the throwing line and tosses another dart. It lands just outside the bullseye. The second one hits the outer bullseye, and the third hits dead center.

Grayson leans in and whispers in my ear, "Kid's a natural."

He really is. The fact that he did so well on back-to-back throws means it's definitely not beginner's luck. His Dexterity must be pretty high for that kind of accuracy.

"Not bad, but what do you say we play a man's game?" One of the mustachioed men steps up behind Dean. He's dressed in all black, and his shirt has an ornamental rose embroidered over his right breast pocket. Tassels dangle from his sleeves. "Let's put your hand-eye coordination to the test." He pulls out a chip worth fifty gold and flips it like a coin.

I move over next to Dean. "Thanks, but we're just here for fun."

"Oh, come one. This is a gambling man's town. The Wild West. If the kid is as good as he claims, here's fifty gold for the taking. I'm always looking for some quality competition."

Dean frowns. "Sorry, but I don't have fifty gold even if I wanted to."

"What's the game?" Grayson steps up beside us, his face set like stone.

The man smiles and his mustache curls up at the edge. "Pinfinger." He pulls a knife from his belt and slams it point down into the table.

Pinfinger. I've never heard of it.

Grayson laughs. "I've played my fair share of pinfinger over the years. It's pretty popular among the sailors."

"How does it work?" asks Dean.

The mustachioed man answers. "It's pretty simple. You place your hand on the table." He presses his palm down and spreads his fingers wide. "Then you stab between each finger from one side to the other. Cut yourself and you lose."

He takes the knife and slowly moves it between each finger, stabbing at the empty space. The tip of the blade taps against the table in rhythmic succession. The pace quickens as he goes from one end of his hand and back, faster and faster until he stabs the blade into the wood between his index finger and thumb.

"What do you say? Up for a challenge?" The man smirks, and his mustache goes lopsided.

Dean stares at the table with a look of confusion. "How do you win?"

"We see who can go the longest before they finally cut themselves. Beat me and this chip is yours." He flashes the chip held between his thumb and index.

"And if I lose?"

He winks. "Then I take your money."

"Sorry, but I don't have—"

"The kid's in." Grayson takes a fifty-gold chip and places it on the table.

I don't know what Grayson is up to, so I pull him aside. "What are you doing?"

"The kid is a natural. Let him play."

"But, Grayson, that's more money than he will make in a year at the mines."

"Exactly." Grayson crosses his arms. "I'm giving him an opportunity to show his skill. If we don't take a chance on our own, who will?"

He has a point. Still, throwing around fifty gold on a single game is ludicrous.

"Fine." I lift my hands in surrender. "It's your money."

Grayson nods to Dean. "Show 'em what you've got."

Dean and the mustachioed man take a seat across from one another at the table.

The mustachioed man pulls the knife free and hands it to Dean. "You can go first. If I beat you, you'll have a chance to outdo me. We keep going until one of us wins." He snaps his finger. "James, you'll keep time."

The other man, James, steps up to the table holding a

golden pocket-watch. He wears a red cowboy shirt and a black bandana around his neck. A thick blond mustache drapes over his lip like a walrus.

Come to think of it, I don't think I've seen so many mustaches in one place as I have in this world. They really do try to make it feel as immersive as possible, unlike in certain worlds where a space knight and a mage can stand side by side.

James lifts the pocket-watch. "I'll start the timer on your first move."

"Show 'em what you've got, kid." Grayson offers his encouragement and then steps aside.

Dean glances at me, and I nod. It's time to see what he's made of.

He takes the blade and taps it between his thumb and index finger, starting the timer. He moves it between one finger to the next like he's done it a thousand times. His eyes are locked on his outstretched hand as he moves robotically.

"Time!" James calls out when a trickle of blood runs down Dean's ring finger. "Twenty-five seconds."

Mustachio extends his hand and flashes a dangerous smile. With the first tap of the blade, James starts the timer.

From the first movement, it's clear that Mustachio is an expert at the game. His motions are precise and fluid, jumping between each finger with ease. He looks Dean in the eyes as he goes, the pattern committed to memory.

"Time! Thirty-seven seconds," James announces.

A tiny prick of blood, almost unnoticeable, sprouts on Mustachio's pinky finger.

He frowns. "Ahh, dammit. Let's see what you've got. Thirty-seven seconds or your friend's gold is mine."

Dean nods but doesn't say anything. His face is set with determination. I'm sure he's feeling the pressure to win back Grayson's bet. I remember the first time I spent a large sum of money after opening the Developer's Chest. I almost vomited from the anxiety.

"Don't worry about it. Just do your best." I try to offer encouragement.

He doesn't acknowledge that I spoke as he takes the knife and begins the next round of pinfinger.

With laser focus, Dean moves the blade from finger to finger. His brow is furrowed as he follows each movement. It's almost as if he's in a trancelike state when he passes twenty-five seconds. At forty seconds, a bead of sweat trickles down his temple.

After a minute, a crowd has gathered, but Dean is so zoned in that he barely seems to notice.

The blade taps in a perfect rhythm as it goes from side to side.

By one minute and fifteen seconds, I'm questioning how he's still going. A minute-thirty and Mustachio looks on in fascination.

When Dean finally nicks his index finger and it glows a bright red, the room erupts in applause.

Mustachio stands up from the table. "I'll be damned. Here, take the chip." He flips the chip like a coin, and it bounces on the table in front of Dean. "If you're looking for a gang to join, we've got room for a sharpshooter in The Wild Bunch."

"Gang?" There's uncertainty in Dean's voice.

"This is the Wild West, make of it what you will. You can help uphold the law, or you can be an outlaw. The choice is yours."

"And which one are you?" asks Dean.

"A little this, a little that." He winks. "If you ever want some real adventure, come find me."

Somehow, I feel like getting involved with a gang is not in Dean's best interest.

The crowd quickly disperses, leaving me and Grayson alone at the table with Dean.

I take a seat next to him. "Wow, Dean. I must say I'm impressed. Where'd you learn to do that?"

"I don't know." His eyes dart to the ground for a moment before he returns my gaze. "I've always been good at games that require steady hands. I got in the zone, and it was like I was a robot."

Grayson slides the chip to Dean. "You put on quite the show. Enjoy the spoils."

Dean picks up the coin and admires it before handing it to Grayson. "You bet on me. It's yours."

"Nonsense." Grayson shakes his head. "You earned it. Now, what do you say we go get you into some real western wear?"

Outside of the Rusty Nail Saloon, a wide dirt road runs through the middle of town. A tumbleweed rolls past, leaving a trail of dust in its wake. Across the street, there's a general store, a bank, and a barber. A little further down, I spot a chapel with a tall steeple and a blacksmith. To the other side, there are a few offices, a jail, and a corral for horses and other livestock. A few houses dot the edge of town, but most of the people I've seen stay in the inn above the saloon.

We head to the general store. Unlike most worlds that would have shops for clothing, weapons, food, and whatever else, it can all be found in one place here.

A porch sits several feet off the ground, making it easier to load and unload supplies into wagons. As we step inside, a bell announces our arrival.

I purchased the clothing I'm wearing through my home portal, so this is the first time I've been in the general store. The entire space is crammed with shelves, counters, and displays showcasing all manner of items.

A giant barrel full of nails sits next to a display of blueprints for barns, houses, and other frontier buildings. Near the back, harnesses and bullwhips hang from the wall next to an assortment of button-up shirts. They have cowboy hats, boots, denim, and khakis. The register is surrounded by a variety of candies, wooden toys, a barrel of pickles, potatoes, jerky, and other foodstuffs. A large bulletin board next to the door displays wanted posters, work for hire, election notices, and other information about the town.

"How can I help you gentlemen?" A weathered voice draws my attention, and I spot an older man with a long gray beard sitting on a stool behind the counter.

"We're looking to get this one outfitted." Grayson gestures toward Dean. "And we'll all need to buy weapons."

The old man gets off the stool. "Follow me this way and I'll show you our starter packs. You get more bang for your buck that way."

Dean follows the man toward the back of the store.

Grayson turns to me. "Do you want to pick a quest off the board for us? That way we can decide what weapons we'll need. I'll help the kid get his gear sorted."

"Will do." I leave Grayson to shop and return my attention to the bulletin board.

It's filled with notices attached by thumbtacks. I disregard the work for hire and stuff relating to the townspeople. We want action and adventure, and the best way to find it is with a bounty. Dozens of posters offer rewards for capturing outlaws wanted for everything from trespassing to murder. I quickly glance through them.

Wanted: *Dead or Alive*
    Peter 'Dust Devil' Griffith
    Crime: *Murder*
    Reward: *$1000*

Wanted: *For Capture Alive*
    Matthew 'Whip' Williamson
    Crime: *Fraud (Selling Harmful Substances as Miracle Medicine)*
    Reward: *$100*

Wanted: *Dead or Alive*
    Jack 'Night Rider' Patterson
    Glen 'Hawkeyes' Hendrix
    Fannie 'the Blind' McConnell
    Elsie 'Faith' Whitehead
    Percy 'Big' Leon
    Crime: *Robbery*
    Reward: *$750 per person*

As I focus on each poster, it enlarges across my vision, offering more detail on each bounty.

. . .

Peter 'Dust Devil' Griffith is wanted for the murder of Ulysses Smith. Griffith murdered Smith in cold blood over a disagreement relating to a game of poker. He is believed to be hiding in Caldecot Cove.

Matthew 'Whip' Williamson is wanted for selling harmful substances under the guise of a miracle cure. After several people became ill, it was determined that Williamson was passing off a mixture that included snake venom as a cure for baldness. He was last seen on the outskirts of town to the west.

Jack 'Night Rider' Patterson, Glen 'Hawkeyes' Hendrix, Fannie 'the Blind' McConnell, Elsie 'Faith' Whitehead, and Percy 'Big' Leon, also known as 'The Rowdy Five', are wanted for stagecoach robbery. Their last-known whereabouts were in the Black Hills, where it is believed they have stashed their loot in the rocky caves.

They go on like this for a while. There are enough bounties to keep us busy for weeks, but I take the one for The Rowdy Five off the board and go find the others. With there being five of them, we have a better chance at collecting at least one of the bounties, not to mention the possibility of finding their stolen loot.

I find Grayson and Dean in the back of the store near the clothing. Dean has a large red-and-yellow poncho draped over his shoulders and a tan Stetson hat. He's also traded his sneakers for a pair of brown boots.

He turns to me with a wide grin. "Pretty cool, right?" He lifts his arms, revealing the breadth of the poncho. "I should blend in pretty well with the sandy terrain." He reaches down and picks up a burlap sack. "I also got this starter pack. It has everything we need to make camp. Plus canned beans and jerky for when we need energy."

"Nice. I found us a bounty. What else do we need?"

Grayson takes the bounty paper and glances it over. "We need weapons, and then we'll need to rent some horses from the stable." He turns to the older gentleman. "Let's take a look at your firearms."

The old man leads us to a glass case filled with various weapons. Several revolvers, a shotgun, and a few different rifles, along with knives of different lengths, and even a slingshot and marbles.

"What can I do for you gentlemen?"

Grayson kneels in front of the display. "It looks like we're setting off in search of The Rowdy Five. We'll capture them if we can, but we need to be prepared for a shootout just in case."

The man shakes his head. "Good luck with that. Many have tried to round them up, but they're a dangerous bunch. They know those hills like the back of their hands." He unlocks the display and reaches inside. "There's a reason nobody has caught them yet. I'd suggest you each take two weapons. But you'll definitely need a revolver in any case." He picks up a handgun with a rotating barrel. "This one should do nicely."

Peacemaker. *Single-action Revolver.*

Ammo Capacity: 6

While they lack the range and firepower of a rifle, the revolver is a staple in every westerner's toolkit. They can be fired with one hand, making them the perfect weapon for firing from horseback or while steering a carriage. They are quick to reload and are accurate in close to medium range.

"Alright, we'll take three of those." I pull out a handful of chips from the saloon. "Tell us about what else you have."

"We'll take four." Grayson takes the revolver from the counter and spins it around his finger. "I prefer to dual wield."

"Very well." The man reaches beneath the counter and pulls out a shotgun. "For close range. Or if you want to pepper something from far away."

Winchester Model 1897. *Pump-action Shotgun.*

Ammo Capacity: 2

The preeminent weapon for close range. The use of pellets over a single bullet provides greater accuracy and damage at close range. They are also excellent weapons for hunting birds and other small game.

"And then we have this if either of you are a sharpshooter."

Spencer Repeating Rifle. *Lever-action Rifle.*

Ammo Capacity: 7

Rifles provide longer range and more firepower than revolvers. Due to the increased damage, they are not recommended for small prey, as they will obliterate the animal, leaving nothing to skin.

. . .

"Dibs on the rifle." Dean picks it up and aims down the sight toward the wall.

I take the shotgun and feel its weight against my palm. "After your stunt in the saloon, I'm not going to argue with you. You have the best accuracy out of any of us. I guess I'll take the shotgun then."

We stock up on ammo, as well as a few other provisions before heading to the stables where we rent three horses for the evening.

Once we're all saddled up, I pull out the wanted poster for The Rowdy Five and focus on it again.

Accept Bounty? Y/N

I accept and a small dot appears on the map in my vision.

CHAPTER NINE

The clop-clop of horse hooves against the sandy terrain is surprisingly calming as we travel across the desert. As I expand the map in the corner of my vision, I notice the dot marking our destination is less precise than it appeared on the mini-map. Instead of it showing a specific location, it's actually a large area nearly a mile wide labeled "Black Hills."

We're definitely going to have our work cut out for us finding these outlaws.

Dean hasn't stopped smiling since climbing on his horse. He holds the reins in his hands, head held high as we trot along. With his poncho and cowboy hat, he fits the part remarkably well.

We all do.

The three of us each have quarter-horses. Dean's is a dark chestnut, Grayson's is black, and mine is a blue roan. The gray coat of my horse appears almost blue in the midday sun. While I don't have the same attachment to it as I do to Fenrir, it's still a magnificent animal. Quarter-horses are decent over long distances, but they really shine in close pursuit. In a quarter-mile chase, they can't be beat.

As the sun dips closer to the horizon, I figure we have a couple of hours before nightfall.

"How do you suppose we go about finding these guys?" I ask. If they are hiding in caves, how the hell are we supposed to find them?

Grayson pulls on his reins and his horse slows until he is on pace between Dean and I. "It's gonna be a tough bounty, which is why it pays so well. It'll be easy for them to conceal themselves among all these rocks and caves, so we'll have to keep our eyes peeled for anything out of the ordinary. With a little luck, we might catch one of them out on a hunt."

Great, so it all comes down to being in the right place at the right time.

"What's that?" Dean points into the distance.

At first, I don't see anything but empty desert and boulders, but then I notice a speck of black moving across the sea of tan.

Grayson winks at me. "And there is our first clue."

We set off in pursuit of the mysterious travelers. As we get closer, a second dot becomes visible. This one is tan and blends into the surroundings better.

The pair don't appear to be in a hurry, and we continue to follow them at a safe distance. As the sky morphs from bright blue to a watercolor of purples and pinks, a gunshot echoes across the vast stillness. The horses snort at the sound, but we whip the reins and rush toward the commotion.

Several more gunshots ring out before we are close enough to see what is happening.

Grayson puts his hand up and brings his horse to a halt. Dean and I follow suit, dismounting and creeping toward the crest of the hill for a better view.

Dead bodies are scattered around the entrance to a cave at the bottom of the hill. A campfire burns at the mouth of the cave, and some small animal roasts on a spit.

A massive body wearing a black poncho stands over the lone survivor with a revolver pointed at her head. I focus on her and her name appears above her head.

Elsie 'Faith' Whitehead

This is it! Someone beat us to The Rowdy Five.

The barrel of the revolver sways back and forth as the man in black says something to her. He wears a black mask over his eyes, and a black Stetson hat pulled low. There is something oddly familiar about him, so I focus on his stats.

Ryken 'The Black Death' Tanaka

I'm so startled that I instinctively grab Grayson by the arm. "What the hell is he doing here?" I haven't seen Ryken since the tournament.

Grayson squints his eyes. "It looks like he had the same idea we did. He's got a kid with him too."

Sure enough, the tan speck we saw traveling ahead of us stands behind Ryken, a rifle pointed at the kneeling NPC.

Dawn Warren

She's dressed identically to Ryken except all her clothing is tan. A blonde braid hangs over one shoulder.

"You know this guy?" asks Dean.

"Yeah, he was kind of my rival in the Developer's Tournament. And my girlfriend's brother. He'll stop at nothing to win."

Realization dawns on Dean's face. "That's right. I thought he looked familiar. He was the death knight that almost beat you! We've got to do something. We can't just let him take our bounty."

"He got here first. There's not much that we can—"

Before I have time to finish, a shot rings out and Ryken drops his gun. He clutches his shoulder and blood seeps through his poncho. His head darts around as he backs toward the cave.

There's a click as Dean pulls the lever on his rifle and takes aim. He fires a second shot, hitting Dawn in the chest. She falls to the ground and crawls toward Ryken. The two of them stumble into the cave and out of sight.

"What the hell was that?" I snap at Dean, who is focused on the cave entrance.

Grayson laughs. "This is the Wild West. Anything goes."

That may be true, but it's not my style. There's no honor in stealing someone's bounty, even if it is Ryken.

Elsie hides behind a boulder as we descend the rocky hill.

"Oh, god. Thank you. He was going to kill me." Tear stains cut through her dust covered cheeks. "He killed all of them."

"You won't be getting any sympathy from us." I hold up the wanted poster with her face on it, pointing to the line "dead or alive." "Keep an eye on the cave while I tie her up."

I search through my bag for the rope from the starter pack. Elsie reaches for Ryken's revolver laying in the sand, but the click of Grayson's weapon being cocked stops her in her tracks.

"Your fate is in your own hands, girlie." Grayson motions for her to step away.

She complies, and I tie her up without incident.

"They're coming out." Dean stares down the sight of his rifle. "Want me to take them out?"

"No, let's see what he has to say."

The three of us stand with our weapons drawn as Ryken emerges from the cave, his hands raised in surrender. Dawn scowls at us from behind his broad frame.

"You have always been a pain in my ass." He sneers. "Tell me, how is my sweet sister doing nowadays?"

"I'd stop right there if I were you." I rest my finger on the trigger, ready to shoot if need be. If anyone would be bold enough to try something against three people with their weapons aimed on them, it would be Ryken.

Ryken lets out a cold laugh. His voice is still deep, despite not having the voice modification of his death knight class he normally uses. "I see things haven't changed. You're still taking credit for other people's hard work."

I fire a warning shot above his head, and Ryken stops moving.

"Looks like I hit a nerve." His hands fall to his sides. "Esil Allen, the supposed hero of the underdogs. Yet all his accomplishments rest on the backs of other people. Funny how that works. You used my sister to win the tournament, even sacrificed a few of her dwarven friends. And now you're here taking our hard-earned bounties. Tell me, Esil, how does it feel to steal from a girl?"

Dawn steps up beside him and I can see an anger burning in her eyes. She looks about the same age as Dean. Whoever she is, hanging around Ryken will not be good for her.

My conviction wavers for a moment, and I take my finger off the trigger. I know he's just trying to get under my skin, but I'm surprised it's working. This whole world is about taking risks. Out here, civilians take the law into their own hands. Ryken would have shot us in the back to take our bounties.

"Sorry, Ryken." I place my finger on the trigger again. "It's nothing personal. To the victor goes the spoils."

"You know what?" He takes a step forward, but before he can finish his sentence, a bullet hits him right between the eyes.

Dawn tries to run. A rifle lever clicks over my shoulder and then she falls face-forward into the sand to the echo of the gunshot.

I turn around to find Dean aiming down the iron sight of his rifle, smirking. He stands tall and stows the rifle over his shoulder.

I shake my head in annoyance. "What were you thinking? We don't just kill people because we feel like it."

My words come out harsh, and Dean takes a step back, his face filled with confusion.

Dean frowns. "He would have killed us if he had the chance. Now we don't have to worry."

I turn to Grayson for support. "Grayson, back me up here."

He shrugs. "You know he would have killed us if he'd had a chance."

Dean scrunches his eyes. "You know this is a game, right? They will respawn."

Some of the tightness in my chest fades. Then I can't help but laugh. "Yeah, you're right. I've spent so much time in the Broken Lands that sometimes the line between game and reality feels a little blurred."

"Is it really that realistic?"

I let out a deep breath. "You have no idea."

After about five minutes, Ryken and Dawn's bodies disappear. The NPCs they killed, however, remain. We search the area around the caves and find two extra horses to tie the bodies to.

The caves are filled with empty bean cans, clothing, and weapons, but there's no sign of the loot they stole. If I had to guess, it's buried in a nearby cave they rarely go to.

Our questioning of Elsie leads us nowhere. She'd die before giving up her hard-earned treasure.

Instead, she rides with Grayson, her hands bound in front of her. He makes sure to let her know what awaits her if she tries to escape.

The sun eventually disappears, leaving us to travel by the starlit sky.

Dean looks at the stars above. "You know, I've never seen stars in real life. Is this what they really look like? They're beautiful."

His comment reminds me of my time before living at Pangea Headquarters. Back when I knew so little of the world outside my box. "Yeah. One day, you'll see them for yourself."

A notification flashes across my vision causing me to stop.

Warning: _It has been a while since you ate. Find nourishment in the next 30 minutes or you will receive a Hunger debuff._

Grayson and Dean must have received the same notice, because they both slow down.

Dean taps the pack hanging from his saddle. "Good thing I bought these."

We find a group of boulders and stop to eat, passing around a can of cold beans and some strips of jerky. We could heat the beans for more authenticity, but this isn't full-immersion, so it's not like we can taste the difference.

After we are done, we're on our way again. The town is eerily dark when we arrive, aside from the light escaping the windows at the saloon.

The saloon doors open and a streak of light cuts through the darkened street. A woman's wailing voice sings of a lost lover. A dark figure steps onto the porch, their face hidden in shadow.

A gunshot rings across the night, and the music abruptly stops.

"Oh, damn," Grayson mutters, and for a moment, I fear he's been shot.

He quickly draws his revolvers and Elsie falls from the horse, landing on the well-trodden street with a thud.

"Easy, old man." Ryken steps into the street. "Those are our bounties. I appreciate you doing us the kindness of bringing them all the way to town for us."

Dawn exits the saloon and stands behind her mentor. A moment later, several more people watch from the saloon porch.

Dean takes aim with his rifle out of the corner of my eye.

"You sure you want to do that, Esil, Junior?" Ryken doesn't seem the least bit concerned that he's being aimed at. "Shoot me in front of all these people and you'll have a bounty on your head. One that I wouldn't mind taking."

Dean glances at me. I nod, and he slowly lowers his weapon.

I urge my horse forward a few paces. "What do you want, Ryken?"

"*We* want our bounties."

"Funny thing, we seem to be the ones with the bodies tied to our horses."

"It sounds like it's your word against mine. In that case, Esil Allen, I challenge you to a duel."

A notification flashes across my vision.

Alert: *You have been challenged to a duel. While within town limits, duels are compulsory. Failure to accept a duel will result in a loss to your reputation and will affect your interaction with locals.*

Dammit. The jail is literally at the end of the street. Why does Ryken always have to be such a thorn in my side?

I don't spend a lot of time in this world, but I can't turn down a challenge, especially from a bully like Ryken. Besides, he's probably streaming this. How would it look if I ran from him?

"Fine. I accept."

Someone on the porch whistles and more people spill out of the saloon. A moment later, the porch is so full that people move down to the street to get a view of the show.

I dismount my horse and hand the reins to Grayson. He and Dean lead the horses to the side of the street and tie them to a post.

A big, burly man with a bushy beard and wearing a white button-up steps into the middle of the street. A gold badge hangs just above his breast.

"You two gentlemen trying to settle a dispute?" he asks. "If you haven't noticed, I'm the sheriff of these here parts. We don't tolerate mindless killing in my town. We do however respect the rules of a duel. So, first off, what is the challenge?"

"That these three stole our hard-earned bounty." Ryken answers.

He looks from me to Ryken. "Each of you have a weapon?"

I nod. The time for talking is over. Let's end this one way or another.

"Yes, sir." Ryken smirks.

"Step on up then." He motions for us to come to him. "Any day now. Don't be shy."

Ryken and I both approach the sheriff.

"Good, now let's see your weapons."

I unholster my revolver and hold it out to him. Ryken does the same.

"These will do. Now each of you holster your weapons and face away from one another. Take ten paces, and then turn around."

The town is dead quiet except for the crunch of our boots with each step and a coyote howling in the distance. I keep my eyes in front of me, refusing to be distracted by the onlookers.

"Now, turn around and face your opponent. You get one shot, whether you hit or not. Any more than that and you'll have a bounty on your own head."

Ryken and I both rest our hands on our holsters. To win, not only do you have to be quick but also accurate.

Ryken's fingers tap against the grip of his revolver like he's playing the piano. One, two, three, four. One, two, three, four. Each finger tapping in turn.

I wait for his pinky finger to tap and draw my weapon. I haven't even raised it past my hip when a gunshot rings out, and I realize my mistake.

My vision goes red as the bullet hits my chest. I stumble back and forth for a moment as my haptic suit clenches around the wound. Then the world fades to sepia and I find myself hovering above my dead body. A timer counting down from five minutes appears in the center of my vision.

Ryken laughs, holstering his weapon. He shot from the hip, and I never had a chance.

He walks over to Dean and Grayson. "I think you have something that belongs to me."

Grayson hands over the reins to the horses with the bandits draped across their backs.

Ryken gives one of the horses to Dawn. "I'll meet you at the jail to claim our reward." Then he turns to Dean. "If you want to enter this tournament, I suggest you find yourself a real mentor. You might think he's a good bet because he came from nothing, but let me tell you. Esil Allen is a leech. Everything he got he took off the back of someone else. I like your spirit. Shooting me out there in the desert, that's something I would have done. Come with me and I'll find you someone with substance."

"That's enough." Grayson takes a step toward Ryken. His hands rest on his holsters and for a moment, I think he might shoot him. "You won the duel. Leave it be and get out of here."

Ryken smiles. It's cold and unsettling. "Alright, old man." He gives one last look at Dean. "Don't say I didn't warn you."

When I respawn in one of the rooms above the saloon, I have half a mind to find Ryken and put a bullet in his head. It'd be worth taking the bounty to wipe the smug look off his face. Instead, I go find Grayson and Dean. They cut their conversation short when I walk up.

Dean looks down at the ground. I'm almost certain he is thinking about what Ryken said.

"Hey, I know how much you want to enter the tournament, but following him, behaving like that, that's not the right way to do it."

He looks up at me with the same fire I saw in his eyes on the day we met. "So, what, I'm supposed to watch an opportunity pass me by because you say he's a bad guy?"

"He'll never understand what you and I have been through. He calls me a leech because he's never had to ask for help. He's always had the solutions right there in front of him. He and Aleesia both came from money, but she understands the value of human connection. That you help those you care about, even when it's not easy for you. Everything is about winning and losing for Ryken."

Dean shakes his head. "What am I supposed to do then? No one else is going to take a chance on me."

"I will." It's not something I would have ever wanted to do—I'm just not wired to be in the public eye—but I'll be damned if I let someone like Ryken bully his way to the top.

The fire fades, and Dean smiles. "Seriously?"

"Seriously. It's going to be tough, and you'll likely lose all privacy, but if you want this, then I'm all in."

Dean rushes over and wraps his arms around me. "You won't regret this."

"I'm sure. Now what do you say we call it a night. Buzz's big tournament is tomorrow."

Dean logs out, and I let out a deep sigh. What have I gotten myself into?

Grayson and I linger for a moment. The street is once again empty and music seeps out from the saloon.

"You sure you want to do this?" Grayson asks.

"Not really, but I need to. Dean has the same killer instinct as Ryken. If I can channel it into a positive direction at all, I want to try."

He nods. "You know I'll help in any way I can."

"I know. See you in Asgard tomorrow?"

"I wouldn't miss it. There's no telling what Buzz has planned."

That's the truth. We say our good-byes, and I log out. My life just got a whole lot more interesting.

CHAPTER TEN

The crowd buzzes like a swarm of bees through the stadium. The constant drone makes it hard to hear anything else. The other riders, their mounts, and the occasional projectile whizzing by all get lost in the ruckus.

For the moment, all that matters is the race. Not the Pro-Am Tournament, not the Broken Lands, only me and my opponents.

A speck of mud flies through the air and lands with a soft plop against my goggles, obscuring my vision. I wipe it away with my thumb and focus on the task at hand. I whip the reins hard, urging my giant chicken to run faster.

As best I can, I tune out the roar of the crowd, focusing on the squawk of the other giant chickens riding my tail.

Position: 3/12

The finish line is in sight. One final stretch of track and two angry chickens stand between me and first place.

I reach into the satchel that hangs around the neck of my chicken, Bobo, and pull out a blue canister. Bobo is seven feet tall with bright blue plumage. A streak of yellow feathers juts out of the top of his head like a mohawk. This is our fifth race together today, and for the most part, we're a pretty good team. I contemplate throwing the canister. It's a great item, and I usually save it for when I'm in second place, but there's no point in holding on to this one any longer. It's time to make moves if I want a shot at winning.

The lightweight canister zooms down the track like a rocket when I toss it forward. It splits open in the middle, and a rope with weighted knots on both ends ejects, wrapping around the feet of the chicken ahead of me. The giant chicken falls to the ground with a squawk, and red feathers flutter into the air. The fall launches the rider headfirst into the mud.

She waves her fist at me as I pass, displaying one brass knuckle with the word "off" engraved on it. My imagination fills in the text from her other knuckle.

Only one rider stands between me and chicken-race immortality.

Okay, maybe not immortality, but between me and the next round of *Buzz's First Annual Chicken Cup Classic*.

Bobo plants his claws in the mud and makes a final push on the leader. I have no idea who the rider in first place is. He wears a golden samurai mask and full body armor, concealing his identity. His chicken is purple with a white head and long golden tail-feathers that whip in the wind.

An item box appears on the track, hovering in the middle just as the leader passes by. These boxes are filled with useful items for attacking opponents. Whenever someone hits an item box, the contents automatically appear in their inventory.

The leader equips a black canister and tosses it to the

ground in front of the item box. Oil explodes from the canister, creating a slick right where the loot box is.

The finish line grows ever closer and I'm no nearer to first place. I need to get that item box, but there's the risk I'll get stuck in the oil. It's a risk I'll have to take in order to win.

Setting our sights on the box, Bobo and I race straight toward our salvation or doom. I urge Bobo to jump and we hit the box square on.

A red canister instantly appears in my hand. Without a second to wait, I toss the canister to the ground before Bobo lands in the oil spill. The canister cracks open as it hits the ground, and a giant flame erupts from Bobo's backside, barreling us through the air and past the oil slick. We continue to soar down the track and are inches from taking first place when the sky suddenly goes black.

You've got to be kidding me.

The leader and I are neck and neck when two giant rods of lightning fork down from the sky. An explosion of white light and deafening thunder hits, forming a crater in the track and immobilizing both me and the samurai. For the next two seconds, we're unable to move, forced to watch helplessly as first and second place go to a pair of gnomes on color-coordinated chickens.

"Dammit!" the rider next to me curses. "It's always the gnomes. Gnomes suck!" He slams his samurai mask on the ground, and I can see that he is actually...a woman.

We creep past the finish line once the stun wears off, taking fifth and sixth place.

"Tough luck," I say, but it does nothing to remove the scowl from her face.

"Just once, I'd like to make it to the finish line without being blown to bits right as I'm about to win. You lead for three laps and then a well-timed item undoes everything. And of course, I'm never lucky enough to have an Infinity Shield." She shakes her head.

"Better luck next time." I extend my hand. "Name's Esil."

She cracks a smile. "I know all about you. I'm sure everyone competing knows who you are. Though, it's a little harder to recognize you without that giant wolf. Name's Sam, nice to meet you."

I check the updated rankings as they adjust to the most recent stats. I'm out of the top ten and won't be competing in the final race.

Oh well, at least I had some fun and can catch up with the others.

"Well, what do you know," says Sam. "Made it by the skin of my teeth."

Glancing at the rankings again, I spot a "Samantha Tarly" in tenth place.

"Well, how about that. I'll be cheering you on in the final race. Best of luck."

"Thanks! Really, though, who would have thought that a bloody chicken race would be one of the most popular games in Pangea?" She beams at me as she walks past to register for her next race.

Over the past year, Buzz has turned his small chicken farm into one of the biggest attractions in Asgard. Between the time he spends in full-immersion and here, I don't know how he has time for anything else. Considering I've barely seen him lately, I guess he doesn't.

A firm hand slaps me on the back.

"I guess you can't win everything." Buzz flashes me a wide smile. "You were really making some moves before that lightning bolt hit you."

"You should really take that item out of the races." I roll my eyes.

"No way. The crowd loves it. You should see their reaction when it hits." He tilts his head back in laughter.

Buzz has been sporting some new threads since opening Buzz's Chicken Races to the public. He's let go of the wolf persona he'd taken on since coming to Asgard. His current outfit can only be described as a cross between a jester and a rogue. He wears the curled shoes and clothing of a jester, but with a dark, motley tunic that is almost somber. Instead of the typical fool's hat, he wears a cowl in the shape of a chicken head. Several daggers hang from his side, each with a hooked talon on the hilt. He still pays homage to the wolves with a small patch in the shape of a wolf head over his heart.

I still can't decide if it's funny or badass.

"Is the turnout everything you hoped?" I ask, but I already know the answer. The stands are full. There are numerous races per hour. This place is booming, and Buzz of all people had a vision for it.

"Business is good. You know, I always had dreams, but it looks like I am finally on the way to becoming the Chicken King. There have been talks with Asgard to have a race in honor of the gods, can you believe that? Loki might even compete." He beams with pride.

"That's great to hear. I'm happy for you." He's come a long way since we both worked in the mines together, mining data for eight hours a day and barely getting by. And in spite of all the challenges, he's overcome them all with a joke and a smile on his face. This truly couldn't have happened to a better person.

Buzz wraps his arm around my shoulder. "They say find something you love, and you'll never work a day in your life. This sure as hell beats mining, I'll tell you that." He turns me around until I'm facing the stands. "I hooked up Grayson and Dean with box seats. Best view in the arena."

"Nice. I'm sure Dean is grateful."

"I can see why you picked him. He seems like a good kid."

"He is. He's got a fire in him, that's for sure. I'm hoping with a little guidance to make it a controlled burn and not a wildfire."

Buzz looks up at the display overhead as it counts down to the next race. It's a busy life running a chicken empire.

"I hate to cut and run, but you know, chicken king duties await."

We shake hands and Buzz disappears into the crowd. I'm glad he has finally turned his small farm into an empire. If anyone is deserving of this much success, it's Buzz.

I head toward the stands to find Dean and Grayson, but the path is full of people moving about during the time between races.

"Esil!" someone shouts nearby.

I search for the person who called my name and spot a hand waving frantically from the stands. Dean beams at me. Grayson gives me a mock salute from behind him.

Dean still wears his new cowboy getup, but Grayson has returned to his pirate outfit. He wears a white vest, halfway unbuttoned, exposing a roaring bear head tattooed on his chest. Several necklaces and amulets dangle from his neck. There's a belt with a revolver on his hip, and two golden battle gauntlets cover his hands. His mustache curls up around the edges, forming two semicircles above a full gray beard.

They jump the railing and meet me among the crowd.

"Man, I totally want to come race chickens some time. It looked like so much fun. You almost had it too." Dean grins.

I pat him on the back. "I'm sure we could arrange that. I hear you guys had the best seats in the house."

Grayson gazes over the massive arena. "It's a far cry from the chicken coop we defended from foxes and frost giants."

"That's the truth. What do you say we explore what Buzzworld has to offer?"

We walk around the stadium, taking in the small shops and vendors that have profited from Buzz's genius. The sudden popularity of the chicken races means that Asgard is no longer primarily filled with warriors carrying large weapons and wearing tunics. Players come from far and wide to witness the mayhem of men and women battling for supremacy while racing giant, rainbow-colored chickens.

"Thank you all for attending my first annual Chicken Cup Classic…" Buzz's voice carries across the stadium. I've heard it all before, so I tune him out and continue exploring.

A concession stand named the Chicken Hut catches my eye and I take a look at what they're selling. It's kind of sadistic that the only options they have are various forms of chicken.

Chicken on a stick. *+10% damage for five minutes.*

Chicken Nuggies. *10% increased movement for five minutes.*

Chicken Pot Pie: *10% increased Stamina for five minutes.*

Chicken Gizzards: *+10 constitution for five minutes.*

Chicken Noodle Soup. *Restores 500 health over 30 seconds.*

****Disclaimer****: Effects are not active while in a chicken race.*

The list goes on and on. Dean buys himself a chicken on a stick. Even though he can't actually taste it, he eats it like a man possessed. He and Buzz have that in common.

There are so many shops surrounding the stadium that I'm sure Buzz is making a fortune just from renting out the locations. I pass a popcorn stand and a booth with cotton candy in every color of the rainbow that grants effects ranging from temporary flight to icy breath. A miniature pub with four barstools catches my eye, and we take the remaining seats next to a stout, red-haired dwarf.

"Esil! By the gods, is that you!" The dwarf bangs his fist on the counter. His braided red beard hangs down into his lap and a mug of dark amber liquid swishes about, foam lingering on the ends of his mustache. "And this one. Grayson! What are the chances?"

"Ordin! It's been a while, indeed. I haven't seen you since, what, the end of the Developer's Tournament?" I give him a friendly slap on the back. The last time we spoke was when I gave him the Developer's Chest that I won in the tournament. If it hadn't been for his help in the final stage, I never would have won, so I figured it was the least I could do. "How have you been?"

He takes a large swig of his drink, finishing it in one gulp and slamming the mug on the table before motioning to the bartender for another.

"Honestly, the life of fame and fortune wasn't for me. After taking on the leadership role after you and Aleesia quit questing with the group, the pressure was too much. I was good for a few weeks making the decisions, but it was a lot. I realized I'm a much better number two. I left the group to Klink and have been exploring on my own ever since. Thought today would be a good day to take in a race or two. Your boy Buzz has really made a name for himself." The bartender hands him another full mug. "Fancy a drink?"

"Why not?" I shrug. "What are you having?"

"Scottish Ale." He frowns, offended that I asked. "It offers a fair amount of buffs to dwarves. Increased healing, strength and defense bonuses. They don't last nearly long enough, but if you ever see a group of dwarves together drinking and they get rowdy, this is the likely cause." He takes another long swig.

"What'll it be?" asks the bartender.

It doesn't really matter to me. It's not like I'll be able to taste it. Not like in The Broken Lands. I don't think I'll ever get over the way full-immersion feels. Indistinguishable from reality. Every sense reporting on what the world feels, smells, and tastes like.

"Dealer's choice, three of them," I say, and the bartender reaches for two bottles—one filled with red liquid and the other blue.

"You've got it, boss."

After pouring the two liquids into a glass, he adds a dash of a rusty brown substance, a sprinkle of white powder, and then muddles a few leaves in the bottom. The concoction begins to bubble and fizz as he pours it into three glasses.

Ordin eyes me warily as I slide my glass closer to me. The blue and red liquids swirl together in the center, creating a miniature vortex.

Substance. Bulwark Smash. *Effect: Aura of Protection. Grants increased Health and Mana Regeneration for five minutes.*

Bonus effect: Aura of Protection is doubled if consumed when under 15% health.

Not a bad recipe at all. I lift my glass to make a toast.

"To finding our happiness." The four of us clink our glasses together, and I take a sip of my cocktail. Immediately, my HP and Mana feel different. I feel more vibrant. "Can I have two more of those?" I ask the bartender.

He makes two more cocktails and I add them to my inventory. They may come in handy in the future.

A horn blares, signaling the start of the next race. Holograms of the race are displayed in countless locations around the track. One appears on the bar between Ordin and me. I spot Sam in the middle of the pack. She tosses a canister, and a violent explosion sends the three chickens surrounding her spinning in place.

Dean and Grayson debate which rider they think will win. I'm not entirely invested in the race, so I make small talk with Ordin.

"Do you mind if I ask what you found in the Developer's Chest?"

"I'd be offended if you didn't," he says gruffly.

He moves his beard to the side, showing me a shimmering amulet hanging from his neck. A blood-red ruby sits encrusted in a gold medallion with a set of runes engraved around the edge. It's one of the most beautiful pieces of jewelry I've ever seen.

"What is it?" I try to focus on it, but like most items in Pangea, if it belongs to another player, I'm unable to see its effects or item details if they are wearing it.

"It's called the Eye of Elaine. It has several buffs, but its bonus effect is what makes it so special. Once every twelve hours, I can double all my stats for sixty seconds. The downside is that all the buffs disappear until the bonus is available again. In a hard battle, it's a game changer. Double HP, attack, defense, everything."

"Wow." That's all I can say. The opportunities that item could have opened up for me are astronomical. Still, I'm glad that Ordin has it. If not for him, I wouldn't be where I am right now anyways. I definitely wouldn't have won the tournament, and that Eye of Elaine would be with someone else.

Ordin drains the rest of his mug and stands up.

"I think it's time for me to be going. I've got a quest to attend to. You're more than welcome to join if you'd like."

"Can I take a rain check? Me and Dean over here are training for the Pro-Am Tournament."

"You don't say? I know who to place my bets on." He winks. "It was good to see you, Esil. Take care."

We grasp each other around the forearm, and Ordin disappears into the crowd. I catch the last of the race, just as Sam crosses the finish line. Good for her.

It's time for us to get going, though. We have a tournament to prepare for.

CHAPTER ELEVEN

When I get home later that evening, I finally send in all the required documentation to enter Dean and myself into the tournament. A few minutes after hitting send, I receive a message from the developers.

Greeting Esil!

Thank you for your interest in Pangea Online's Pro-Am Tournament. Over the next few hours, we will be confirming that your apprentice has not competed in an official Pangea Online tournament. Once this has been confirmed, you will be officially added to the contestant list.

Since the Pro-Am Tournament is an opportunity for young players to compete alongside our great winners of the past, the stages will be constructed so that all entrants have a fair chance at the prize. For this tournament, levels will not matter. One's ability to win will be based on their use of items, abilities, and natural skill. The tournament will consist of three stages, each one building on the last, wherein a winner will be crowned on the final stage. Once entry is closed, the first stage will be revealed.

Thank you for entering the Pangea Online Pro-Am Tournament, and as always, never stop leveling!
-Pangea Online Developers

Well, that doesn't tell me much. How am I supposed to plan our training if I have no idea what we're up against? At least it puts all the competitors on the same page.

Before heading to bed, I reach out to Aleesia, Buzz, and Grayson about teaming up for some training tomorrow afternoon. Maybe one of them will have a better idea of where to start.

I wake up to a slew of messages. Buzz and Grayson both say they can't come because of orientation for the new full-immersion units. I search through my messages for the details about orientation, but I can't find anything. I do, however, have a message from Benjamin.

Esil,
Stop by my office in the morning. There is something we need to discuss.
-Benjamin

My stomach drops. No message about orientation and Benjamin wants to meet with me. This can't be good. There's no way they would kick me off the beta team, is there? I've done everything they've asked of me.

I quickly glance over the message from Aleesia saying

she'd be happy to join us. I'm too rattled to focus on anything at the moment, so I throw on some clothes and rush toward the main building.

Benjamin's door is closed when I arrive. I knock and the door opens with a whoosh. He places his tablet on the desk and motions for me to take a seat.

"Good morning, Esil." His voice gives nothing away.

"Good morning." The words come out as a croak as I take a seat in the polished leather chair. My hands are sweaty as I grip the armrests, leaving a trail of moisture every time I move.

I don't know what I could have possibly done to make them take me off the project. Too friendly with the NPCs perhaps, but wasn't that the whole point?

He stares at me for a moment, and then flashes me a smile. "I heard through the grapevine that you're entering the Pro-Am Tournament."

I nod. "You heard right." Is that why they don't want me around anymore? Did agreeing to mentor Dean cost me my job?

"With a kid from The Boxes as your apprentice, no less. The public is going to love it. You really know how to set yourself up for the spotlight, don't you?"

I almost snap at him, but I rein my temper in. "I never asked to be in the spotlight. Not then, and not now. No one else was going to take a chance on him, so I felt it was my responsibility. Who else is going to look out for those in The Boxes?"

Benjamin raises his hands in defense. "Easy. I'm not criticizing. I think it's a great thing that you're doing. The reason I asked to meet with you is so that I could tell you this in person. We're going to have to take you off the beta team while you're in the tournament."

"Why? I can train for the tournament and still help with the Broken Lands."

He frowns. "I don't doubt that you could. Unfortunately, that's not going to be possible. There's not much I can say on the matter, just know it's nothing personal and it has nothing to do with your abilities. You have been a valuable asset for our full-immersion testing and we will be happy to have you back once the tournament is over. Let's just say that we can't have you having a conflict of interest."

"Conflict of interest?" I scrunch my eyes. Does that mean that the Broken Lands will play a part in the tournament?

"I think you can put the pieces together yourself. I'll be rooting for you during the tournament, Esil. Now, if you don't mind, I have a lot of work to get done."

I leave Benjamin's office and walk down to the laboratory. My mind is full of questions. About the tournament and the Broken Lands. Does this mean there will be a full-immersion stage, or are the Broken Lands being added to Pangea?

Even though it's only been a couple of weeks since they shut the program down, the laboratory looks completely different. The giant vats we used to submerge ourselves in are gone, replaced by dozens of much smaller units, each one about the size of a coffin. They're polished and sleek, with a transparent top.

No one is down in the lab. The viewing deck, however, is packed with people in lab-coats. I spot Aleesia's messy bun as she stands on the far side taking notes. How much has she known about all of this?

She's already agreed to hang out tonight, so I'll fish for information then.

I have most of the day to kill until Dean is finished with school, so I wander aimlessly around the headquarters, drifting through the various parks and botanical gardens.

When I finally return home, I start researching some of the more skill-based worlds across Pangea. If the tournament is discounting our levels and current abilities, then we'd get the most benefit from exploring worlds where everyone is on the same page.

Personally, I like worlds where I can witness my avatar grow and level over time, but some people like the challenge of beating level after level.

I get so caught up in my research that before I know it, I have a message from Aleesia telling me to meet her in her home portal.

I strap into my haptic suit, toss Fenrir a few treats in my own portal, and go to meet Aleesia. After entering the code, I find her inside, sprawled out on a luxurious leather couch in the center of the room. I haven't been in many people's home portals, but I have a feeling that hers would put most of them to shame.

A spiral staircase leads to a loft that overlooks the main room. I can barely see the top of her four-poster bed up above. A crystal chandelier casts sparkles across the room. Mannequins span the perimeter, displaying copies of her best pieces of clothing, armor, and accessories. A symphony plays quietly in the background, and a display on the wall follows her unicorn as it prances in an open field. Everything in here screams royalty.

"How long have you known that the Broken Lands were part of the new tournament?"

She grimaces. "Sorry, I've known for a while now, but I was bound to secrecy. I wasn't even sure if you would be competing and I didn't want anything I said to influence you. I'm surprised they waited so long to tell you, though. I guess they wanted to wait until you officially entered."

I cross the room and give her a kiss on the cheek. "It seems a little soon to be taking full-immersion mainstream, don't you think?"

She shrugs. "I don't know. While we were perfecting the AI in the Broken Lands, another team was working on a more portable form of full-immersion. This is going to be big, Esil. Once this goes public, Pangea will never be the same."

"What do you mean?"

Aleesia sits up off the couch, her eyes wide with excitement. "They've found a way to experience full-immersion with nothing but a helmet."

"Wait, what? I was at the lab and I saw dozens of pods."

She grins. "Here's the best part. Those are for extended play. There's a nanobot gel that can keep the body functioning for days without having to eject. But the helmets by themselves are rated for up to six hours of immersion at a time."

I'm frozen for a moment as I take it all in. "So you mean to tell me that full-immersion is almost ready to come to all of Pangea?"

"In time. There's a lot of coding to get all the game worlds up to par, so it'll take time. But this tournament will be the big reveal."

I take a seat on the couch beside her. Any chance I had of keeping a low profile is over. With this kind of announcement, everyone across Pangea will be tuning into the tournament.

The loud gong of church bells announces a visitor, and

a hologram appears in the center of the table. Dean looks around nervously in his cowboy outfit.

"Let him in," she says, and a door opens, allowing Dean to enter.

He gawks at the lavish accessories before walking over to us.

"Nice to meet you. This place is amazing."

Aleesia offers him a warm smile. "Thanks. I don't spend as much time here as I used to, but it was my sanctuary for a time."

We engage in small talk for a bit before I get down to business.

"If we're going to have a shot at this tournament, we need lots of practice in different worlds. We want to be as well-versed as possible so that we can handle any challenge they throw at us."

Dean nods along as I speak. "So where are we going first?"

"Street Brawl. It's a two-dimensional world where we fight our way through levels, clear bosses, and try to reach the center of town."

We open an exit portal to Pangea's game worlds, and an endless expanse of destinations floats before us.

Welcome to Street Brawl! The city of Greendale has descended into anarchy. Thugs have taken over the streets and neighborhoods throughout the city. Fight your way downtown and rescue the Mayor so that he may call in reinforcements and bring safety to the city once again.

. . .

The world before me is full of flat surfaces and bright colors. Tall buildings stretch on each side of the road, forcing us down the path before us. The spaces between buildings ends with a walled-off alley. This is a far cry from the open worlds I'm used to. The street we stand on is littered with trash, broken-down vehicles, and burning dumpsters. In the distance, hooded individuals wearing ski masks walk back and forth holding chains, tire irons, and pieces of wood with nails in them.

My own body is two-dimensional and flat, like an animated version of me, but when I twist my arm, it's like I'm a piece of paper. Every time I take a step there's a barely audible beep. Techno-inspired music plays quietly in the background.

Dean and Aleesia have gone through the same transformation, each of them cardboard cutouts of their avatars.

"Whoa!" Dean flips his two-dimensional hand back and forth, amazed by the physics. "This is crazy. I'm moving like normal, but it feels different. I can't quite explain it."

"Don't worry about it." Aleesia tests out her own movement. "It's just your mind trying to make sense of everything. You'll get used to it shortly."

"So what do we do?" Dean looks to me for answers.

"We need to pick our weapons, and then make our way to the center of town." I point to a collection of potential weapons scattered on the street before us. A slingshot. A baseball bat. A yo-yo.

"Ladies first." I motion for Aleesia to choose her weapon.

"Hmm. I think I'll take the yo-yo." She picks it up and places the string around her finger. Then she flicks her wrist, and the yo-yo shoots out and retracts. She tries a few different tricks, spinning the yo-yo straight in front of her, and then doing an around-the-world where it goes in a complete circle over her body.

"Dean, you're next."

"Definitely the slingshot." He holds it out in front of him and pulls back on the sling, taking aim down the street. "Nice."

If his slingshot skills are anything like his darts, it'll be the perfect weapon for him.

"I guess that leaves me with the bat." I pick it up and take a few swings. It moves effortlessly in my hands. "Follow me. This first level should be pretty easy. The enemies get stronger as we progress, so it's important to get a hang of things early on."

The thugs pace back and forth as we approach. Even after passing where a normal human would see us, they don't look in our direction. Once we're about ten feet out, the closest two grunt and charge toward us.

Dean fires a pellet from his slingshot and the first thug shatters into pixels. A gold coin hovers in the area where he fell. Aleesia swings her yo-yo, knocking the second one out. Another gold coin appears.

The three thugs behind them continue to pace, oblivious to what just happened. Once we're close enough, they turn on us. I rush in and clobber the thug wearing a bright orange vest with my bat. Two coins sprout up from him as the avatar dissipates into hundreds of pixels. Aleesia and Dean finish off the other two.

A chain-link fence that was blocking the road now opens, allowing us to pass to the next level. I collect the coins from the enemies I downed. Most are worth five coins, but one is worth ten. There's a cha-ching with each one I pick up, along with a counter in the top right of my vision.

"That was easy." Aleesia reaches for one of the gold coins, and it vanishes as soon as she touches it. "What are these for?"

I read a brief summary of the world, so I know some of the basics. "We'll be able to upgrade our weapons once we find a shop."

The second level is more difficult, with each thug taking two hits to kill. Dean shoots each thug once before moving on to the next one so that when they get close enough, it only takes one hit from Aleesia or me to finish them off.

Things get more interesting once we reach level three. New enemies appear. This time, there are women throwing rocks at us in addition to the thugs.

The rocks travel slow enough that we can dodge them, but once multiple rocks come sailing in, we're forced to choose between dodging their attacks and fighting.

I swing my bat at one of the incoming rocks and it explodes into pixels.

"If we hit the rocks, then they vanish."

"Good to know," says Aleesia as she hits one with her yo-yo.

Dean attempts to hit the women with his ranged attack, but their rocks block his shots, disintegrating both projectiles.

"Let's take out the thugs first, then we'll deal with the others." I move forward and a rock barrage comes barreling in my direction. I smack the first one, but two more hit me before I'm ready to attack again. Techno chimes echo around me with each hit, and my health bar drops by a third.

I take a few steps back and the rocks spread evenly between us once again.

Aleesia hits one with her yo-yo. "They focus on whoever is closest. Looks like we'll need to press at the same time to keep them from focusing on one of us."

We push as a team, and the projectiles come at us at an even rate, allowing us to destroy them as we push. Once we are close enough, the thugs rush us. A few feet separate each attacker, giving me an idea.

"If we attack them at the same time, we should be able to kill them faster. We'll take some damage, but less than if we fought them individually."

As the first thug lunges at us with his tire iron, Aleesia hits him with her yo-yo. I quickly follow up with a swing of my bat, dropping the thug. Aleesia has enough time to block the rock thrown at her, but I'm not so lucky. My vision flashes red and I lose another chunk of my health bar.

"You hit them first next time so that you can block the rock," Aleesia orders. "I'll take the damage."

Dean continues to fire from a distance. His long range gives him time to shoot and then step aside, avoiding the rocks entirely. He manages to take out a thug on his own in the same time as Aleesia and me.

Aleesia and I are down to half health by the time we clear the thugs. Three women in the back continue to throw rocks in a steady stream.

We press on them at the same time. As we block each rock, I notice that our attacks are slightly faster than the women's. Once we're close enough to attack them, it gives us a slight edge. I block the rock, and just as the woman winds up to toss another, my bat explodes her into pixel dust. Dean and Aleesia both receive gold coins, but an orange soda hovers in front of me.

Orange Soda. *Restores 50HP.*

I down the soda and my health bar shoots up to seventy-five percent.

"Well done!" I congratulate the others. A new fence opens, revealing a street with a dumpster in the middle. This one isn't on fire like the others. The word "shop" hovers in the air above the dumpster.

"Nice, we can finally spend our coins!" Dean runs past me.

I focus on the dumpster and a screen appears in my vision. There's a picture of me, my health, and my weapon on one side. On the other are the items and upgrades.

Orange Soda. *Restores 50HP. 5 coins.*

Roasted Turkey. *Restores full HP. 20 coins.*

Weapon Upgrade. *"Nailbiter." Doubles damage of baseball bat. 50 coins.*

Extra Life. *Respawn at the beginning of the previous level. 100 coins.*

It's a pretty simple setup. We buy items to heal and upgrade our weapons to deal more damage. I confirm with Aleesia and Dean that they have the same options.

"How many coins do you have?"

"One-fifteen," says Dean.

"One-twenty," says Aleesia.

"I have one hundred and ten myself. I say we definitely go for the weapon upgrades. The extra life won't mean much if we can't deal damage." I focus on "Nailbiter" and as soon as I accept, my weapon transforms. Long nails jut through the tip of the bat, making it a destructive force.

"Nice, now I have two yo-yos." Aleesia flicks both wrists and a yo-yo dangles from each.

"What about you, Dean?" I ask.

"I got bigger pellets for my slingshot. They deal double damage." He grins.

I buy two turkeys and spend the rest of my coins on sodas. It's more likely I'll need to top my health off gradually than refill it all at once.

Once we've spent all our coins, we step into the next level.

There's a loud screech, and the fence on the far end bursts off of its hinges. A red truck rams through, with two men standing in the bed of the truck. One swings a chain and the other holds a Molotov cocktail in his hand.

They zoom up and down the street before spinning out in the middle of the road. The man holding the Molotov cocktail tosses it in our direction. It explodes on the pavement in front of us and a wall of flame erupts. It lasts for five seconds before fading away.

The man raises a fist at us. "You may have made it past the lackeys, but good luck getting past us."

The dialogue is nothing to write home about, but I guess some people enjoy this more classic adventure.

Tires screech and the truck comes barreling down the street. The other man swings his chain in a circle on the left side of the truck. I'm not quick enough to move and it hits me in the shoulder, taking out a quarter of my health.

Dean shoots the truck with his slingshot, and its health bar drops a smidge. "I think we have to destroy the truck, and then we fight the thugs."

I chug one of the orange sodas to replenish my health just as another Molotov cocktail explodes behind us. The truck makes another loop, but the fire wall blocks our retreat. I smash the truck with my bat at the same time as the chain hits me. Aleesia and Dean are able to get in a hit as well, and we come out slightly ahead on the encounter. Even so, the truck has way more health than we do, and I don't know if we have enough items to outlast them.

"Try to hit the Molotov as he throws it next time." If we can disrupt it, then it'll at least give us enough room to dodge the chain when the truck drives by.

The thug winds up, and Dean lets his pellet fly. It hits the Molotov just as it releases. Instead of vanishing, the Molotov explodes in the back of the truck, setting both thugs on fire. Unable to escape, they die in the flames.

"Nice!" Aleesia runs toward the burning truck.

"Wait!" I shout, but it's too late.

Even though we took out the two thugs, the driver is still alive. He floors the gas and hits Aleesia square on. She loses half her health from the hit.

"Go back and heal," I order. "Dean, let's finish this."

He shoots pellet after pellet, slowly dropping the truck's health. The next time it comes barreling by, I get in a good hit with my bat. Without the two thugs in the back, we have no problem avoiding being hit. After healing, Aleesia is back in the fight, hitting the truck with double yo-yos as it passes by.

Without the two passengers, there is little the driver can do other than attempting to run us over. We're nimble enough to avoid him as we constantly attack any chance we get.

When the health bar reaches zero, the truck bursts into flame and the next level opens up.

"Check this out!" Dean points at three hearts that hover where the truck once stood. "An extra life."

We each take an extra life, and a small heart appears in the top of my vision next to my gold coins.

The next level is easy enough. There are more thugs,

and the back line has ranged attackers throwing Molotov cocktails, but our newly-upgraded weapons and a little strategy have us turning down a new street in no time.

The town hall where the mayor is being held hostage is only a few blocks away. The top of the dome shines brightly over the surrounding buildings.

We pass a street filled with chain-whipping thugs on motorcycles. I almost die due to being in the center of the road as two pass by on each side, but Aleesia and Dean take them out before they make another loop. We also have difficulty on another level where ranged attackers hide behind barricades. Some artful dodging allows us to flank them and pass through. Finally, we arrive at the town hall.

Women line the steps, each one holding a rock. More women than we have faced at any level. They easily outnumber us four to one.

The door to the town hall opens and two men step out, one is bound with rope. The other wears all black and has slicked black hair.

"Good job making it all the way to town hall, but you'll never make it up the stairs." The comically-evil villain holds the mayor by the arm. "Finish them, ladies."

I almost laugh at how absurd this situation is but when I glance at Dean, he's all smiles as he aims his slingshot.

The ladies stand four wide and three deep, blocking the stairs. In unison, they each toss their rocks at us. We hit the first wave of rocks, minus one that catches me in the shoulder. But then two more waves pummel us before we have time to react.

"This isn't good." Aleesia looks at me with wide eyes. "Any idea how we are getting past this?"

I don't have a clue. There has to be a strategy, but

there's so much to dodge and not nearly enough space. Before I have time to answer, they are already throwing more rocks.

The rocks are hurling toward us when an idea pops into my head. "Get behind me."

Aleesia and Dean do as I say. I hit the first rock, Aleesia hits the second, and Dean finishes off the third. The other projectiles go soaring by on both sides of us where they once stood.

"Nice!" Dean shouts, but there's already another wave on the way.

I don't know if it's me, or if they are throwing faster and faster. This time, all the rocks are aimed at the center, funneling toward us in a cone. The women are tossing the rocks at wherever we are standing when they release them. We split to two sides, and they all go sailing by.

The next round comes even faster, targeting both sides of the street. Before these rocks have even hit, they're already throwing the next round. We hit what we can, but there are just too many.

We try to form a line again, but the rocks are coming too fast. We block one rock each, but two more hit us before we can block another. Dean runs and several rocks that should have hit go sailing by. While he's facing the sides of the level, his avatar is paper thin. It gives me an idea, but my vision flashes red as I'm hit again. I'm hit several more times before I hear a loud "wonk-wonk" as my health drops to zero and my arms dissipate into pixels.

The heart in the top of my vision disappears, and I find myself at the entrance to town hall once again. Aleesia joins me a few seconds later, followed by Dean. He takes a step forward, eager to get back to the action, but I stop him.

"This is our last life. We need a plan if we're going to win this."

"What do you have in mind?" Dean asks.

"I noticed something right before we died. When you turned sideways, most of the rocks missed you."

"Yeah, well, they still got me in the end, didn't they?" He frowns.

Aleesia's eyes light up. "But if we used that tactic from the start, then maybe we could get to the stairs before they are throwing so fast."

I tap the side of my head. "Exactly. Here's what I'm thinking." I tell them my plan, and then we step into the final stage once again.

The terrorist and mayor appear at the top of the steps. He gives his stupid speech, and then we square off.

"Ready?" I ask, hopeful that this works, because we don't have any more lives.

"Ready," they say in unison.

The first rocks soar toward us. We step aside and turn sideways at the last moment, and they all go flying past. We quickly face toward the stairs again and run as far as we can before the women toss their next wave. We make it halfway to the stairs before turning sideways and dodging the next wave.

The women ready their rocks faster, but we're already on the stairs. We each take out one of ladies on the first row. Two rocks hit me, turning my vision red, but I stick to the plan. We move up the stairs, eliminating the next row, and I take another rock to the face. Each of our health bars drop again, but we take out three more enemies.

Only three remain, making it much easier to dodge

their final attempt before sending them to the pixel underworld.

A helicopter roars to life behind the building, and as it takes to the air, the terrorist waves his fist in our direction. "This isn't the last you've seen of me. You may have won the day, but Greendale will be mine."

Phase 1- Complete

The alert flashes across my vision just as the mayor stumbles out of the building with his hands still bound.

"Thank you for your service to the great city of Greendale. I fear that the terrorists will return, but for today, the city is safe. Now, I must free the others." The mayor disappears back inside the building.

A second prompt flashes across my vision.

Phase 2- Begin?

"As much fun as that sounds, we need to get Dean home in time for dinner." I turn toward my apprentice. "New world tomorrow?"

He grins from ear to ear. "I can't wait."

Dean logs out, leaving Aleesia and I standing alone on the stairs.

"That was fun." She smiles.

Even her two-dimensional smile disarms me.

I take her hand in mine. In spite of the physics of this world, I can still feel the pressure of her hand against mine.

"I'm nervous," I confess.

"Why?"

"It's not life or death like it was with Buzz's mom, but I don't want to let Dean down. The last thing he needs is more disappointment." Not to mention the people I could help with the charity donation.

She squeezes my hand. "You can't put that kind of

pressure on yourself, Esil. Enjoy the experience. Let Dean enjoy it. Everything else will fall into place."

"I hope you're right. Will you join us tomorrow?"

She shakes her head. "I wish I could, but we're about to be incredibly busy in the lab. Besides, it'll be good for you to do this on your own. Learn to work together. You'll be all you have when the tournament starts."

She's right. Pretty soon, it'll be me and Dean versus the world.

CHAPTER TWELVE

"What's your goal?" I ask Dean.

He pulls down the black cowl covering his face. "What do you mean?"

The moonlight gives his face a silver glow as we rest on the bank of a tranquil pond. We're both ninjas, deadly assassins who just completed a mission taking out a powerful businessman responsible for the deaths of a member of our clan's family.

"With the tournament. What are you hoping to get out of it?"

He looks at me with a confused expression. "A scholarship. A chance at a better life."

I decide to push him a little harder. If he's going to give this his all, especially when things get difficult, then he needs to know why he's doing it.

"Why though? What do you want to do with the scholarship?"

He sits in silence for a moment before answering. A frog leaps into the pond with a splash.

"I want to create games. To do that, I need to get my foot in the door."

Now we're getting somewhere. For the past few weeks, we've traveled from world to world in an attempt to experience as many different game worlds and play styles as possible. We've mostly avoided talk of the tournament, though, because it's all speculation at this point. I know it will incorporate full-immersion, but aside from that, we don't have much to go on.

"Why do you want to create games, Dean?"

He frowns and turns away. "Why do you want to know so much?"

I can tell I've struck a nerve. It's not easy for someone like him, like me, to open up about their dreams. He's probably never even said them aloud out of fear that they might disappear into the ether.

I decide to let it go. "I'm sorry. You want to create games. That's enough of a reason."

"I just—" He sighs. "I just want something that is mine. Something that I have control over."

I know exactly what he means. Growing up in an orphanage, nothing is truly our own. Only the thoughts inside our heads.

I put my arm around his shoulder. "Tell me about this world you want to create."

His lips curl at the edges. "Well, it'll be set in ancient —"

He lets out a grunt as a shuriken hits his shoulder. There are whispers in the shadows just before a gleam of silver flashes in our direction.

Dammit! I knew we shouldn't have rested so soon. I pull Dean aside, and the second ninja star skips across the pond.

"They've tracked us down. We need to move."

Dean pulls up his cowl, and I pry free the weapon buried in his back. We both activate Shadow Step and moved in a shadowy blur into the bushes.

We're concealed for the moment. I listen for signs of movement, but all I hear are rustling branches.

"How many are there?" Dean whispers.

"I don't know. One, maybe two. If there were more, I'm pretty sure we'd be dead."

"Kaze!" someone shouts from the darkness.

I know what's coming next, so I channel my ki into my forearm. I say the Japanese word "shīrudo," and a translucent shield forms in front of my arm. A gale of wind blasts through the bushes with enough force to rip the leaves from the branches. My shield holds, blocking the damage, but we're sitting in plain view of our assailants, surrounded by skeletal bushes.

Dean curses under his breath. We need to move, and quick. Right now, we're sitting ducks.

Two shuriken cut through the darkness toward Dean and I. I activate Smokescreen and then Shadow Step again, bringing my ki reserves down to half as I search for an advantage. The smoke conceals us for a moment as Dean and I split up. While still in shadow form, I scale the wall of a nearby building and attempt to flank our attackers.

I spot one standing on his tiptoes, balanced on an outstretched tree branch as they throw another shuriken. Dean comes out of his shadow form in a nearby tree, but our attackers anticipate his move. The shuriken are already thrown before Dean reveals himself. One buries itself in Dean's neck and he falls to the ground.

"Dammit," I mumble under my breath.

Both ninjas turn their heads in my direction. If I'm

going to go out, I should at least go out in style. I burn through the last of my ki activating Shadow Step and then Doppelgänger. I have enough ki that three separate shadow versions of me spread through the night.

While my attackers follow the moving shadows, I stand still. Once I know their attention is gone. I launch myself at the nearest one. Mid-jump, I pull out my katana and bury it in the back of the ninja. His final words gurgle out of his mouth.

Without any ki, I can only rely on my own skill for what comes next. Unfortunately, it's not enough with the remaining ninja using his own Shadow Step, appearing behind me, and burying a dagger in my throat.

Blood stains my vision and a moment later, I find myself in the empty room where our quest first began. Moonlight glows from outside the sliding door, and a branch sways in the night breeze gently scratching the window.

I search for Dean and find him in a corner with his eyes glazed over.

"They got me too," I say.

A moment later, his eyes return to normal. "Check your messages! There's a tournament update!"

Greeting Esil!

We are happy to announce that you and your apprentice Dean Wilmington have been approved for the final five hundred contestants in the Pangea Online Pro-Am Tournament. With two-hundred and fifty champions and an equal number of wards competing for the top prize, this is truly the best Pangea has to offer.

We will be announcing the first stage of the tournament tomorrow morning, along with introductions to the competitors of past and future. Please be in your home portal with your apprentice at 10:00am for a brief interview. Highlights of your win in the tournament have already been gathered.

We look forward to your contribution to the tournament, and as always, never stop leveling!

-Pangea Online Developers

Wow! Five hundred people competing in the tournament. I honestly don't know what to expect. The second stage of the Developer's Tournament had one hundred people and it was insane. This sounds like it could be a bloodbath.

My pulse suddenly thunders in my ears. This is getting more real by the day.

"We're in!" Dean shouts, harboring none of my anxiety. He runs toward me, hand raised, and we high-five.

"We're in." I echo. I don't want to put a damper on his enthusiasm, but our chances of beating out four-hundred-and-ninety-eight other competitors are slim to none. "I hope you're ready for a wild ride."

"I can't wait!" He grins. "Just wait until the others see."

I take a deep breath. The whole world is about to be watching.

CHAPTER THIRTEEN

I have dinner with Buzz, Grayson, and Maria the night before the big reveal. I try one last time to pump them for information, but to no avail.

Buzz shoves a heaping mound of mashed potatoes in his mouth. "Bro, it's going to be awesome," he says between bites. "That's all you need to know."

"Grayson? Any last words from you?"

The fragile old man smiles. He has the same fiery eyes as his avatar, but his body is a lifetime away from the brawny pirate of Pangea. "We have been sworn to secrecy. But let's just say you'll have a fighting chance."

"Enough talk about the tournament," scolds Maria. "It'll be here before you know it. I suggest you get a good night's sleep, Esil. You don't want to have bags under your eyes for your big interview."

Despite my best intentions, I toss and turn for most of the night. I don't know why I'm so nervous. It's not like anyone's life is on the line, but I'm still riddled with anxiety. I finally decide to put my time to use and pull out my tablet. I go to the site for the tournament, hoping to learn a little bit about my fellow competitors. Just my luck, though, the contestant list hasn't been posted. I guess they're planning to make a huge event of tomorrow. I could go through the list of previous tournament winners, but over the past few years, there have been hundreds of tournaments across Pangea. None as popular as the Developer's Tournament, not until now.

Eventually, sleep wins out. It feels like I'm only out for a minute before a gentle ring wakes me as my alarm goes off.

I make sure to eat a hearty breakfast, not knowing how long the introductions will take. By the time I log into my home portal, Dean is already waiting outside.

I buzz him in, and Fenrir immediately pounces on him, licking his face and disheveling his already-messy black hair.

"How long have you been waiting?" I ask.

Dean crawls to his feet and attempts to slick his hair down. "I didn't want to be late."

I can't help but laugh. I still remember the excitement of the Developer's Tournament. Even though I was doing it for Buzz and his mom, it was still a dream come true. I'm sure Dean feels the same way.

"Have a seat. We still have a few minutes before things kick off."

I tap a button on the wall and a giant screen descends from the ceiling, taking up nearly half the wall in front of the sofa. I tune into the official Pangea Online stream, where two reporters discuss the upcoming tournament.

A man in a blue suit with neatly-parted hair stares into the camera. "We're only a few minutes away from the start of the first ever Pro-Am Tournament. No one knows what awaits the challengers, but it's sure to be exciting."

"Exciting is an understatement," his co-anchor chimes in, a woman with a towering afro wearing a high-necked red dress. "This will be the best of the best competing alongside the newest of the new. I can't wait to see how this all unfolds."

A timer at the top of the screen counts down, currently at three minutes and twenty-one seconds. Three minutes until playtime is over and we live and breathe this tournament for the next few weeks.

When the timer hits zero, the screen goes black. A tiny pinprick of white forms in the center of the screen. It slowly expands, filling with greens and blues until it forms a planet with one giant landmass surrounded by deep blue oceans.

The landmass splits into several continents and they spread around the planet. Mountains rise, deserts and lakes form, and then the planet expands again, doubling in size before it breaks apart into hundreds of shards, each one reflecting images of the many worlds of Pangea Online. Warriors fight, spaceships race, kingdoms battle one another in open fields.

The shards continue to spread until they take up the entirety of the screen. Then, in a flash, they all retract into a tiny white dot once again. After a moment, it fades into the darkness. There's a shimmer as words begin to form in the darkness, dark gray then slowly brightening until they are silver.

Pangea Online

The World is Yours

The words fade, and hundreds of rectangles form across the screen, each one filled with videos playing simultaneously. A flash of green catches my eye and I notice one of them is a clip of me from the Developer's Tournament. I'm standing next to Aleesia as a giant tornado of fire rips through Ryken. Each clip must be from a tournament winner.

A speeding motorcycle overtakes another at the last second before crossing the finish line. A tennis champion lifts a trophy. A woman wearing a jetpack holds a ray gun in one hand and tosses a ball at a large net hundreds of feet off the ground. A lone minotaur stands atop a hill surrounded by the bodies of his enemies.

This time, when the screen changes, Benjamin smiles at the camera. He is as polished as ever, wearing a black suit and not a strand of hair out of place.

"Hello, I am Benjamin, President of Pangea Online, and welcome to the first ever Pro-Am Tournament. If you looked closely, you may have noticed some of the winners of past tournaments in the intro clip. No need to fear though, you'll be introduced to all of our two-hundred and fifty champions over the course of the day, along with their apprentices. The apprentices will be competing for a chance at an internship at Pangea Online Headquarters. But it wouldn't be fair to leave out the champions, now would it?" Benjamin winks at the camera. "The pro who takes home the trophy will be winning a donation of one hundred thousand to the charity of their choice. Now, without further ado, let's send you over to Nancy, head of Pangea's tournament division. She'll be introducing you to our contestants, starting in alphabetical order with Annabelle Akron and her apprentice Kirsten Hoffman."

I take a deep breath. If they are going in alphabetical order, then we should be up soon.

Just as I suspect, I receive a notification telling me to prepare ourselves, because we're up next.

Benjamin vanishes and the screen splits in half. On one side is Nancy, who hosted my own tournament. She's a valkyrie, wearing shimmering silver armor. Her blond hair dangles from the sides of a winged helmet. I remember her riding a pegasus through the air before stage two of the tournament.

On the other screen, two women sit inside a room full of pink and neon green lights. Graffiti covers the wall behind them, depicting a crown and a dagger. The women could pass for sisters, and I'm not sure which is the champion. They both have black hair, pink skin, bangs that cover their eyes, and a face full of piercings.

Nancy smiles for the camera. "Annabelle won the most recent Brawl Busters tournament. Check out her amazing combo that took home the trophy."

We zoom in on a fighting arena in the center of lush forest. Annabelle wears black boots, tight jeans, and a leather jacket. She twirls a chain as she faces off against a woman in tights with legs so thick, they look like they could crush watermelons. Their health bars and ki bars are at the top of the screen, both HP bars nearly depleted for each fighter.

The woman in tights lunges for Annabelle, but she jumps at the last second, leaving the woman grasping at air. She flips over the woman's back and performs a leg sweep, knocking her on her back. The kick moves her ki bar to full and it pulses with energy. Annabelle leaps into the air and spreads her arms wide, a swarm of missiles shooting in from off screen.

"KO" flashes across the screen, and Annabelle raises her fist into the air in celebration.

"Quite the tactical performance, Annabelle. Do you have any words for the viewers at home?"

She looks into the camera, her face showing no trace of joy or excitement. "Kirsten and I are here to win. By any means necessary."

Dean laughs and looks at me. "This has got to be some sort of show for the cameras, right?"

I shrug. "You never know. For some of these people, they live and breathe these tournaments.

"...and next up, is Esil Allen and his apprentice Dean Wilmington."

While Nancy introduces me and goes over my highlights, I receive a request to join the video chat. The next thing I know, Dean and I are on the split-screen with Nancy.

She smiles at the camera. "Now, if this isn't a great story, I don't know what is. We all remember Esil's rise to fame during the Developer's Tournament, when it was revealed that he was in fact the son of deceased developer Howard Allen who had somehow found himself growing up in an orphanage in The Boxes. Esil has spent the past year working at Pangea Headquarters, but he never forgot where he came from. His apprentice is a young man by the name of Dean, an orphan at the very same group home where Esil grew up. So tell me, Esil, what made you want to partner up with someone from The Boxes for this tournament?"

There's something about the way she harps on and on about the orphanage and The Boxes that rubs me the wrong way. Like they're using my story, and now Dean's, for ratings. Well, if they're going to use us, then I'll make sure to use them too.

I don't smile when I answer. I look directly into the camera without blinking. "Because who else would?"

She stutters for a moment, caught off guard. "Whatever do you mean?"

"I had no intention of entering a public tournament ever again. Dean reached out to countless champions, asking for them to take a chance on him. Do you know how many even so much as offered to meet him? Zero. But here's the thing, Nancy. We're not just some sob story for people to rally behind. We're real people stuck in a place that most of you couldn't even dream of. Real people with dreams and talents and skills that this world could use. We could do so much more than mine and die while living in a metal box. Dean has ambition, and he has skills that some of these champions wish they had. So, you want to know why I partnered up with Dean? It's because I'll be damned if he doesn't get his chance."

I cut the feed, and half of the display goes black. I don't know why I'm so angry, but I start pacing across the room. Fenrir raises his head, watching me before letting it fall back to the floor.

Nancy looks stunned for a moment before regaining her composure. "Well, there you have it, folks. Esil Allen and his apprentice are sure to shake things up once again."

She introduces the next champion, a gnome who wields a battle-axe twice the size of his body, but I shut off the display and it retracts into the ceiling.

"Hey, I was watching that!" Dean objects. "And thanks for letting me speak."

I turn around, ready to snap. "You don't get it—"

Dean's death stare has me swallowing my words.

"I'm sorry. You're right. I've made a better life for myself, but it's still raw at times. It's like anytime we do anything worth notice, it's not about the act itself. It's about someone from The Boxes doing it. This was supposed to be your day, your tournament, and I made it about me. It was wrong of me to take away your moment to speak for yourself."

His face softens. "You know your little outburst is only going to have more people watching us, right?"

I sigh. "I suppose you're right."

"You might be a drama queen," Dean laughs, "but if it gets people to notice me, then maybe my only way out of The Boxes won't be by winning."

"But you're still gonna give it your all, right?"

He looks offended that I even asked. "What is it that Grayson said? That sometimes those of us in The Boxes only get one chance, if that. You think I'm gonna waste that because you don't know when to shut up?"

I gently shove him in the shoulder. "Easy there, I'm still your mentor."

"Glad to hear it. Now, do you mind if we watch some of the other challengers? I, for one, would like to know what we are up against."

I turn the display back on just as a vampire explodes into a swarm of bats. A bolt of lightning crashes into the spot where the vampire once stood, scorching the earth. A second later, the bats rush back together and the vampire forms once again, just in time to pull a sword stabbed in the earth. "Victor" flashes across the screen before it shifts back to Nancy.

"Quite a narrow victory for Lyle Hagan, but impressive ingenuity nonetheless."

Lyle's home portal mimics an ancient castle. Stone

walls surround him, lit by flickering candles and adorned with oil paints of him in various poses. His skin is a pasty white and his black hair is slicked back. He wears Victorian-era garb complete with ruffles and a tailcoat. When he smiles, his incisors jut down farther than the rest of his teeth.

Next to him stands a young woman wearing a red corset with silver clasps across the front. Her curly brunette hair drapes over her shoulders, and a silver dagger hangs from her waist. Her gaze is fixed as she stares at the camera.

I can't help but laugh at the notion of a vampire and a vampire hunter teaming up together.

"How did you decide to take on Aliya as your apprentice?" asks Nancy.

Lyle smirks at the camera before answering. His red pupils pulse in an eerie way. "I had a little tournament of my own. I invited anyone on Darkwood to travel to the Village of the Night. I offered to mentor the first eligible person to kill me. It took her a week, but Aliya here finally got the job done."

Over the next few hours, I learn about more champions than I ever cared to. Human is by far the most common race for avatars, but we see a fair amount of fantasy and sci-fi races, even a few robots and cyborgs.

Dean and I are still laughing at a rainbow-colored clown that managed to win a racing tournament driving a tiny car, and his apprentice, a pink unicorn centaur, when the next challenger is announced.

The camera pans over a vast valley that stretches before a castle. A dark cloud of smoke moves across the landscape, and a thunderous roar emanates from within. Several hundred yards away, an army stands in position outside of a medieval city. Blue banners wave in the wind. Rows of knights are positioned at the front, followed by those on foot. Drums of war compete against the oncoming thunderous cloud.

As the cloud of darkness travels toward the army like a sandstorm of death, it leaves a trail of decay in its wake. The green fields are left blackened and charred, as if every bit of life had been ripped from the soil.

The knights charge into battle, vanishing in the depths of the cloud. Amidst the crack of thunder, a buzzing fills the air. The soldiers press on, but some on the back lines turn and run.

As more and more soldiers rush into the darkness, it pulses with dark energy, growing in size.

The hair on my neck stands up as I realize what has happened. The gates to the kingdom are closed, preventing the turncoats' retreat, and the darkness swallows them as well.

The buzzing and crackling fades, and the cloud begins to disperse, revealing an undead army of thousands upon thousands. A chasm forms in the center, and a small speck of orange moves through. The camera zooms in, revealing a black horse with a fiery mane, tail, and hooves. A nightmare. Fire explodes from its nostrils as it neighs. Upon its back sits a behemoth of a man wearing heavy black armor. The ominous armor has skull pauldrons and a breastplate engraved with two skulls facing each other. A helm with two horns that curl around the side conceals the rider's face, but I would never forget this armor, not in a million years. Two orange eyes glow brightly beneath the helm. Skeletal fingers hold the reins in one hand and the other holds a broadsword that nearly touches the ground.

Dean sits on the edge of his seat, watching the action

unfold.

The image splits to one side of the screen as the castle gates open.

Nancy grins at the camera. "And there you have it folks, our next challenger needs no introduction, but he'll get one anyways. He's won more tournaments this year than any other challenger. And in the clip you just witnessed, Ryken became the first player to overtake the Valmar Kingdom without forging a single alliance. Here's Pangea's very own Ryken "The Black Death" Tanaka and his apprentice, Dawn Warren."

Ryken and his army of death fades away, replaced by the death knight sitting on a throne in his home portal. The throne is as black as night, carved from obsidian. A row of skulls with jeweled eyes top the backrest, the eyes glimmering in the light of the candle chandelier above.

I roll my eyes. Of course he has a throne. He fancies himself as the greatest player to ever grace Pangea.

Dawn sits at his feet, clad in black armor in the same style as her mentor. Hers is more ornately designed, with black roses on the pauldrons and two foxes facing one another on the breastplate. A helm with a thin slit in the eyes sits at her feet, a black feather protruding from the top. If not for the fact that we knew she was a woman, one could never tell by the armor alone.

They're a far cry from the cowboy clothing we last faced them in. I'm sure part of the reason for Ryken's success is the intimidation his look and class bring.

Ryken's eyes glow a menacing orange as he stares at the camera.

"Well, Ryken, you're one of the most popular streamers around and a favorite to win the tournament. Do you have anything to say to the people watching at home?"

He clenches his hand into a fist and leans forward. When he speaks, his voice is deep and cavernous, like it's bouncing off the walls of a cave. "Enjoy the show. We're here to win, and I will take out anyone who stands in our way."

"And what about you, Dawn? Any words for those watching?"

She smirks as her gaze finds the camera. "I prefer to let my actions do the talking."

"Gah, these two are annoying," Dean grumbles. "I hope I get a chance to shoot them all over again."

I can't help but laugh. For whatever reason, Ryken is a popular streamer, but he has a certain unlikable quality about him that I just can't get over. Is it sullied by our first encounter? Maybe. But truth be told, the guy is a bully and a giant dick.

Maybe his followers use him as some kind of wish-fulfillment fantasy as he travels from world to world, destroying everything in his path and winning tournaments, but with an attitude like that, I very much doubt they would like him if they actually met him.

As I stew on my disdain for Ryken, Nancy interviews the next challenger. Her home portal is filled with plants and tree limbs that stretch from one end of the portal to the other. Large jungle cats perch on its branches. A dark-skinned woman sits on one of the branches, gently stroking a large jaguar.

Dreadlocks drape down the side of her face, and she wears a very simple outfit of tan cloth. Golden arm bangles wrap around her biceps, but aside from that, she is very rustic and plain. Yet there is an intensity that burns in her eyes. An intensity that I've seen before.

"Wait!" I say to myself more than anything. "Is that

Talia?"

"Who?" asks Dean.

"I used to play Team Deathmatch with her on Space-world. And she helped Buzz with a quest that allowed him to upgrade his chicken farm. She always wore the advanced spacesuits back then. I never would have expected her home portal to look like this."

Dean squints as he examines her before shrugging.

On the other side of the jaguar, a shirtless young man with an afro looks uncomfortable as he stares at the camera. He fidgets with his thumbs, before fixing his gaze on his dangling feet.

"Talia Tate," Nancy begins. "I think I speak for everyone when I say this is not the portal I envisioned for the reigning champion of Spaceworld Solo Deathmatch."

She sits up straight and winks at the camera. "You know what they say, Nancy. You can't judge a book by its cover."

Nancy laughs. "Very true. Now tell us about your apprentice, Chadwick Tate."

Chadwick looks up once again, his eyes wide.

"Chadwick is my brother, if you couldn't tell by our last names. We aim to show the power of family pride to all of Pangea."

They both form their arms in an X and tap them twice against their chest. Chadwick suddenly looks a little more relaxed.

I turn to Dean while Nancy continues the interview. "This is good. We'll at least have one other friend to lean on during the early stages of the tournament."

He cocks an eyebrow. "You sure about that? I wouldn't trust anyone but my partner in a tournament like this."

I understand his hesitation, especially considering his

upbringing. "We wouldn't be here if I didn't trust people. Talia is a good friend. And she's one of the most honorable people I know."

"If you say so."

By the time the interviews are over, it's nearly 8pm. After watching Talia's interview, Dean and I played ping pong and foosball for most of the remainder. I hope I never have to sit through something so boring ever again.

After the last interview is completed, Nancy sends the broadcast back to Benjamin.

"There you have it, folks. The complete list of challengers in the Pro-Am Tournament. I hope you're as excited as I am to watch these titans compete against one another. As much fun as it was to get to know the competitors and newcomers, I'm sure you're dying to know about the stages. To keep the tournament as fair as possible, we've decided not to announce the stages ahead of time. Each stage will be revealed at the moment all five hundred players enter the portal." He pauses for a moment, letting the words sink in. "How's that for a game changer? What I can tell you is this—there will be three stages, and one of them will be unlike anything you have ever witnessed. As for the first stage, I see no need to wait a week for the action to start. Competitors, be in your home portal at eight a.m. tomorrow morning. All weapons, items, levels, and abilities will be stripped from your avatar upon entering the gameworld, so bring your wits and determination, for that is what you'll need to win."

He winks at the camera and the feed goes back to the Pangea Online reporters. They looked as shocked as I am. I don't think anyone expected the tournament to start a day after interviews. For something this big, usually there is at least a week of buildup.

"I don't think anyone saw that coming." The woman in the red dress turns to her co-anchor. "I've got a feeling this tournament will be full of surprises."

The man nods. "Sometimes we all want to eat our dessert first. And it looks like we'll be digging into it first thing in the morning. Stay tuned as we turn the broadcast over to our analysts as they reveal their favorites to win the tournament and dissect all of today's news only on the official Pangea Online stream. As for us, we'll be back here bright and early for the first stage of the Pro-Am Tournament. For Cynthia Blackstone, I'm Greg Orwin, it's time to level up."

I turn off the feed as it transitions to a table with four analysts. The last thing I need is to hear their thoughts and predictions.

"I hope you're ready, Dean. Because tomorrow will be unlike anything you've ever experienced."

His face is grave as he stares at me. "I'm as ready as I'll ever be. Let's show them what The Boxes are really made of."

"We will. Now go home and get some rest. I need you at your best tomorrow."

After Dean leaves, I sit on the couch to the sound of Fenrir's snoring. We have some stiff competition. The odds are definitely not in our favor, and I don't even want to know who the analysts have their money on. Probably Ryken. I can't let Dean down, though, so I'll be going at this with everything I've got.

I sound like Ryken as the thought crosses my mind, but two words stand at the forefront.

No mercy.

CHAPTER FOURTEEN

When I arrive home, I send a message to Buzz, Grayson, and Aleesia telling them not to worry about me, but I'll be muting all incoming messages for the night—for everyone except Dean, but I don't tell them that. If he needs me, I'll be there, but I want time to myself to get in the headspace for the tournament. I know the others will want to wish me well, but the last thing I need is encouragement.

I expected to have more time. For what, I'm not sure. Dean and I have spent weeks training on so many different worlds just to get a feel for what may come, but the truth is that we have no better idea than anyone else. Well, that's not entirely true. I have one advantage that others don't. I know that full-immersion is coming.

Will it be unveiled from the start or is going to be in a later level? Will the Broken Lands be a part of the tournament? If so, will Carter and the others be a part of it?

I lay down in my bed and stare at the ceiling. More questions than answers. The story of my life.

Closing my eyes, I try to quiet the voices in my head,

to silence the worries. If I'm feeling this stressed, I can only imagine how Dean is feeling. If he is stressed, he does a good job of hiding it. Maybe he's better suited for this tournament business than I ever was.

The dull ring of my alarm slowly amplifies, gently waking me. I eat, shower, and strap into my haptic suit. Fenrir greets me enthusiastically as I enter my portal and a few minutes later, Dean arrives.

My jaw hits the floor when he steps into my home portal. Instead of going home and getting rest, it looks like he spent the evening shopping for a new outfit. His cowboy outfit is gone, replaced by something resembling my own.

He wears a red tunic, hemmed with black. A golden axe is embroidered on each collar. A golden wolf buckle stands out prominently against his black belt. Black pants tie the whole thing together. His outfit is practically identical to the one I'm wearing, but in a different color.

He looks at me expectantly. "What do you think?"

My face flushes, and I'm suddenly aware of just how much this means to him. I could make a joke about how we look like a better combination than a warrior and a cowboy, but I don't want to downplay what he's done. "I think we look like a damn good team."

A grin spreads across his face. "Yeah, but we both know I wear it better."

"Ha, whatever you say, kid. Just know I'm the original."

Dean plays tug-of-war with Fenrir while we wait for instructions about the tournament. The giant wolf slings him around my portal like he weighs nothing.

A few minutes later, I receive a notification, detailing a special portal and the code to get in.

Dean and I go to the coordinates listed and input the code. We materialize inside of a massive white room.

You have entered The Vacuum. All abilities, levels, weapons, and items have been stripped of their power upon entering.

I open my inventory and sure enough, every item is grayed out and unusable. We all have our clothing, but any stats associated with them have also been removed.

Several hundred challengers are already here, and more materialize by the second.

Dean looks on in awe beside me. "This is a lot of people."

Standing so close together, the competition finally settles in. Many of the faces around us are just as awestruck as we are. Two gnomes get lost among the host of large bodies. A giant with a young boy perched on his shoulder has the best view around.

We have quite a road ahead of us.

Off to the right, Ryken and Dawn stand with their arms crossed. A skeleton walks up to Ryken, says something, and then abruptly takes a step back.

"Esil!" A hand grips me firmly on the arm and I turn to see Talia. Her brother stands sheepishly behind her. "I was surprised to see you show up in the interviews. I thought your tournament days were behind you."

I wrap my arm around her, giving her a half-hug. "So did I. But here we are." I glance around the crowd. "It's good to see a friendly face, though. I hardly recognized you in your new setup. Talia, this is Dean. Dean, Talia."

"Nice to meet you. This is my brother Chadwick." She spreads her arms wide, showcasing her tribal outfit. "You know I enjoy the spaceworlds, but in my free time, I like to get back to my roots. Maybe we can all keep an eye out for one another when the time comes."

To our left, a group of beast people have huddled around one another. A couple of minotaurs, a centaur, others with the heads of lions and tigers. Are they forming alliances already or admiring one another's avatars?

"I don't think you're the first person with that idea. We need—"

A gust of wind sweeps over the crowd as Nancy enters through a portal in the sky. Her pegasus flaps its massive wings as she hovers in the air above us. Her silver armor glimmers as it reflects the whiteness of our surroundings.

"Greetings, challengers, and welcome to the Pangea Online Pro-Am Tournament. I'm going to keep this short and simple. Your journey begins here. Complete stage one and you will move forward in the tournament. Fail, and your journey is over. In the end, only one team will be victorious. Good luck, challengers!"

She snaps her fingers and bodies begin to dissipate all around me. The next thing I know, everything is black.

CHAPTER FIFTEEN

There's blackness everywhere. I wait for my eyes to adjust, but it never happens. A faint beeping echoes in the distance. My feet are on solid ground, I can tell that much, but that is the only thing I know for certain. Extending my arms, I feel the space around me. My fingers graze a cloth-like material.

"AHHH!" someone yells.

The scream carries as something firm swats at my arm.

"Esil, is that you?" Dean's voice is higher-pitched than usual.

"Yeah, it's me." I breathe a sigh of relief. We're together, so this is clearly stage one of the tournament.

The ground shakes, and I wobble to find my balance in a world where I can't tell up from down. The space around us rumbles to life and dim lights flicker all around us. A pathway ignites beneath our feet in orange neon and a hatch suctions shut behind us.

It looks like we're inside some kind of spaceship. Panels and pipes run along the walls. Machinery hisses and grunts on the other side of the walls.

"Where are we?" Dean asks, his face bathed in an orange glow. His new clothing has been replaced by a gray unitard and matching gray boots.

I'm wearing the same thing.

In answer to his question, a prompt appears in my vision. Digital neon letters hover in the air before me.

In the year 2525, while passing through an interdimensional wormhole, the megatransport ship CS Lancaster *disappeared while on a supply run to the intergalactic front. While the weaponry and armor on board are vital to our efforts to hold our territories from foreign invaders, there is a greater threat upon the ship. A rare artifact which could prove disastrous if it falls into the wrong hands. For twenty-five years, its whereabouts have remained unknown.*

Until now.

The CS Lancaster *has appeared just outside of empire territory, emitting a distress signal. All attempts to contact the crew have failed. An extraction team was sent to investigate and recover this valuable artifact. Upon entering the spaceship, the alpha team discovered that the ship had been overtaken by beings from foreign dimensions. Their attempts to make it to the control room failed.*

Your research vessel has been commandeered for the good of the empire. While reinforcements have been sent, it will take days for them to reach your location. We must not allow the CS Lancaster *to fall into enemy hands! You must take the control room at all costs, clearing the ship of any foreign inhabitants that stand between you and your goal. The fate of the empire depends on it.*

Your team has docked at the lowest level up the ship. In panel A75, you will find an extraction kit hidden away for extreme circumstances. Equip the kit and fight your way to the control room, gathering weaponry and armor as you do so, and bring the CS Lancaster home.

"Sounds like a classic tower climb to me." I turn to Dean. "We fight our way through each level, getting better gear as we go along. If we reach the control room, we're on to the next round."

Dean looks down the hallway. "Do you think the others are here? Or are we each playing our own version?"

"I have no idea. In the Developer's Tournament, we each had our own first stage, but then we were all together in the rest. This ship could be the size of a small city for all we know, so I guess we're just going to have to find out."

"Then we better get moving." He takes off down the hallway.

The grates beneath our feet clink with each step, sending ominous echoes down the empty tunnel. The dim lighting and winding corridor does little to put me at ease.

Each panel we pass is labeled with faded paint. A27. A49. A67. A75. Bingo.

Dean opens the panel. A tray slides out topped with two black boxes. Two latches run along the sides of each box. We each take one and sit in on the floor in front of us.

Out of curiosity, I open panel A74 to see if there are other hidden items, but it's filled with breakers and wiring.

"Let's see what we're working with." I return to the box, flipping the latch and opening the lid.

There's a slight hiss as the interior of the box rises and then expands. On each side, there's a silver helmet with a mirrored faceguard. In the center, two gleaming white chest plates reflect the dim light. Beneath them sits a badge with a barcode. I assume that's how we're making our way through this ship.

Dean's box is much smaller. Inside, there is a futuristic pistol, an item that looks like the hilt of a sword, and two small metallic orbs.

He picks up the pistol and it whirs to life. A glowing streak of light runs down the side of the barrel. "Well? Are you gonna stare at it all day or are we going to try and win this thing?"

The entire thing is sleek and polished. If I had to guess, it's some kind of energy weapon.

I put on one of the helmets. It fits snugly to my head and an augmented reality overlay pops up on the inside of the faceguard. A health bar appears over Dean and when I look at his weapon, stats appear in digital green letters.

Weapon. *Plasma Pistol.*

The sword hilt turns out to be a plasma sword. It feels natural in my hand, and when I activate it, a beam of hot white energy shoots out about two and a half feet long.

"Badass!" Dean's eyes light up as I slash the sword in front of me.

I can toggle the blade on and off as needed. There's also a detailed reading of my own health on the right side of the faceguard, displaying a map of my body segmented into different regions. Currently, they are all green, but I expect that it will change if I'm injured.

The two orbs are plasma grenades.

I pick up the chest plate and press it to my body, it opens at the edges and strips of kevlar-like material wrap around my back and sides.

Armor. *Flex-armor. Level 1.*

I focus back on the badges.

Key card. *Technician. Level 4 access.*

Interesting. Does that mean we'll have to find other key cards as we go along?

Dean follows my lead, putting on the helmet and then the armor. He picks up a plasma grenade and surprisingly, it sticks to his chest plate like a magnet. I test it out my own armor with my sword and it clings just the same. Not a bad place to store items in a pinch.

"Are you cool taking the pistol?" I remove the sword and feel its weight against my palm. "Your aim is better than mine."

He pries the weapon from his chest and spins it around his finger. "Is that even a question?" He squeezes the trigger gently and the strip of light glows brighter as it charges for a pulse shot. "I've seen you play. It's like watching a barbarian, the way you charge into battle. The sword will suit you just fine."

"Alright, alright." I roll my eyes. "Let's get this show on the road."

With our weapons at the ready, we make our way down the empty corridor until we come to a door. Dean reaches up to scan his badge, but I stop him.

"Wait a second. We need a plan first. We don't even know where we are going."

"Maybe we can find a map somewhere."

"Wait, that's a great idea." I play around with the AR overlay on my helmet. There are options for notifications, appearance, voice commands, and much more. I could spend a lot of time setting it up to my exact specifications, but we don't have time for that. We just need it to do the minimum to get us to the control room. After some trial and error, I pull up a map of the ship. "Go to your settings on the helmet. I think we just hit the jackpot."

A blue hologram of a giant spaceship hovers in front of

me. It's shaped like a giant block with rounded edges. A half-dozen massive thrusters protrude from the rear, surrounded by an equal number of smaller thrusters. More run down the sides, top, and bottom of the cargo ship.

I reach out and touch the hologram. It spins with the movement of my fingers. When I push them together, it zooms in, and when I pull them apart, it zooms back out. A tiny red dot shows my location on the bottom. As I zoom in on the holographic blueprint, I'm able to see numerous cargo bays, hundreds of floors, tunnels, and rooms. This ship is bigger than I ever imagined.

Dean moves his hands back and forth as he examines the map. "How are we supposed to get through all of this? If we take our time, it could take days to fight our way to the top."

I enable voice control on my helmet so that whenever I touch the side of the helmet, it responds to my voice. "Search for control room." A section of the ship near the upper front glows yellow. "Display the quickest route to the control room." A zig-zag line forms from our location to the control room.

Add route to display? pops up in my vision. I accept and a highlight forms along the floor leading from where I'm standing to the door.

"Alright, scan the badge."

Dean swipes it, and the door opens with a hissing sound. My eyes adjust as we step out into a brightly-lit hallway.

Where the one we came from was some kind of maintenance shaft, this one is clearly for transport. It's wide enough to fit a vehicle and several lifts are parked to the side. Lights flash along the walls, but there is no sign of life.

I take an instinctive step back when a loud screech exits a vent overhead. Heavy thumps echo, and the metal sags as something crawls down the shaft.

"What the heck was that?" Dean stares at the vent.

"No idea, but it didn't sound friendly. Let's get moving."

We follow the display route from the helmet as it guides us down the hallway. After we pass through two gateways, I begin to wonder if we're going to face any obstacles. That thought comes to a halt when Dean scans us through the third gateway.

The gate slides open, but the passage is blocked. A thick wall of a golden translucent substance distorts the area beyond. A skeleton floats inside the outer edge of the substance. My helmet beeps as it analyzes the substance.

Foreign Lifeform. *Slime. Slow, deadly, and unintelligent. Slimes absorb the life force of any living creature trapped within its gelatinous confines.*

If these are anything like the slimes I've encountered in other worlds, then they are slow but dangerous. While they are easy to evade, getting caught inside one is almost certain death. The floating skeleton is reminder enough not to underestimate the slime.

Considering it's blocking the entire entrance, we need to find a way through or around. Ripples travel through the slime as it wobbles, making the lights on the other side bulge and shrink with the movement.

"How are we getting through?" asks Dean.

"I don't know, but the path leads through here and we don't know that there won't be something equally as dangerous if we try to detour. Maybe we can try to lure it toward us."

"Or..." Dean raises his plasma pistol and fires a shot at the slime.

The white beam pierces through the slime, turning the translucent yellow a deep brown and charring it black at the edges. Steam pours from the hole as it slowly closes before returning to a calm amber.

Dean shrugs. "It was worth a shot."

"Wait, it wasn't a bad idea." The way the slime charred at the edges, if the beam was wider it might stay open for longer. "Try to hit it with the pulse blast."

He holds his finger on the trigger and the strip of light down the side of the pistol glows brighter. Once the brightness peaks, he pulls the trigger and a blast much larger than the previous one shoots out.

Instead of being a single beam, this one is shaped like a ball. It tears through the slime, leaving a hole the size of my head in its wake. The slime turns dark brown once again, this time taking longer to regenerate to its normal state.

"Hmmm. If we could make a hole big enough, we could probably sneak through." I equip my plasma sword and head toward the wall of slime.

I'm unable to tell if there is more slime beyond this construct or if it has all migrated to the gate. I activate my plasma sword and a beam of energy flares to life.

The slime stands tall as I move several feet away from it. It continues to wobble but doesn't move toward me. Slimes are not intelligent creatures, but that doesn't mean they can't be deadly. Water can be deadly to someone who can't swim.

As I raise my sword, the slime blisters at the heat, turning an angry brown. I stab the sword into the slime and it sizzles, charring the gooey creature as it melts its gelatinous body. I attempt to carve a makeshift tunnel when Dean's panicked voice startles me.

"Run! It's falling."

I look up just in time to witness the top of the slime peeling away from the ceiling. It arches like a wave about to crash all around me. I stow my sword and sprint toward Dean.

My haptic suit jars my back as the slime crashes into me. Luckily, only the topmost edge hits me, so instead of making friends with the skeleton inside, I'm knocked forward and fall on my face. I crawl to my feet and turn to see a two-foot-tall blob of slime blocking the entirety of the tunnel. There's no way we're making it through this way.

The slime creeps toward us an inch at a time.

I shake my head at our misfortune. "Looks like we're going to need to find an alternate route."

"Wait, I think I know a way we can get through here." Dean flashes me a mischievous grin.

"And how's that?" I ask, raising one of my eyebrows.

He pulls the plasma grenade attached to his chest plate and holds it up.

"We might need those later," I counter.

"Yeah, we *might*. But we actually need one now." He spins the gleaming grenade in his palm.

"Alright, this is your show. If you want to use it now, I support you." I'm here to help Dean and guide him to the best of my ability, but I've decided that he will always get the final say. His future is the one on the line, after all.

He taps the grenade with his index finger, and it begins to glow while also emitting a faint beeping sound. Dean holds on to it for a second and then tosses it into the center of the slime. The grenade bounces on the gelatinous body before being absorbed inside.

I turn my head away, expecting a splattering of exploded slime guts to rain down upon us, but the explosion is soft. There's a wave of heat, and when I turn back around, there are only a few remnants of slime that slowly crawl across the floor toward one another. Dean quickly disposes of them with his plasma pistol.

"Nice job!" I slap him on the back. He really has a knack for innovative solutions.

With our path cleared, I follow the guided route into the next section of tunnel. We find more slimes in the following tunnel, but they are spread out and easy to eliminate. Several tunnels diverge up ahead, but we stay true to the route and follow a ramp that leads up to the next level.

At the top of the ramp, my headset guides us through a door and into a storage area. Hundreds of metal crates fill the dimly-lit room.

"What do you think is inside?" asks Dean.

My first instinct is to tell him it doesn't matter, but then I remember the prompt. *Fight your way to the control room, gathering weaponry and armor as you do so.*

"Let's take a look."

It takes both of us to pry the lid off the crate, but it's a good thing we do. As we move from one crate to another, they are filled with weapons, armor, and attachments.

"Now, this is cool." He lifts a weapon that looks like a crab claw. There's a grip in the center, and two tiny nodules facing one another at the tip of each claw. When his fingers wrap around the grip, the weapon comes to life and a streak of plasma energy connects the two nodes.

Weapon. *Plasma Rifle.*

I search through the contents of the crate, finding

some extended energy mags, a sniper rifle, and an armor upgrade that adds a plate on our backs to attach more items.

We both switch out our armor and open a few more crates. In the end, we find several more plasma grenades, pulse grenades, and a plasma shotgun.

I go for a plasma rifle, which can work at close to medium distance, and elect to keep the plasma sword. Dean discards his pistol and takes the plasma rifle and the plasma sniper rifle. I'm not sure how useful a sniper rifle will be on the ship, but it's massive, so there is no telling. We cover the rest of the open space on our armor with as many grenades as we can carry.

"Not a bad haul." I attach the last pulse grenade to my chest plate, excited to use them later. Each one pulls nearby inanimate objects toward its center before detonating. "Ready to see what's up next."

Dean charges his weapon for a moment, watching the plasma dance between the nodes. "Let's do it."

Our route leads out of the storage room and into another tunnel. Dean scans his badge, and as soon as we enter the tunnel, there's an odd clicking noise. I recognize the whir of a weapon being charged and push Dean back into the storage room just as the door closes. A beam of energy hits the crease between the two sides of the door and sparks jump through the other side.

I take Dean's badge and open the door again. The unsettling clicks continue to ring out from the other side. I try to peek around the edge to see what we're up against, but my head barely emerges before another shot sends sparks raining down.

"What is it?" Dean asks.

"I don't know. I can't get a good look."

"Lay down some cover fire, and I'll take a look."

I creep up to the door frame and extend my plasma rifle around the corner, firing off a stream of plasma. Dean pokes his head around like a gopher and retreats just as quickly before another barrage explodes against the door frame. He takes his badge back and closes the door again.

"What is it?" I ask.

His face is stark white, mirroring the kid behind the avatar. "Robots. Only, there is something off about them." His lips curl up like he's seen something disturbing.

"What do you mean? It can't be that bad."

"They're like spiders. They have these long metal legs that they are using to cling to the walls. And in the center, they're humanoid, but like a gaunt skeletal body, except it's all metal. Then there's a head...with glowing red eyes that they shoot lasers from." He shivers, rocking from side to side.

No wonder he's freaked out. I still remember the spiders from my days at the orphanage. Their glowing red eyes. At least it explains the clicking I heard.

I pat him on the shoulder. "It'll be okay. They aren't real. We just need to find a way to get past them and we'll be on to the next horrifying monster."

He laughs. "Right."

"How many did you see?"

He grimaces. "At least four."

"And they are all on the walls?"

"Three on the wall, one on the ceiling."

"Not the best odds, but we're well-stocked as long as we're in here. Is there anything we can use for cover in the tunnel?"

Dean frowns. "I'm not sure. Open the door and I'll take another look."

We're pressing our luck by constantly opening the door, but we need to know what we're working with. Not having windows makes these doors great for keeping items stored away but terrible for fighting our way through the ship. I take the badge and swipe it in front of the reader.

I fire a few rounds into the tunnel as Dean scopes out the landscape. He ducks back in, and I close the door as more sparks rain down.

He keeps his eyes focused on the door, as if it might spontaneously open at any moment. "There's not much. A few overturned crates and a transport cart. The good news is that the robot spiders don't seem to be moving any closer. They just kind of move around where they are."

"I don't know if I would trust that once we're out in the open, though." A shiver runs through me as I visualize being pinned to the ground beneath one of the gruesome creatures.

"What if we could lure them off the wall? All four of them at once."

"And how exactly do you plan to do that? It's not like we have any way of forcing them down."

He flashes me a grin. The one I've learned to mean he has something up his sleeve.

Dean pries a pulse grenade from his chest plate. "They aren't living creatures."

"I like the way you think." I prop my plasma rifle on the floor and dig through one of the crates until I find what I'm looking for. I toss Dean a plasma shotgun and take one for myself. "If we're smashing spiders, we need power over precision."

We go over the plan and once we're ready, I open the door. Dean activates two pulse grenades and tosses them into the tunnel. They glow a bright blue as they soar through the air.

Beams blast toward our location once again.

"Alright, get out and hold on tight," I order.

We rush through the door just as the pulse grenade activates and head for cover behind an overturned lift. An errant beam catches me in the shoulder before it's ripped off its trajectory. I catch a glimpse of the deformed robot spiders as they are pried from the ceiling, pulled by the gravitational force of the pulse grenade. It sucks them in like a vacuum. Sparks fly as lasers cut through pipes and wiring on the ceiling. There's a loud crash inside the storage room as crates are launched against the wall by the pull of the grenade.

Dean and I are just out of its range, though I can feel the grenade pulling the shotgun against my grip.

"Fire!" I shout, and we both pull the trigger.

A blast of plasma erupts from each of our shotguns, peppering the area with white energy where the spiders are pinned in place by the pull of the grenade. The spiders screech in defiance as their limbs are blown apart. Laser beams shoot out in random directions like some grotesque light show. I charge the blast and fire another one as the pulse grenade explodes, finishing off the spiders.

Metal legs and shrapnel litter the tunnel. Dean kicks one of the spider's metal skulls and it skids across the floor, the red eyes fading as its energy source depletes.

"Good job, Dean." I extend my fist to him and he returns the gesture. "That's the kind of thinking that will get us through this challenge."

He grins. "I'm just glad I didn't kill us both."

"No risk, no reward." I wink. "Now, let's finish up here and get moving."

Back inside the storage room, several crates are over-turned, spilling their contents against the wall from the pull of the grenade. If not for the wall preventing them from exploding with the grenade, we'd probably be space dust right about now.

We exchange our shotguns for plasma rifles. While the shotguns came in handy against the robot spiders, the plasma rifles are more practical going forward. They offer better fire rate and more utility. I still think Dean should take the shotgun over the sniper rifle, but it's his choice.

Our helmets guide us down the tunnel, through a dimly-lit stairwell, and down more tunnels. Aside from a handful of slimes, we go unmolested for a moment, though the rhythmic tapping of spider legs can be heard on the other side of doors, setting my hair on end. The occasional creature crumples the air ducts that wind like a maze throughout the ship. Each time, we hurry past, careful not to linger in the presence of what may be inside.

The tunnel ends at a large elevator shaft. According to the map of the ship, it's going to take us up five floors.

Dean scans the badge, and we both have our plasma rifles pointed at the elevator door as it opens. The elevator is empty, but its insides are coated with some kind of webbing. Thick ropes of gray material drape like curtains along the walls. It's almost like a giant cocoon that has been ripped open.

"I just hope it's not more spiders." Dean shakes his head, finally lowering his weapon.

"I second that." I fight back the shiver that threatens to weasel through my body.

Inside the elevator, the webbing is too strong to tear through with my hand, so I use my plasma sword to cut a hole so that we can access the interface. After scanning the card, a touch screen asks for our destination. I input the floor number, and we begin to rise.

The elevator groans as we slowly ascend. A large thirty-three flashes across the screen, and we come to a jerky halt.

Something lands on the roof of the elevator with a thud, and I instinctively press the screen to keep the doors closed.

We rock back and forth as whatever creature wreaks havoc overhead. The cables whine as we're jostled inside. Dean's eyes are panicked as he holds on to the webbing for stability. After a moment, the elevator quits rocking, and we sit in silence.

Dean and I both sigh at the same time. He must notice, too, because our eyes meet and he smiles. Even though we both know whatever creature looms above can't truly hurt us, the fear of the unknown is still very real. It calls to our primal instincts.

I reach for the control panel. "Time to find out what abomination is waiting for us on the other side."

Dean raises his weapon, and I press the button to open the door.

Before I even have a chance to raise my own weapon, a giant insect the size of a dog launches through the door. Dean blasts it and green ichor splashes on me, covering my faceguard in a thick layer of guts. I quickly close the door as the dying insect writhes on the floor, its abdomen split in half.

"Holy..." Deans words drift off.

The insect's mandible clenches open and closed before it finally quits moving. Six barbed legs curl up from its upside-down body. A thick black carapace with a green sheen is covered with barbs around the edges and a dangerous ridge running down the center of its back. Lacy transparent wings peek out from underneath the shell.

I kick the dead bug to the back of the elevator. "Before this thing flew in here, were you able to get a look outside?"

"Barely. I saw a lot of this webbing stuff. It might be some kind of nest."

"Great. We're stuck between a rock and a hard place. We could try to find another way, but based on what we've seen so far, we're screwed no matter where we go."

"So what do we do?" Dean crouches and examines our dead friend.

"We fight our way out and continue on the shortest route possible. At least we know we're not fighting more enemies than we have to." I don't like the thought of fighting our way through a nest of giant space insects, but at least we know what we're dealing with. "Get ready."

Dean raises his plasma rifle, his finger resting on the trigger. This time, when I scan the badge, I rush into position as the door slides open.

Dean was right, the hallway is filled with the same webbing type material. A buzz fills the space before us as dozens of winged and barbed beetles fly toward us. Our plasma rifles whir to life and beams of hot plasma rip into the swarm. Guts and hollow body parts explode around us, obscuring my vision as my visor is once again coated in a thick layer of green. We're ankle deep in exoskeleton when I realize there's no way we're making it out of here.

I close the door, but three insects manage to make it inside. Dean shoots them with pinpoint accuracy, and one is severed in half by the closing door. Its head falls to the ground, still clenching its pincers. Several thuds continue to beat against the door as insects crash against the outside.

I stomp the head of the severed insect before it pinches my boot. "This isn't going to work. There's too many of them."

I pull up a hologram of the ship and instruct my helmet to reroute us. The map shows a stairwell entrance from the floor below that should reconnect with our original route after bypassing a large section of the tunnel.

I press the icon, and we slowly descend. When we come to a stop, whatever creature that has set up shop on top of the elevator grows restless again, rocking us back and forth before settling down.

"What are we doing?" asks Dean.

"Hopefully finding a safer route. It seems like the smart option considering what's waiting upstairs."

He nods and raises his weapon, pointing it at the exit. I open the door. An empty hallway greets us, and we both visibly relax. The overhead lighting is dim and flickering, as if this section is running on backup power.

We exit the elevator cautiously. The hallway may be quiet, but there could be dangers all around us. There are no giant bugs and no killer robots, but something feels off. We turn a corner for the stairwell marked on the map.

Sparks jump out from an open panel in the wall. A body lies on the ground, long decayed, but it's evident from the gash in this person's clothing that they were attacked. The contents of a box of tools lay scattered around the corpse.

I crouch beside the body and roll it over. A hole runs from their back through their chest.

"Gored." I've seen enough blood and guts throughout

my time in Pangea that the wound doesn't bother me. The creature that caused it is another story.

Dean kneels beside me. "Whatever it was, it wasn't the bug creatures. This was done by some kind of horn or spear, not by a pincer."

"You're right. We should get out of here before it decides to come back."

Dean scans his badge to enter the stairwell, but the door doesn't open. "He must have been trying to repair it."

"Wait, try this." I grab the badge clipped to the repairman's chest. "Level-ten clearance."

Dean swipes the badge, but the door still doesn't open.

I take a look at the open panel. A couple of wires appear to have been severed. Thick gashes run through the metal door that covers the compartment. If we can use the tools to reconnect the wires, maybe we can fix the scanner and be on our way.

A shudder runs through me as I pry the rubber gloves from the corpse's hands. "Keep an eye out for anything coming down the hallway while I try to get this running."

Dean drops to one knee and focuses his attention down the hallway.

Trying not to think about where the gloves have been, I slip my hands inside. I don't know much about electrical repair, but this seems simple enough. Something ripped through the wires, so I need to put them back together.

The sparks are caused by two severed wires that are barely touching one another. I pry them back and the sparks stop. The overhead lights also quit flickering and go to full-backup power, which is much dimmer.

I search through the contents of the toolbox, finding a pair of pliers with insulated handles, a wire stripper, and a box of plastic connectors that I assume are for pairing the wires together. The wiring is mangled from whatever tore through it, so I use the wire stripper to remove enough of the insulation so that the metal ends can connect to one another.

Next, I take the two same-colored wires and press them together. The wiring sparks as they touch, and the lights flicker to life overhead. My rubber gloves protect me from any voltage they might produce. I use the pliers to twist the wires together and then place the connector over the exposed wiring.

Something crashes down the hallway, and Dean stiffens. The lights coming on must have disturbed whatever caused this mess.

"We've got company," he whispers as thunderous steps echo down the hallway.

I run the badge over the scanner, but the door doesn't open. "I need another minute to connect the second set of wires."

"Hurry up," Dean snaps. "I can't see it yet but it's coming."

I quickly strip the last two wires and press them together. As I'm twisting the wires, Dean has a sharp intake of breath.

"This is not good." He says it so low I'm not sure if he's talking to me or himself.

I take a quick glance down the hallway just in time to see a massive beast taking up the majority of the tunnel and running toward us. It has a metallic silver body and eyes as red as rubies. Massive hooves thunder against the floor. Its head rocks from side to side, a shimmering horn reminiscent of a rhinoceros swinging like a pendulum.

As soon as the wires are wrapped, I don't even think

about applying the connectors. I scan the badge and thank my lucky stars when the door opens.

"Inside, quick!" I pull Dean in behind me as I rush into the stairwell.

The door shuts moments before the space rhino smashes its horn into it, leaving a dent the size of my body in the metal. My pulse thunders in my ears as I take a step back and lean against the wall.

"Close call," I say between breaths. My fingers shake from the adrenaline pumping through my body. Funny how the excitement in my body outside translates in-game.

"And not a moment too soon." Dean grins. "That thing would have flattened us for sure."

The creature rams into the door again, startling Dean and leaving another giant dent.

We hurry up the stairwell as the thuds crash against the door below, echoing all around us. We pass exits on each level until we reach the floor marked on the map. There are doors to both sides. The one on the left empties into the web-infested corridor. The one to the right parallels it with several storage rooms and stairwells connecting the two. If we can make it down the hallway to the right, we can reconnect with our original route after bypassing the nest.

On full guard, we exit the door to the right. It's void of killer insects and stampeding rhinos. Empty carts litter the hallway. They aren't overturned or otherwise molested, just parked aimlessly. Even though it seems safe, I refuse to let my guard down. Dean and I keep our weapons raised as we hurry down the hallway, scanning entry into a storage unit.

Without waiting, Dean immediately starts opening the crates.

"Nice." He moves on the next one. "Nice!" He closes the lid and moves to another. "NICE! Esil, we just hit the motherload!"

"What are you talking about?" We've barely gone through any of our grenades and are well-kitted with the weapons we have now. I lift the lid and immediately see what he is talking about.

Weapon. *Plasma Minigun.*

Only two of the miniguns fit inside the crate. Long slate-gray cylinders poke out of what looks like a miniature jet engine. There's a handle on top and a trigger mechanism at the rear. The portable turret looks like it could wreak devastation on anything in its path.

Even though it's powerful, the weapon is way too cumbersome and would only be practical against an unintelligent horde.

The second crate only has one weapon inside. It's bigger than the minigun and has a base for mounting.

Weapon. *Plasma Turret.*

The turret is even better than the minigun for stationary fighting because it can turn on a swivel, and due to not having to carry the weight of the weapon, it can be more precise and easily maneuvered.

The final crate is filled with weapons no one would ever use on a spaceship.

Weapon. *Missile Launcher.*

Several long cylinders are packed to one side. Each one is mounted with a digital display for tracking enemy movement. Half a dozen rockets are placed vertically in foam. These are clearly designed for targeting aircraft or vehicles, not for fighting in close combat on a spaceship. One of these could probably rip a hole in the hull.

I close the lid and turn back to Dean, who has pulled

the turret base from the crate and is trying unsuccessfully to lift the turret itself.

"What do you have in mind?" I have an idea of what he's planning, but I want to let him formulate it himself before I offer any input. I reach into the crate and grab the other side of the turret, helping Dean mount it on the base.

"I think the turret is our answer to clearing the hallway." He checks the clamps on the base and moves the turret back and forth on the swivel. "If we position it in front of the door then we'll be able to rip through the swarm as they come in. One of us can stand behind and take out any stragglers that might slip through."

"What about the other weapons?"

He shakes his head. "The minigun is too bulky. If one of us got swarmed, then we'd be dead weight. With the turret, it's easy to abandon if we have to. And the rockets are just as likely to blow us up as they are the insects. What do you think?" He looks at me expectantly.

"Sounds like a mighty fine plan to me. So, who's taking the turret?"

He grins. "I really want to let this baby sing."

I laugh. "Go for it." I equip my plasma sword. "I'll handle anything that makes it past you."

We slide the turret to where it's positioned directly across from the door and move the rest of the crates against the far wall. It's about to be open season on anything that steps inside. Dean takes position behind the turret. One hand rests on the trigger and the other on a handle for aiming. A digital sight sits on top of the turret for advanced aiming.

"Are you ready?" I ask.

Dean nods, and I scan the badge. The door slides open

with a whoosh and for a moment there is nothing but silence. I activate the blade on my plasma sword and take my position to the right of Dean. I'm strictly support in this scenario. If anything makes it past the turret, I'll slice and dice it.

A faint buzz comes from down the hall, growing louder by the second. All of the insects must have been waiting outside of the elevator shaft expecting us to return.

Before they even enter the room, Dean already has the turret whirring to life. After a second, the turbine emits a bright glow and I'm forced to look away. As the turbine spins, it spits out beams of plasma in a cylindrical pattern. At full speed, the beams look like a continuous stream of glowing white energy.

The first insects to enter the doorframe are obliterated instantly. Flakes of shell flutter through the air like ash on a windy day.

The turret lets out a dull whine as it sprays plasma like a water hose. Dozens of insects die in a flash, vaporized by the steady beam. I'm sure that even if they wanted to turn away, the brightness of the plasma draws them in like moths to a flame.

One insect flops to the floor, its body severed in half by the turret. It crawls forward on its two remaining legs, pincers grasping. The tips of its wings were also incinerated, making it impossible to fly. I stab it in the head just as another half-incinerated beetle clanks against my helmet.

The turret rattles and Dean curses as the steady stream of plasma grinds to a halt. Beetles flood the enclosed room and I slash at everything within striking distance. The air is so dense with insects that I can't even see Dean among the chaos.

My plasma sword cuts through the bugs with ease, but there are so many that their severed body parts make it impossible to move without falling. Green ichor obscures my vision and the health readings inside my helmet flash orange and yellow along my exposed limbs. My haptic suit clenches around my arms and legs as pincers catch me in their violent grip.

The turret was a good plan, but we didn't anticipate it overheating. Dean can't be faring much better. I listen for his screams, but I can't hear anything over the scraping of carapaces and the fluttering of wings.

I struggle as my health readings continue to plummet, but I know it's useless. We didn't even make it through the first stage of the tournament. Dean is going to be so disappoint—

There's a loud crash of splintering wood and the familiar whir of a turret cannon. Beams of plasma speckle through the insectoid horde.

Drawn by the light, the beetles release me and surge toward its deadly embrace. I finish off the lingerers with my sword and slash at those hovering in the air nearby.

I crawl to the door and scan the badge, stopping the influx of beetles, though I'm sure there can't be many more outside. The floor is a slushy mixture of guts and shell, both crunchy and slippery at the same time. I take a moment to regain my composure and search for Dean among the chaos.

I'm unable to spot him, but I do find the source of the plasma beams. They shoot out of an exploded section in one of the crates.

Genius! He must have blown it apart from the inside.

Thirty seconds later and we've finished off the last of

the insects. When the whir of the minigun fades, it's eerily quiet.

My boots slosh with each step until I'm hovering over Dean. He breathes heavily, lying on his back with the minigun draped across his torso. He pushes it aside and I extend a hand to help him up.

"How'd you manage to pull this off?" I ask.

He slouches against the crate. "I panicked. I couldn't find my weapon. I tried to escape through the other door, but you had the badge." He shakes his head. "In that moment, I just wanted to be safe, so I climbed into one of the crates."

He frowns. I know that look. He's disappointed with himself in spite of it all.

I place my arm on his shoulder. "Hey, it doesn't matter how you ended up in there. It saved both our asses."

"Easy for you to say. You didn't run like a little kid. Everyone watching is going to see it."

I shake my head. "Don't sweat it. You ran. So what? If you decide you want to keep streaming after all of this, your viewers are going to see you make some big mistakes. But this isn't about them. This is about me and you. Sometimes you have to run so that you can live and fight another day. You want to know the truth? When I was buried under that mountain of creepy crawlies, I gave up hope. I thought we were out of the competition. I thought it was over. And then you saved us. Whether you planned to or not, you're the reason we're still in the tournament. Now, let's grab our gear and finish this thing."

He stares at me with a blank expression for a moment, then his mouth curls at the edges. "You're right. You might want to clean up a bit, though."

I look down at my body. My bodysuit is in shambles,

pieces of ripped cloth hang off me in ribbons. I'm covered in enough slime that I could probably slide on my stomach down the tunnel. The gray material is stained green and red as my blood mixes with the insects'. Dean has fared much better standing behind the turret and minigun.

I do my best to wipe the slime from my faceguard. "Gather your weapons. We need to finish off the last of the bugs on the other side, then we can get going."

We gear up and exit into the web-covered tunnel. The remaining insects are easy enough to finish off with our plasma rifles. The entire corridor gives me the creeps with the way the webbing drapes over everything like a sinister snowfall.

My helmet guides us down the tunnel and eventually, the webbing fades away. Creatures scramble in the vents as we pass underneath. A blob of slime blocks the entrance to a stairwell, but our plasma grenades clear the area with no resistance. We climb a few dozen floors before being led into a new tunnel.

This one is slimmer than the others, clearly not designed for transport. Sleek white walls stretch in perpetuity to both sides.

I stop in front of one of the many doors lining the corridor. "These look like rooms for the crew."

Each door has a scanner and a peephole. I attempt to enter one of the rooms, but I'm met with "Access Denied." Apparently, level-ten access isn't good enough to enter personal quarters.

"You think there's anyone inside?"

"Of the original crew? I doubt it. Otherwise, we wouldn't be here. Who knows what kind of creatures could be hidden within."

We're making our way down the corridor when something rams against one of the doors. The sound is so unexpected that I jump. A moment later, something smashes against the door to our right.

"That's our cue to get moving." I take off running down the corridor.

Dean follows closely at my heels. More rumblings thunder all around us as creatures wreak havoc on the other side of the doors.

Then a bone-chilling sound stops me in my tracks. A loud hiss lingers in the air as the doors behind us open simultaneously.

A large figure steps out into the hallway. A reptilian humanoid with slick green scales looks in our direction. It has a thick tail that touches the ground, black claws on the tips of its fingers, and a head reminiscent of a T-Rex. It flashes rows of dangerous teeth as it snarls.

As we stand frozen in shock, more of the creatures step into the corridor. Tongues lash out at the air as they taste our scent.

"Run!" I yell.

I pry a plasma grenade from my vest, activate it, and toss it over my shoulder. I glance back just in time to see it explode, knocking several of our reptilian pursuers against the wall.

"Toss everything you've got behind us. We can't stop and fight, but we can slow them down." I activate another grenade and let it fly.

"On it!" There are faint beeps each time Dean activates a grenade.

Every few seconds, an explosion rumbles behind us. I don't dare to look, only focused on the map before us. If we can make it to the end of the corridor, there's a stairwell waiting for us.

Growling and hissing mixes with the sounds of explosions and bodies hurled against the pristine white walls. Dean's feet patter behind me. The beeping of plasma grenades speeding up just before they explode might be the final note to a chaotic symphony if not for the thunderous pulse pounding inside my ears.

A dark figure emerges into the tunnel a hundred yards in front of us. A scaled version of a wolf with barbs running down its spine lowers its shoulders as if ready to pounce.

Please don't move, I pray silently to myself. The creature is far enough away that we'll be able to make it into the stairwell, but not if it attacks us.

The closer we get, the deeper the creature sinks into a pouncing position. Its shoulders rock back and forth as it watches us hungrily. I can sense an impending lunge.

We're a few yards from the stairwell entrance when the creature lunges. I activate my plasma sword in one hand and equip the badge with another.

The cat-wolf-reptile is mid-air when I drop to one knee. The green ichor from our battle with the beetles allows me to slide with surprising speed along the slick floor. I use my free hand to scan the entrance to the stairwell and extend my sword, ripping into the creature's body as I pass underneath. The creature collapses to the ground, and Dean makes it safely inside.

He stands in the doorframe with the door propped, waiting for me. I crawl to my feet and run to him, ready to unload my plasma rifle on the pursuing reptilians, but they swarm the dead creature, feasting on the easy prey.

The door closes with a clank, and I lean against the wall.

"Another close call." Dean squats and presses his head

to his knees. "This is way more intense than any of the training we've done."

"No, it's not." I shake my head. "We've battled aliens, escaped from dinosaurs, hell, we even fought a dragon. Not that it ended well. The only thing different is the pressure you're putting on yourself. This is still just a game."

"I know. I just—" He stands back up. "I just really want to win. I want to prove that I can be more than what I am."

"Hey." I step in front of him and my faceguard isn't more than an inch from his. "You are more than you think you are. Regardless of how this ends. Just take it one step at a time. I know it's easier said than done, but try to enjoy the experience. This is your first tournament, after all."

He takes a deep breath and then slowly releases. "Alright, one step at a time."

I can't tell if my words sink in or not, but I know if he keeps putting so much pressure on himself, eventually it will take its toll.

After checking our gear, we're both out of plasma grenades. We have a few pulse grenades, but they only work on inanimate objects. Aside from my tattered body suit, the chest and back piece of my armor are holding up fine.

My helmet guides us up the stairwell, past two more floors of crew quarters. Above that is a mess hall and entertainment section. I'm almost tempted to check them out, but we don't have time for side quests.

We stop in front of an exit where an echoing clank beats in rhythmic succession from the other side. Once we're certain it's not a threat, we head up several more levels and exit the stairwell into an enormous open bay filled with all-terrain vehicles.

Hundreds of vehicles are parked in neat lines, ranging from small one-man ATVs to tanks large enough to run down trees in a forest. There are motorcycles, trucks, and armored vehicles topped with plasma turrets. Almost anything an army would need for a land invasion.

Too bad there's nothing that's going to help us fight our way through the ship. Even if we took one of the motorbikes, we've had to weasel and wind enough that they wouldn't last us long. What we need are more grenades.

"Is there anywhere we can replenish our plasma grenades on our current route?" I ask the helmet AI.

A room lights up green on the hologram. It's a side room a few floors up along our current route so it'll be an easy stop.

I close the hologram. "They've been the most useful item we've found so far. It makes sense to replenish them if we can."

Dean nods. "I'd love to take one of these babies for a spin sometime." He runs his hand along the side of a bulky tank with a flame thrower mounted to the front.

"Let's try to beat this stage before we start thinking about joy-riding."

We're running between a row of ATVs when I spot something out of the corner of my eye that forces me to do a double-take. I stop running and Dean plows into my back, nearly knocking me over.

He instinctively raises his weapon in the direction I'm looking.

"What is it?" he whispers.

"Behind those trucks. What does that look like to you?"

His eyes go wide. "You've gotta be kidding me. Are those mech suits?"

We make our way to the six mechanical exoskeletons parked against the back wall. They are so far back that I nearly missed them. Each one is slate gray and about ten feet tall. Big enough to make it a formidable force, but not too big that we couldn't operate them in most of the tunnels. We'd be banned from stairwells, but cargo elevators should work nicely.

I run my finger along the slick exterior. "What do you say we take them for a ride?"

"Hell yes!" Dean doesn't waste a second, running to the closest mech unit.

He presses his hand against the chest piece and the mech splits down the center along the chest and legs with a hiss. The head area flips backward, and plates extend outward and away, making room for him to climb inside.

Dean removes his weapons from his chest armor and climbs into the mech. There's a seat and footrests to support him, with each appendage being about two feet longer than his own. When he inserts his arms into the arm slots, the machine beeps to life. Straps extend from small compartments, holding him in place. He moves his arm and the helmet clamps into place, concealing his head, followed quickly by the legs and chest plate.

"Dude, this is so cool!" a mechanical voice booms from the mech. "This thing is loaded with weapons."

He takes a step forward and the unit hisses and groans as gears and pistons maneuver the giant machine. A panel opens in each arm, revealing a Gatling gun and a flamethrower. A missile launcher emerges from each shoulder, armed with a half-dozen missiles each.

Dean jumps and the mech soars several yards through the air before landing with a thud and shaking the ground.

While he tests out the unit, I activate my own and climb inside. It's surprisingly comfortable to be so bulky. I slip my hand into one of the arm holes and the unit pairs with my helmet, opening a slew of new commands. A video feed gives me a view of my surroundings. Thin green boxes follow Dean as he moves around, constantly alerting me to his location.

Activate Unit? *Y/N*

I accept and the mech comes to life. Pistons activate as the mech stands.

Mode: *Standby.*

Weapons: *Standby.*

When I focus on Mode, I'm given several options. Peacekeeping, Agility, and Heavy Artillery.

For Weapons, there is the option for manual or automatic. When I select manual, I'm given an interface with all the weapon attachments available.

There's the heavy firepower of the Gatling gun, flamethrower, and homing missiles, but there are also plasma beams, stun beams, heat-seeking missiles. There's also an option for EMP, an electro-magnetic pulse that disables the mech and all other technology within a hundred-yard radius as a last resort.

Better than having it fall into the wrong hands, I suppose.

I cycle between the various modes. Peacekeeping switches to non-lethal stun weapons. Agility engages thrusters along the legs, back, and arms, making it possible to maneuver mid-air. And Heavy Artillery equips all the weapons at once. There is also an option for a custom setup, but we don't have time to do that.

I switch to Agility mode and jump. At my peak, I engage the thrusters and rocket over Dean. Despite its weight, my mech lands without jostling me. Then I switch to Heavy Artillery, and the weaponry springs to life.

The mech unit is surprisingly easy to control. It responds to my movement like a second layer of skin, and even though it's bulky, the feedback never feels cumbersome.

"Route us to the control room using only tunnels and cargo elevators," I order the AI, and a new route appears on the map. This one avoids stairwells and anywhere that the mech wouldn't be able to fit. "Lock and load, Dean. Time to bring this baby home!"

Dean activates his flamethrower, and a cone of flame pours out in a steady stream. His normal voice cackles with laughter inside of my mech's speakers.

I keep my mech in Heavy Artillery mode in case we run into any enemies. It doesn't take long before we are tested.

Green squares appear in my feed as it locks onto something moving down the tunnel. Dark amorphous blobs glide from one wall to another. They look like slimes for a second, but I've never seen slimes move that fast. And the way they are constantly changing shapes is unsettling. They switch from blobs to humanoids to different depictions of beasts, like it doesn't know what it wants to be.

"What are these creepy things?" Dean asks.

We're too far out to analyze them, but as we move down the tunnel, they eventually become identifiable.

Foreign Lifeform. *Ooze Beast. A sentient and more*

dangerous cousin to the slime, an ooze beast is capable of trans-forming into lifelike forms and launching acidic projectile attacks.

"I wonder how well our mechs will hold up against acid?" I say it more to myself than anything.

Dean switches his mech to Agility mode and his thrusters carry him down the tunnel. He grinds to a halt once in range and extends his arm. The Gatling gun emerges from the mech's forearm and fires a burst of plasma beams into the oozes. The beams rip through their bodies the same as our weapons did to the slimes. Without a concentrated burst attack all it does is distort the ooze for a moment before the holes repair themselves.

I catch up to Dean just as the oozes begin to group up in front of him. One of them transforms into something resembling an elephant and shoots a blob of acid from its trunk. The acid hits Dean's mech and slides off without so much as a scratch.

"Haha!" he shouts. "Let's go!"

Dean runs into battle, punching and kicking, and firing plasma at the oozes. They assault him with acid, but it has no effect on the mech.

They fight, neither one gaining the upper hand. This is nothing more than a waste of time.

"Dean, if they can't hurt us, we should just bypass them." I activate Agility mode and launch myself forward.

"Oh no. I think I pissed them off."

I'm confused as to what he's talking about until I notice that the dozens of small green squares on my screen have morphed into one large square. The oozes have bonded together into a giant ooze. Combined, they dwarf our mechs.

One of the giant ooze's appendages extends and engulfs a forklift, wrapping around it like a sledgehammer.

Dean fires at the giant, but his plasma beams have no effect aside from rearranging the ooze.

The ooze beast lifts the forklift and smashes it into Dean, sending his mech crashing against the wall. One of the missile launchers on the mech's shoulder snaps and hangs at an odd angle. The beast stalks toward him, forklift raised and ready to strike.

I switch back to Heavy Artillery and unleash a combination of plasma and fire. The plasma gains its attention, but the fire actually causes the ooze to melt and lose its grip on the forklift. The heavy machinery crashes to the floor.

"Fire!" I shout. "Kill it with fire!"

A stream of fire shoots from Dean's left arm. The ooze recoils, but its massive leg is already weakened, causing it to collapse to one side. The ooze attempts to change form into something more bestial, but we press our attack. Giant sweat beads and blisters form along its outer layer as it melts and evaporates. We continue our assault, and the ooze shrinks by the second, shriveling until there is nothing left.

"Nicely done!" Dean raises his mech's hand for a high-five, but I don't acknowledge it.

"Did you forget that we are a team?" He can't see my face, so I do my best to show my disapproval in my tone. "You could have let me know what you were thinking. This isn't the first time you've rushed into battle without telling me. If you want to make it through this, then we have to work as a team at all times. Playing catchup means I'm always one step behind, and that might get us both killed."

His mech stands like a silent sentry before he eventually speaks. "You're right. I don't know what I was think-ing. That could have ended very badly."

"Don't sweat it." I soften my voice. "Just keep me informed the next time you think about diving in head-first."

We make our way down the tunnel and take a freight elevator up several floors, exiting into another insect-infested corridor. Our flamethrowers have no problem burning through webbing and setting the entire tunnel ablaze. Crispy carapaces crunch under our feet as we walk through.

My mech's AI notices something crawling through the vents and locks on to its location, but it's unable to iden-tify the creature without a clear visual. I could blast it with a missile, but it's better to let sleeping dogs lie.

We enter another hangar filled with fighter spacecraft. None of it is practical for what we're doing here, so we hurry past and into the next transport tunnel. Our guide leads us to an elevator that's too small for our mechs.

"What do we do now?" asks Dean.

"Looks like it's the end of the line. We're near the control room, but I think we'll have to finish on foot."

"Aww man, I was hoping we might get more use out of these." His mech opens, revealing a disappointed teenager inside.

"They got us this far, so I'd say that's a win." I disen-gage my own mech and climb down. Then I realize our mistake. "Dammit!"

"What is it?" Dean's head swivels as he looks for the source of danger.

"Our weapons. We had to leave them when we took the mechs."

He pats his chest plate and reaches around at the piece

covering his back, grasping for weapons and grenades that are no longer there. "Are we screwed?"

"No way. We've gotten out of stickier situations than this, we just need a little ingenuity. The control room is only a few floors up."

We enter the elevator. Nothing looks out of order, which is all the more reason we should keep our guard up. After an agonizingly slow climb, we exit onto the level where the control room is located.

The hallways are very businesslike and our steps clack as we walk. Occasionally, something moves in the ducts overhead. Pictures of men in military garb hang along the walls. Two navy stripes run along the outer edges of the light gray floors.

Our level-ten badge gets us through two gated entries, but when we arrive at the control room, our access is denied.

The octagonal control room is surrounded by massive panes of tinted glass on all sides. I can make out several monitors, and a ring of consoles with glowing buttons and switches. There's a hologram of the ship in the center, flashing red in numerous spots. Could that be all the areas that have been taken over by alien lifeforms?

Next to the hologram is a podium topped with a cube that hovers in mid-air. Some sort of alien runes or letters are engraved in each of its sides. They shine with a brilliant internal energy. I have no doubt that that is the powerful artifact we were sent to retrieve.

The bodies are so still that I almost don't notice them lying on the floor. They don't appear to show any signs of trauma. A skeletal figure leans forward in the captain's seat, head nestled between its knees.

"This is creepy." Dean's lip curls up in disgust. "What do you think happened to them?"

"No idea. Maybe it has something to do with that cube. Or the reason why so many different types of aliens are on the ship. Maybe they locked themselves in the control room when the ship was overrun. Who knows?" I kick hard at the glass door blocking our way, but it doesn't budge. It's clearly made of something stronger than pure glass. "We need to find a way in."

We circle the perimeter of the control room, searching for any signs of weakness, until Dean and I reconvene on the other side.

Dean presses his hands to the glass and looks into the control room. "Gah, we're so close! Maybe we have to go back. Either find a badge with higher clearance or a weapon capable of getting us inside."

I ask the helmet AI to search for a higher clearance badge but receive an error notice. It can only route us to things labeled as part of the ship's layout or inventory. I place my hands to the glass and join Dean. Maybe there's something inside that will give us a clue.

I scour the room but come up with nothing. "We can work our way back and check any rooms we have access to until we find something useful."

I don't like the idea one bit, but there's little else we can do under the circumstances. We've made it so far to have to start backtracking now, but I don't let my frustration get to me. I need to stay positive for Dean.

We step into the hallway and something scurries through the duct overhead.

"Wait! That's it." I grab Dean by the shoulder. "If we can find a way into the air ducts, there has to be one that empties into the control room!"

He grins, but it slowly fades into a frown. "But what about whatever is…" He points up at the ducts. "Up there."

I hadn't thought of that. We've heard something moving through the ducts since we first started. There's no telling what it could be, but it's not like we have any better options. "We'll just have to deal with it."

I instruct the AI to route us to the nearest maintenance closet, where we find a toolbox that will hopefully get us into the air ducts. We have to backtrack to one of the main hallways before we find an accessible entrance into the ventilation system.

The vent comes off easy enough, revealing a square duct that goes in for a few feet before angling straight up. There's enough space to crawl on our hands and knees, but once we reach the vertical area, it's too high to reach from a standing position.

"Climb on my shoulders and I'll boost you up. Then you can pull me up." I press my body against the metal duct and brace myself.

Dean grabs my shoulders and places his feet on my thighs. It's a tight fit, but he's able to leverage his back against the other side of the duct and weasel his way upward. Once I feel his feet pressing against my shoulders, I step back, giving him a better angle to climb to the next level. The metal creaks and groans as he climbs, but eventually, his weight vanishes and his feet disappear over the ledge.

There's more groaning as he contorts himself in the tight space before his head pops out and he extends a hand to me.

Dean leans down as far as he can without losing his balance, but he's still about two feet out of my reach. "You're going to have to jump."

And hope that I don't pull him down when I grab hold.

A loud groan echoes through the ducts, and Dean whips his head around.

"Was that you?" I ask, but I already know the answer.

He's wide-eyed as he shakes his head.

"Hold on a second. I'll be right back."

I drop to my knees and crawl back into the hallway. Inside the toolbox, I grab a hammer and a screwdriver. They're not great weapons, but they're better than nothing.

Dean wears an anxious expression when I return, but he keeps quiet.

"Here, I'm going to toss these up to you first."

He catches the tools and places them next to him before extending his hand once again.

I take a deep breath and jump as high as I can. My hand clasps around his and I press both legs against the walls of the duct. Dean's face goes red as he tries to pull me up, but I'm not moving. This is our best chance, so I can't let go.

I dig my feet into the metal and try to shimmy by back up a few inches at a time. Once my legs are extended as far as they can go without losing my grip, I put all my weight onto Dean and lift my legs as fast as I can. Dean grunts as my weight pulls his body to its limits.

I shimmy up the wall again and repeat the process until I can see the open duct in front of me.

"Alright, I'm going to make a move and I need you to pull with everything you've got. On three. One. Two. Three."

I launch myself toward the open duct and my chest slams against the ledge. For a moment, the only thing keeping me from falling back down is Dean's strength. My feet slip against the metal as they try to find grip before I'm able to press them against the back wall and push myself forward.

I lean against the cool metal of the duct, gasping for air. "We did it," I manage to say between breaths.

Dean crawls backward through the duct until we come to a section where four ducts converge. I pull up the hologram of the ship and find the route that will take us to the control room.

"Do you want to lead or me?" I ask.

Dean backs into one of the other ducts and motions me forward. "Just don't fart in my face, please."

The metal thunders around us with every movement we make. I try to crawl faster in the hopes of making it to the control room before anything notices our presence.

We're not so lucky.

The metal ducts wobble around us as some monstrosity approaches. It's impossible to know where the creature is because the ventilation shaft in front of us splits into a T about twenty yards ahead. I imagine some deformed snake slithering through the vents.

I grip my screwdriver and wait for the creature to reveal itself.

Dean taps me on my calf. "Slide over. I want to see."

I scoot to the left, giving Dean a view as we wait anxiously. Whatever we're waiting on, it moves slowly. The metal pops and echoes, growing louder by the second. The duct at the intersection sags slightly, revealing the monster's location.

I take a deep breath, wishing I had anything better than a screwdriver to fight with.

The metal pops again and a small pink bunny hops into view. Its head turns in our direction, revealing a gray horn protruding from its head and dark red eyes looking at us with curiosity.

Something is off. The duct sinks around the bunny like it weighs hundreds of pounds.

It hops toward us and the entire structure feels like it could collapse at any moment. The helmet AI analyzes the bunny, but it only leaves me more confused.

Foreign Lifeform. *Nimbus Dragon. The nimbus dragon travels through space and time, feeding off of energy-rich planets. Nimbus dragons are incredibly dense and often polymorph into local fauna to avoid suspicion as they drain planets of their vital aura.*

You've got to be kidding me. We're trapped in a ventilation shaft with a dragon capable of destroying planets that just so happens to be in the shape of a pink bunny.

"Back up," I whisper.

Maybe if we can get out of sight, then the dragon-bunny will go on its merry way.

Dean squirms backward and I do the same. The ruby red eyes of the nimbus dragon stare at us as we go. It sits back on its haunches and wiggles its nose before rubbing one tiny paw against its eyes.

The bunny raises its nose into the air, as if sniffing our scent, and I swear it licks its lips before taking a step forward. The metal sinks and the pop echoes all around us.

"What's going on? Is it chasing us?" Dean's voice is high-pitched once again.

The bunny takes another step, sending another resounding echo.

"No, it's just slowly walking toward us," I lie. It could have been my imagination, but I'm pretty sure this cute little dragon wants to eat us.

"Well, do something. We're sitting ducks here."

I could be wrong and the dragon isn't dangerous at all, but I'd rather not take any chances. Dean's right, and there's no way we're escaping while trapped in these vents. If only there was some way to weaken the ducts so that the dragon's weight could dislodge it.

The dragon takes another step and I know that if I don't act, we're going to be screwed. I scan the inside of the ducts for anything I can unscrew, but there's nothing. It must all be fixed from the exterior.

"Dean, hand me the hammer." I extend my hand behind me and he places it in my hand.

The dragon continues its slow prowl toward us. I take the screwdriver in one hand and smash the hammer into the butt of the handle. A dent forms in the metal and a second hit punctures through. The bunny cocks its head before taking another step.

I move the screwdriver and smash it with the hammer again, this time harder. It pierces the thin metal of the duct in one hit this time. Quickly, I form an X pattern with holes and continue to slide backward.

The bunny hops again, causing the entire shaft to shake. We continue to back up until we're almost back to the intersection. The bunny stops and shifts its head from side to side. It looks like it's about to turn and walk away when I take the hammer and throw it.

The bunny turns and screeches, and for a moment, the shadowy silhouette of a dragon shrouds the bunny, revealing a spectral image of its true form. The dragon lowers its head, teeth bared as it roars in our direction. Shadowy flames brush against me, surprisingly cool against my skin.

The shadow disappears and the bunny hops toward us quickly, the metal creaking with each jump. It hits the hole-marked X and loud snaps echo as the metal rips from hole to hole. The bunny sinks through the ventilation and falls to the floor below.

The hole in the duct is only about a foot wide, so I creep back over and peek through.

Down below, a black dragon speckled with spots of purple, blue, and white thrashes back and forth. As it moves, the scales give off the appearance of a galaxy. Black flames pour from its mouth, setting aflame everything in sight.

"We need to go!" I shout, scurrying like a cornered rodent down the shaft.

Our movement echoes around me as we make our way to the end and take a right. With the apex predator out of the way, I don't dally. I follow the guide until we're over the control room.

I have to kick several times before the screws give way and the vent opens.

We lower ourselves from the vent and drop into the control room. "Complete" flashes across my vision and suddenly I'm looking at the scene in third person—as if hovering above the room watching myself and Dean as we remove the skeletons from their stations and take control of the ship.

Dean presses a few buttons, and I slide a lever. The ship jumps into hyperspace, and all I see are stars.

CHAPTER SIXTEEN

We materialize back in the whiteness of The Vacuum.

Dean wraps his arms around me, squeezing tightly. "We did it! We made it through the first stage."

He smiles broadly before releasing me and taking a step back, as if suddenly realizing what he's done. He looks around to see if anyone saw him, but the other contestants are focused on the massive feeds displayed in the sky.

I place my arm around him and pull him in. "And quicker than most of our competitors, it seems."

A few dozen challengers stand around watching the video feeds. Far less than were here this morning. We're all back in our normal outfits again. A leaderboard in the sky tells us that we were the sixtieth team to finish.

A slender elf and a burly dwarf materialize out of thin air.

The dwarf pushes the elf in the thigh. "Stupid! I told you not to run in like that. I knew I should have taken your sister instead." He turns to the rest of us. "Screw you! All of you."

A portal opens and both the dwarf and elf step through. I guess we won't be seeing them in the next round.

Ryken and Dawn stand by themselves at the far end, huddled together and whispering. I should have known they would be one of the first ones through. I search the leaderboard for their position. Tenth.

Nancy hovers in the air on her pegasus. A camera with miniature thrusters floats in front of her as she comments on the main Pangea Online feed as it cycles through various players' streams. The camera is more for appearance than anything, or possibly to let her know when she's being recorded.

I focus on the feed, but it's hard to tell who it's following with everyone wearing the same gray unitards and their faces covered with helmets. The current feed follows a pair as they maneuver a large tank down a tunnel.

"That's the one I wanted to drive!" Dean rocks on his feet excitedly. "I knew it would have fit in the tunnel."

Nancy offers commentary as the tank spits out a stream of fire from the mounted flamethrower. "—and look at it go. Paul Campbell is putting those flamethrowers to use, completely incinerating the ooze beasts before him."

The feed shifts to a team ducking behind a corner as a door explodes. "It looks like we have our next set of victors. That satchel of plasma grenades came in useful for Talia and Chadwick Tate. With fifty of them, they just blew the door to the control room clean off its hinges!"

"Oh! That's not good." It cycles to the next feed and Nancy places a hand over her eyes as a group of lizard people pry off the helmet of some unlucky soul and devour him. "It looks like we've lost another competitor. They're dropping like houseflies. How many remain? How many will survive until the next stage? Stay tuned to the official Pangea Online stream to find out. Now back to headquarters for more in-depth coverage."

The feed zooms in on a table of analysts as they discuss those still competing. I tune it out. There will be plenty of time to catch up on everything once the results are finalized. A few of the other teams disappear through their own portals, so I assume it is safe to leave.

"What do you say we get out of here?" I ask Dean.

He shrugs. "Don't you want to talk to any of the other teams? We could probably learn something."

I look around, but there's no one who interests me. We'll study them behind closed doors. "This stage is over, and all that matters now is the next stage. I'll reach out to Talia later and see what she thinks about everything, but as far as the rest of these people, they're our competition. Don't forget that. We'll learn more than we'd ever want to know about them in the coming days. For now, I'd like to sit and gather my thoughts. And I know the other kids will be dying to hear you tell them all about today."

Dean grins. "Alright, captain."

I open a portal to get us out of here. Right before Dean steps through, I call to him. "You did good today."

He nods. "Couldn't have done it without you."

Dean steps into the portal and disappears. I follow behind him, and a moment later, I'm in my home portal being licked vigorously by Fenrir. I play tug-of-war with him for a few minutes before finally logging out.

Back in my apartment, I strip out of my haptic suit and lay on the couch. For a few minutes, I just close my eyes and listen to the birds chirping outside my window. This is one of the few peaceful moments I'll have over the next few days. Everything has come full circle, and now I'm right in the middle of another tournament.

My tablet beeps, letting me know I have a new message, but I don't move. It's been a long day, and we're just getting started. It beeps five more times, but I just roll over.

Pounding at my door finally forces me to get up. I creep over to the door still wearing my underwear, and bright light blinds me as I crack the door.

"Dude!" Buzz rushes in past me. "What are you doing? It's time to celebrate! You made it through the first round."

"What are you doing? I figured you would be working with the tournament in full effect."

He cocks an eyebrow at me. "You know I'm not supposed to talk about that with you." He plops down on the couch. "But it's an off day for the testers. The programmers are working on the back end as things are finalized."

"That quick?" It feels like it hasn't been that long since I was testing the old version of The Broken Lands.

Buzz leans back and props his feet on the edge of the sofa. "I wouldn't call it quick. We've had testers cycling in and out twenty-four hours a day for weeks now. It's crunch time, but we aren't cutting any corners. You're gonna love what they have planned."

"And you can't tell me anything about it?"

"My lips are—" He claps his hands together and barks. "—seals. My lips are seals."

I roll my eyes at his terrible pun. "Don't quit your day job."

"I wouldn't dream of it." He sits up and taps the sofa

beside him. "So, tell me all about it. How's Esil Jr. holding up?"

"Don't call him that." I scowl at Buzz. "Let me throw on some clothes before we start talking business."

I toss on a pair of sweatpants and a hoodie and join Buzz on the sofa. "Dean's good. Much better than I was when I first got into Pangea. He's smart. A little too reckless at times, but he's saved my butt just as many times as I've saved his. We've got some tough competition, but I think we've got a real chance."

"I don't doubt it. Grayson wants to get together later and go over some of the footage. To talk about where you could improve and go over some of the alternatives other teams took." He pats me on the knee. "The old man's taken a real interest in this. He's been glued to the feeds all morning following yours and half a dozen others taking notes."

I don't know where I would be without these two. "I think being put in the mine with you and Grayson was probably the greatest thing to ever happen to me."

Buzz grins. "Well, duh. What would your life be like without me in it?"

I shove him in the shoulder. "I'm starving. Want to go grab a bite to eat?"

Buzz jumps to his feet. "Have you known me to ever turn down a meal?"

We arrive at the cafeteria, where feeds of the tournament are displayed all around the room. I better get used to it because there will be no escaping this madness until a victor has been crowned.

I grab a burger and Buzz takes two. I give him a questioning look and he just shrugs.

"What? I'm a growing boy."

"You'll be an expanding boy if you keep it up."

We take a seat across from one another underneath one of the TVs. At least that way, I don't have to watch it.

My tablet beeps again, and I remember I never checked my messages from earlier. Buzz shoves food in his mouth as I pull them up.

The first two are from Buzz.

Esil, I see you're done with the tournament. Want to hang out? -Buzz

Screw it. I'm coming over. I hope you're dressed. -Buzz

The next two are from Grayson and Aleesia.

Good job, kid. You two are quite the pair. Let's meet up later and go over strategy. -Grayson

Esil, I'm so proud of you. Work is super busy at the moment, but I've been following along. Can't wait to see you soon! -Aleesia.

And then there are several from various Pangea departments.

Esil Allen,

Congratulations on completing round one of the Pro-Am

Tournament! You will be contacted over the next few hours regarding scheduling for interviews and post-stage conferences. We're excited to follow your journey through the next stage of the tournament. And as always, never stop leveling!

-Pangea Online Developers

Esil Allen,

Congratulations on making it through stage one! We would like to schedule your first interview for this evening at 17:00, where we will be asking you and your apprentice questions about what it took to make it through stage one.

-Pangea Communications

I set the tablet on the table and groan.

Buzz looks up from his food. "What is it?"

"We have our first interview tonight."

He dips a fry in ketchup and points it at me. "Mr. Allen, tell me, what's it like being one of the most famous streamers on the planet?"

I smack his hand away. "Oh, shut it. I had my five-minutes of fame during the last tournament. I don't even get half the followers Ryken or some of the others get."

He stuffs the fry in his mouth. "That's because you do the bare minimum. Who wants to follow someone who only streams for an hour every other day?"

"Meh, I'm just not an entertainer. I did what I had to do to get to where I am. Nothing more than that."

Buzz grins. "And that's why people love you. The reluctant hero."

"Eat your other burger and shut up." I dig into my own

and for the next few minutes, all we hear is the sound of chewing and slurping.

When we're done, I message Dean, telling him to meet me at my portal ten minutes before the scheduled interview. Then we head back to Buzz's place, where Grayson is sitting in front of a monitor with sixteen feeds going simultaneously.

"I never took you for a fanboy," I tease.

He hands me a tablet without looking away from the monitor. "You'll be thanking me if any of this comes in useful."

I glance through it. He's labeled every team and left detailed notes, ranging from their route, the weapons they picked up, even the monsters they fought. These are probably better notes than the analysts have.

"Have you taken a break at all?" I ask.

"I'll rest when I'm done."

I sit down beside him. "How valuable do you think any of this stuff will be? It's not like any of this carries over into the next round."

He types a new note as one of the teams swap out their weapons in a storage room. "That's where you're wrong. You can learn a lot about someone just by watching them play. The way each team interacts here is likely how they will behave going forward. For example, Ryken always takes the lead. He's fearless. He's doing this more for personal glory than to help the girl he is with. And the two gnomes, they made it through without fighting anything. They're crafty. You'll want to watch your back around them."

"What about me and Dean?"

Grayson cocks his head to the side before turning around. It seems I've finally gotten his attention.

His mustache curls up at the edges and I can tell he is smiling. "You're a special case. More like two solos who happen to be playing alongside one another. You both go in half-cocked more often than not, especially the kid. You both have good instincts, but they will only take you so far if you don't learn how to work together. This—" He taps at the tablet I'm holding. "—just might keep you in the running until you do. Now, if you don't mind, I have work to do. I'll have you a full write-up by the time you're done with your interviews."

He resumes his diligent note-taking, and I'm left there speechless. He's right. More than I'm willing to admit. Even by standing aside and offering to play support as Dean led the way, we were never truly in sync. We reacted to one another, because that's what we've done all our lives. We've reacted to everything around us, never able to blaze our own trail.

I glance at the clock on the wall. There's still a couple of hours until the interview. If Dean and I really want a chance at this, then we need to be a real team.

I stand up from the sofa and head for the door. "Sorry, to head out so soon, but there's something I need to take care of."

"Is everything okay?" asks Buzz.

I nod. "Yeah, I'm going to see if Dean wants to move in with me until the tournament is over."

CHAPTER SEVENTEEN

I rush back home and call Dean for a video chat. He looks confused when he answers. Several children sit behind him in the background.

He furrows his brow. "What's going on? I thought we were meeting up in a couple of hours for the interview."

"Everything is fine." I wave at a young girl peeking over Dean's shoulder. "I actually have a proposition for you. We're going to be spending a lot of time working together and strategizing in the next few days. I thought it might be better if you came and stayed with me until the tournament is over."

His mouth drops and he stares at the camera for a long time before speaking. "Are you serious?"

I can't get a read on what's going through his mind. "Absolutely. So, what do you think?"

"Uhm, yeah, that would be great." He seems a bit awestruck. "I've never been outside of The Boxes before. How do I get there?"

"I'll send a pod to pick you up. Don't worry about bringing your haptic suit. I'll pick up one from headquarters for you to use. Go pack your things, and I'll get every-thing else taken care of."

He flashes me a wide grin. "Yeah, sounds good. I'll get right on it."

He ends the call, and a strange sense of relief washes over me. I call Mr. Green to make the arrangements with the orphanage and put in orders for the pod and haptic suit.

By the time Dean arrives, I have the couch converted into a makeshift bed, and a second haptic suit set up next to mine in the other room. The fridge is stocked with food and snacks in case he gets hungry. Preparing the place for a guest feels nice. And with this being his first time out of The Boxes, I want him to feel as welcome as possible.

I meet him out front of the main headquarters build-ing. Dean climbs out of the pod wearing his hazmat suit and face mask, carrying nothing but a small backpack. His head turns on a swivel as he takes everything in.

I extend my arm, offering to take his bag. "You can take that off. The air is safe to breathe here."

He's hesitant, but he eventually removes his mask, closing his eyes and taking in a deep breath. "So that's what fresh air smells like?"

He climbs out of the hazmat suit. Underneath, he's wearing gray pants and a matching shirt. The only outfit most people in The Boxes can afford.

"We've got about an hour before the interview. Do you want to get settled in? I'll give you the tour tomorrow."

He nods. I get the feeling he's a bit overwhelmed by all the sensory input. Birds chirping, drones buzzing, blue skies, and real plants. Not to mention all the people walking around as they please. It can be a lot to take in for someone who's never experienced it.

I keep quiet as we walk, letting Dean bask in the wonder of it all.

I remember the first time I came here. The pod door opened and I freaked out because I didn't have my mask on. Nowadays, I can't even remember the last time wearing a filtration mask crossed my mind. Probably when I visited the orphanage, and that's about it. I've gotten so used to luxury that it's become the norm.

I stop in front of my apartment. "Well, here it is." We step inside and I lead Dean to the living room. "This is where you'll be sleeping. I have our haptic suits set up in the next room. Bathroom is over there, and my bedroom is down the hall. Feel free to grab whatever you'd like from the kitchen and there's always the cafeteria in the main building as well."

Dean just stares at me.

"What?" I ask.

"It's so..." His words trail off.

"Different?"

He nods. "Yeah, that's one way of putting it. It's like being in Pangea. So detailed and full of color. I always wondered what it was like out here, but I never imagined it would be like this."

I look around at our surroundings, remembering how much of a change it was for me. "It's a different world, that's for sure. Do you want to go meet Grayson and the others before our interview?"

He agrees and we head over to Buzz's apartment. Maria, Buzz's mom, lets us in. Grayson is still working on his notes and Buzz is fast asleep on the couch, a bead of drool dripping down his chin.

"You must be the famous Dean I keep hearing about."

Maria smiles. "You did a great job today. Would you boys like to stick around for dinner?"

I wrap my arm around Maria and pull her in. "Unfortunately, we can't stay long. I just wanted to give Dean a chance to meet everyone before our interview."

Grayson stands up, finally taking some time away from the feeds. He extends his hand, and they shake. "You did good in there today, kid. I can't wait to see what they throw at you next."

"Thanks. You look different from your avatar. I'm not sure what it is. Similar, but different."

Grayson laughs. "Old age catches up with us all eventually."

"Wasgoingon?" Buzz stirs on the couch. "Whos'ere?"

"Ah." Grayson turns toward Buzz. "Sleeping beauty has arisen."

Buzz wipes his eyes with his fist like a small child and sits up. "Are you Dean?"

Dean nods.

Buzz jumps from the couch and wraps him in a bear hug. "Welcome to the family. It's taken a while but people from The Boxes are finally making our mark on the world. I hope you and Esil crush it."

Dean's face is bright red once he's released. "We're going to do our best."

I'm sure he's not used to human touch at the orphanage. Or praise. I know I wasn't. I'm still not in a lot of respects.

"What are you working on?" Dean points to the feeds Grayson has been following.

"Oh, just taking some notes for you guys to look over later."

Dean's eyes light up. "Mind if I take a look?"

Grayson looks to me as if waiting for permission.

"Have fun. I'll check it out later."

Buzz and Grayson take a seat around the monitor while Buzz, Maria, and I sit at the table.

Maria leans forward, her voice barely above a whisper. "Are you sure it was a good idea bringing him here, Esil?"

"What do you mean? This is beyond anything he's ever experienced. Don't you think it's good for him to know there is more out there?"

"What happens when he has to go back? Back to the world you fought so hard to escape." Her face is kind, but intense.

"I hadn't thought about that." Could it be that offering him a taste of this life will only make it worse when it's over?

"Don't listen to her." Buzz waves his hand through the air. "Just being here, it'll give him a goal to work toward. It won't make him any more miserable when he goes back."

Maria purses her lips. "I hope you're right."

Before I know it, it's time for us to leave. Our first post-stage interview awaits.

Dean and I sit in my home portal waiting for our interview to connect to the display along the wall.

"How's the new haptic suit feel?"

Dean wrestles with Fenrir on the floor. The massive wolf lays on his back toying with Dean as he paws at him.

"It's good. Fits like a glove."

The display blinks and Nancy's face appears as she thumbs through a tablet. She must be putting in the hours during this tournament. I just hope the questions are geared more toward our performance and less about our origin.

She looks into the camera. "Alright, gentlemen. We'll be going live in ten seconds. Standby."

There's a beeping as a timer counts down on the screen. When it hits zero, Nancy smiles.

"Thanks, Janine. As we continue our interviews for the day, here we have a name that needs no introduction, Esil Allen. Esil and his protege, Dean Wilmington, took an unconventional route into the control room, climbing through the vents and bypassing a Nimbus Dragon. Only one other team thought to use the vents to their advantage. So, Esil and Dean, what made you want to take the road less traveled?"

I answer this one. "We didn't really have much of a choice. We were out of weapons due to taking the mech units, so it was just as big of a risk to go back and try to find more. We had to work with what we had."

"And it worked out pretty well indeed. You're not the only ones to encounter that problem. The mechs were designed as a risk-reward scenario. They can get you through some sticky situations, but at the cost of being unarmed on the final stretch. Now, Dean, this was your first tournament. Tell me, what was it like?"

He sits up straight and brushes the hair from his eyes. "It was amazing. Better than I could have ever imagined. It was a real roller coaster of emotion as we overcame one challenge after another. I can't wait to see what's next."

"And neither can we. We'll be announcing the next stage first thing in the morning but before we get to that, let's dive a little deeper into the first stage. Ninety percent of contestants unlocked the helmet's automated system, and many of them elected to take the shortest route as you did. When things got tough, you pivoted your plan of attack. Can you speak a little more to how you adapted to each situation?"

I glance at Dean before answering. "I think we both just followed our instincts. If I learned anything from the last tournament, it's that there's more than one way to succeed. And there's no shame in changing tactics when things aren't working."

"I know this is a sensitive topic for you, but do you feel your upbringing has given you any advantages or disadvantages during the tournament?"

Dean and I sit in silence. I knew that these questions would come. For some reason, it doesn't set me off like last time. Maybe because it's a genuine question and not a story byline.

Dean clears his throat. "How could it not? Growing up in The Boxes, I never had access to all of Pangea, not until Esil came along. I've had to learn in a few weeks what most of these people have been discovering their entire lives. But I don't want anybody's pity. The one thing we know better than anyone is how to survive."

I wrap my arm around Dean and look straight into the camera. "Yeah, what he said."

For the next few minutes, we answer questions about specific instances, going into detail about our thought process and how we survived. All in all, it wasn't a bad interview. Aside from the one question, there was no talk of The Boxes or my family. Maybe we can actually focus on the tournament going forward.

When we log out, it's late, but not late enough to go to bed.

"What do you say we chill tonight? We can focus hard

on the tournament tomorrow once we know the next stage.”

Dean plops down on the couch. “Sounds good to me.”

“Excellent. You pick out a movie. I’ll grab the ice cream.”

CHAPTER EIGHTEEN

"Esil. Esil, wake up!" Dean's excited voice shouts from the doorway.

I open my eyes and it's still dark outside.

"What is it?" I prop myself up, wondering what he could possibly want at this hour.

"Stage two! Check your messages."

I use voice command to turn on the lights and find my tablet on the bedside table. Sure enough, I have a message from the developers.

Greetings Esil,

After yesterday's exciting events, we're happy to announce that one-hundred and sixty-three teams have made it through to the next round. In three days' time, you will be embarking on the next stage of the tournament. Without further ado, here are the details regarding stage two:

Location: Raceworld's Portal Pass

Teams: 163

Positions advancing: 100

Good luck with your preparations and as always, never stop leveling!

-Pangea Online Developers

I sit up in bed. "Portal pass? Is that the racetrack that takes you through different worlds using portals?"

Dean nods. "Yep, and it's not a new stage so that means we can go practice!"

"Right now?" I haven't even gotten out of bed and he's ready to hit the ground running.

"Yeah, come on." He taps on the doorframe. "We need to get there before everyone else."

Welcome to Raceworld. While in an active race, users who are not spectating must be on a mount at all times. More than thirty seconds spent on foot will result in disqualification from any race.

A wall with dozens of video screens stands before us. On each screen, there is a different type of race. Cars, planes, animals, hoverboards; if you can ride it, there is a race for it. In the middle, there is a slightly bigger screen that reads "Portal Pass."

I focus on the image to enter Portal Pass and receive a notification.

Error: *Server full.*

I try again and receive the same message.

That's odd. "Dean, are you getting an error notice?"

He frowns. "Yeah, what the heck?"

"Looks like we're late to the party?" a familiar voice calls over my shoulder.

I turn around to find Talia and her brother Chadwick. They're both dressed in their tribal garb and carry spears tipped with some dark metal. They wear plain leather clothing with golden jewelry. Chadwick stands a few feet behind Talia wearing a necklace with a large claw that dangles on his chest.

"Hey! Congrats on making it through. What's going on here?" I ask her.

She presses her fingers to her temples and massages. "Clearly, the developers didn't think this one through. Once stage two was announced, users from all over flooded Portal Pass to race alongside their favorite challengers. There are normally a hundred instances going at once and now all of them are full. Only a handful of actual contestants have been able to get inside."

"So what are we supposed to do?" Dean tries to enter Portal Pass again. "We're the ones who need the practice."

Talia shrugs. "I don't think we have much of a choice. We have to wait for them to sort it out, which I don't imagine will take too long. Want to go check out another race while we wait?"

I look over our other options for something similar to Portal Pass. "Might as well. There are a few things I want to discuss with you. How about this one?" I point to Hoverworld. It's the closest thing to Portal Pass since it uses hovercraft, but it's far more limited in items and abilities in-game.

We all enter Hoverworld and are presented with numerous options for mounts. There are single-rider hoverbikes and two-seaters with options for side-by-side or front-and-back layouts. Some are built for top speed, while others have faster acceleration, tankiness, or maneuverability.

"Take your pick, Dean?" I motion toward all our options.

He looks them over before stopping in front of a sleek black hovercar. Silver spikes jut out around all four sides, making it a dangerous weapon in its own right without even counting the turret mounted on the back. There's no roof. One seat faces forward with the steering wheel and another faces the rear to aim the turret.

"This one has good acceleration and is built like a tank. The top speed isn't that great, but it's good for bullying in the early part and can handle corners pretty well." He climbs in the back seat. "Dibs on the gun!"

Talia and Chadwick take a long, slender hovercraft. It's red with a black stripe running down the center and has the highest top speed of any of the options. Both riders face forward, one behind the other, but the back seat has a display for aiming the gun mounted on top of the roof. Unlike our hovercar, this one can aim in all directions.

Talia climbs inside the front seat. "Want to run a few laps and then we can talk?"

"Sounds good." I pull our hovercar up to the starting line.

30 seconds until next race flashes across my vision. I rev the engine and blue flames shoot from the thrusters as the engine whines. Talia winks at me as she revs her own.

Something rumbles behind us, so deep and sonorous that I can feel in my chest.

Two more vehicles have joined the race. One is a small halfling riding a hoverbike and wearing a billowing cloak. The hoverbike doesn't have a weapon, but two canisters hang from both sides. The second is a truck with two tall smokestacks attached to the bed. A steady stream of smoke billows into the air. A black-bearded dwarf sits in the driver's seat while a minotaur stands in the bed pointing a turret in our direction.

A map of the track appears in the top right of my vision, along with a timer, a position counter, and how many laps we've completed. This race is set to be three laps.

I look over my shoulder to Dean. "Looks like we already have a target on us. You ready?"

Dean smiles as he points his turret at the minotaur. "I was born ready."

The timer hits zero and the roar of thrusters and weapons firing fills the air. The halfling zooms past us, cloak whipping as she does. Chadwick tries to blast her with the turret but misses, damaging the energy shield surrounding our own car. He grimaces and raises a hand in apology.

I fall into second place as Dean and the minotaur exchange fire, the energy beams canceling out one another mid-air.

The truck and Talia are neck-and-neck when Chadwick sets his aim on the minotaur. The dwarf swerves hard to the right, ramming the massive truck into Talia and Chadwick as we take the first curve. The hit from the truck causes the red hotrod to spin out.

The halfling on the hoverbike is nowhere to be seen. Dean and the minotaur are locked in a stalemate as they continue to shoot at one another, but neither one is able to land a direct hit.

Something small and black sits in the middle of the track up ahead. I swerve to the left to avoid it, but the box explodes, sending us screeching against the metal railing of the track. Hairline fractures splinter along the edge of our forcefield as we crash. The truck passes us by as we are forced to slow down. I punch the acceleration as we hit the first open stretch of road. Wind whips against my eyes and a loud roar passes us by as Talia and Chadwick catch up, their car finally hitting top speed.

"Dude, we're in last place. Catch up!" Dean yells from behind me.

Talia is forced to slow down to take the next turn. Our car has much better handling, so I only slow down a fraction, hitting the top of the embankment and accelerating as I maneuver to the bottom as we exit the turn. I pass Talia just as we hit another stretch.

Up ahead, the halfling swerves from left to right as the minotaur showers the road with energy beams. One catches the hoverbike in the rear, forcing it to spin out. The truck is about to make a break for it when the halfling pulls a mine from her satchel and tosses it in front of the truck. The dwarf slams on the brakes, but it's too late. The mine explodes, knocking the truck hard into the wall.

This is our chance. I try to thread the needle between the two downed vehicles. Both are just getting up to speed when someone shouts.

"Not so fast!"

The tip of Talia's car appears in the corner of my vision right before it smashes into us. The shield on their car falters as our spiked exterior dishes back damage. The halfling lets out a yelp as we crash into her. Metal grinds against the exterior wall as the truck takes the opportunity to ram into Talia's car, pinning us and the hoverbike against the wall.

Dean grunts as he struggles behind me. "Ugh, I can't turn the turret to hit anything."

Dean fights with the weapon while I try to reverse us out of this situation, but we're stuck between the other vehicles. The truck backs up and I think we have a shot to escape, but it plows forward, hitting us again. Talia's shield cracks and smoke flows freely from the thrusters. She smashes her fist to the steering wheel as her engine dies.

Our position changes from 3/4 to 3/3.

"Sorry, dude." Dean turns his turret away from the truck and points it at the halfling.

The halfling opens her mouth, but the words never come out as Dean opens fire. The positioning changes again to 2/2.

I try to maneuver us free again, but our spikes are lodged in the downed car and hoverbike, not to mention the truck still pressing us against the railing.

Our shield collapses and the exterior of the vehicle begins to crumple. The engine whines as I press the gas and attempt to jerk us free.

Our spikes rip free and I'm able to reverse us out. The truck does the same, but we're already screwed. I attempt to use our maneuverability to position us so that Dean can aim, but the minotaur has positioning. He shows me a rude gesture and opens fire.

My vision flashes red and a notification appears in front of me as we're blown to bits.

Eliminated!

I let out a long sigh as the truck drives away. This certainly bodes well for our chances in the tournament.

After a moment, Dean and I materialize at the starting line. I catch sight of the halfling just before she logs out. Talia and Chadwick sit on the concrete wall to the left of the track.

I hop onto the wall and take a seat. "I thought we would at least make it through the first lap."

Talia frowns. "Yeah, we're going to have to do better if we want to make it through to the final round. So, what was it you were wanting to talk about?"

The truck comes blazing around the corner. As it passes by, the minotaur aims the turret in our direction and fires. We all flinch, but the beams pass straight through us. The minotaur tilts his head back and boisterous laughter fades as they zoom away.

"What a jerk!" Dean raises his fist at our tormentors.

I return my attention to Talia. "I was thinking it might be a good idea to form an alliance. With over a hundred and sixty teams, we could watch each other's backs, give us a better shot at making it through."

She sits in silence for a while before whispering something in Chadwick's ear. He nods and then covers his mouth so I can't see what he is saying. The two carry on with this back and forth before turning to me.

"We're in, but we have conditions." She hops down from the ledge.

"Okay, let's hear them."

She stands right in front of me. "No one else gets in on our alliance. You're the only one I trust in this whole competition, and I don't want to be stabbed in the back by someone I haven't fought beside in battle."

I nod. "Sounds good. What else?"

"We train together in Portal Pass." She winks. "We can set up bots to go against us."

I look to Dean and he nods his acceptance.

"I think we can manage that. If we can ever get inside."

She extends a hand to help me down. "We better get moving then. Chadwick just checked the forums and everyone has been purged from Portal Pass. Only those in the tournament are allowed to train there for now."

We log out just as the hovertruck makes another lap. The main lobby of Raceworld is crowded. Dozens of people stand in front of the entrance to Portal Pass.

"Oh, come on! Why can't we get back in?"

"This is some Grade-A bullshi—"

"Let's get out of here. What a waste of time."

We press our way through the crowd until we're able to see the screen.

"Hey, I know you. You're that kid from—" Someone grabs me by the shoulder, but before they have time to initiate a conversation, I'm already entering Portal Pass.

I select a separate instance for us to enter. The system confirms that I'm in the tournament, and then allows me to invite the others. A moment later, they all materialize inside of a showroom.

Inside of the showroom, dozens of vehicles hover in the air rotating in a circle. The walls of the showroom display various stages, and a long counter shows all the items and abilities each stage has to offer. Next to them, miniature holograms show how they work on a model hovercraft.

Talia stands in front of one of the location displays, swiping through each stage. "Hey, Esil. Can you give me admin access? I'd like to set up some test courses."

Pretty soon, we have a test track created with ten different stages. She randomizes the items and adds one hundred bots to the race.

Finally, it's time to train.

CHAPTER NINETEEN

After our fifteenth race of the day, we stop for a break at the finish line. The bots dissipate as they finish the race, leaving Talia, Chadwick, Dean, and myself in a sandy clearing in the middle of a lush jungle.

Large ropes run along the edge of the sandy track, keeping us from venturing into the jungle. Birds and monkeys play in the trees, filling the air with noise. Somewhere in the distance, a waterfall gives off a low roar.

"This is crazy." Chadwick hops out of the rear seat of the bug-shaped car and kicks at the sand. Painted red, the car looks like a ladybug as it hovers a foot off the ground. "We haven't finished in the top ten once. Can't you make them go a little easier on us?"

Talia unbuckles herself and climbs out of the front seat. "You think our opponents are going to go easy on us?"

He scowls at her. "No, but how many times are we going to get blasted? This isn't fun."

She crosses her arms. "Until we stop getting hit. And it's not supposed to be fun, we're training. So that you can get that scholarship you want so badly."

I try my best to ease some of the tension. "Hey, at least there's no elimination on this one, so it doesn't matter how many times we get knocked down. As long as we finish in the top one hundred, we'll be through."

"I get what he's saying, though." Dean joins Talia and Chadwick in the sand. "This is intense. There's too much to learn in such a short time, and I'm sure the developers will throw some kind of twist on what we're expecting. But geez, how many times are we going to get hit with an ice beam?"

Talia shrugs. "I know it's not easy. But we need to figure out what works. Each elemental projectile has a counter that nullifies it. We just need to get better at using those to our advantage."

On paper, this seems like a simple race, but the sheer number of item combinations makes it difficult to formulate any kind of plan until the race starts. Items spawn randomly on the track, so aside from vehicle choice, it's all about adapting to the situation at hand. So far, we've done a pretty poor job.

I'm confident we'll come up with some good ideas the more we practice. "We still have a few days to work on things, and I'm sure we'll get it figured out. Dean and I have to bounce, though. I promised Grayson we'd go over some of his research. Want to meet up again later tonight?"

Talia extends her fist and taps it against mine. "Sounds good. We'll see you later. Chadwick, let's run it through one more time."

A few minutes after we log out, there's a knock on the door. Dean answers and lets Grayson inside.

"Alright, let's get straight to business." Grayson sits down at the kitchen table and pulls out his tablet. "I've gone over everything I can find about Portal Pass. It's an interesting raceworld since it essentially blends multiple tracks together using portals to connect each stage. Some of the stages have death traps or falls that can set you back a great deal. My guess is that they'll throw in a few tricks that no one is expecting. How did the trial runs go?"

Dean takes a seat next to Grayson and answers. "Not good. Even with Talia and Chadwick watching our backs, we never did all that great."

Grayson nods. "She's a good one to have on your side. If you were going to pick an ally, she's the one to go with. I'm assuming Esil is the driver, and you're the gunner?"

I join them at the table. "You assume right."

"Aside from the portals, the thing that really sets this race apart from the others are the elements each gun uses. As you pass over certain areas of the track, you gain elemental charges for your weapons, this is in addition to any items you have. You can store and cycle through the elements at your disposal, three charges per gun if I recall correctly. This is what will offer the most strategy. The most common elements are fire, water, ice, wind, electricity, earth, and poison, but there may be new ones in the next round. Each one has a counter, but more importantly, they can also pair together to make different outcomes. Do you know why this is important?"

Dean shrugs. "I don't know. It's not like we can fire two guns at once."

Grayson stares him down. "Come on, kid. Use your brain. Why is this important?"

Dean scrunches his eyes as he thinks it over. "Because of target fire?"

"Exactly!" Grayson grins. "For one, you can fire at someone who is already being targeted to activate a bonus effect. But most importantly, if you are able to stay close to Talia, then you can coordinate together."

"That's not a bad idea." I chime in. "We should probably get a list of how all of the elements work and counter one another."

"No need. Check your messages." Grayson winks.

I open my tablet and find a message from him. Inside is a list with each element's counter as well as how they gel with other elements.

"Wow!" Dean scrolls through his tablet. "Lightning and wind make a lightning cloud? And wind and poison make toxic gas? I was wondering why our shield was draining when we weren't actually covered in poison. This is so cool!"

Grayson opens another document on his tablet. "I'm glad you find it helpful, but what I really want to talk about is the competition. You need to know what to expect with these people."

I lean in a little closer. "What have you got?"

Our competition hasn't crossed my mind much since the initial interviews. Now that we're about to enter the PVP section of the tournament, it's time to learn as much as possible.

A second message pops up with a copy of Grayson's list.

He taps the tablet as he shows it to us. "I've put together what I think are the strongest teams, but I've got notes on just about everyone. Let's start with the gnomes, Benny Reid and Yvonne Powers. If you recall, they were the only ones to make it to the control room without engaging in combat at all."

"How did they manage that?" asks Dean.

"Here, activate share screen and I'll show you."

I receive a notification for Grayson to share his screen with me, and I accept. A video appears on my tablet and starts playing. Two humans wearing the same gray unitards sneak between a line of tanks.

"Wait, I thought you said they were gnomes?" Dean looks confused.

"They are normally, but everyone was given a human avatar for stage one. Now watch." Grayson taps his tablet and the video plays. One of the figures activates a pulse grenade and tosses it between a group of parked hover-craft. After a short delay, the grenade activates, pulling all nearby vehicles toward one another. The loud crash lures the ooze beasts from the tunnel, and they are able to bypass them.

A new clip plays, showing the pair stuck in the tunnel between the lizard people and a spiky cat-wolf creature. They activate a handful of plasma grenades in the hall-way. After they explode, the doors to the crew quarters open and lizardfolk spill out into the hallway in the direction of the noise. The two sneak behind one as he rushes toward the crash and lock themselves inside the quarters as the lizardfolk and cat-wolf devour one another.

"I looked up their history, and Benny has won several puzzle and strategy tournaments. They use distraction and their surroundings to their advantage. I'd be careful of these two. They might not fight you directly, so be wary of getting lured into a trap. You can watch the clips in detail later, but you get the picture."

He closes out the clip and opens another. "These two are pretty genius as well. Lyle Hagan and Aliya Diaz. You may remember him as the vampire who gave his apprenticeship to the first player to kill him. Check this out."

Lyle and Aliya sit in an armored tank as it drives through a wide tunnel. Dozens of hairless, bear-like creatures cling to the tank. Lyle drives the tank into a hangar filled with more vehicles and parks it in the center. A silver glow surrounds the tank as they activate a pulse grenade inside. A moment later, the surrounding vehicles are pulled in violently, crushing the bears beneath their weight.

"Holy..." Dean's voice trails off. "That was brutal."

We go over numerous highlights, and by the time we're done, I feel like I finally have an idea of how some of the teams operate. The majority have one person calling the shots, usually the champion, while the apprentice follows orders, but a few operate as a team, letting each other's strengths guide their decisions.

Dean is a valuable asset, so I want to make sure that he's given the opportunity to shine. With his accuracy and precision, having him on the gunner is the smart choice.

We finish up with Grayson and after a quick break for dinner, we spend the rest of the evening with Talia and Chadwick. Our new info comes in useful, and we're actually able to put some of the combos to use. For the first time, one of us makes the top ten.

"Nicely done!" Talia congratulates us. "Let's end on a high note. I think we might finally be making progress. See you in the morning?"

"We'll see you then." I clasp her around the forearm.

Chadwick and Dean high-five as we say our good-byes.

My notifications flash, and I'm surprised when I receive a message from Aleesia. With the tournament in full-effect, I've barely seen her the past few days.

. . .

Esil,

It's been a crazy week but I finally have some free time tomorrow if you want to grab dinner. I'd love to finally meet Dean in person.

-Aleesia

I can't help but smile. Aleesia has always been a comforting presence for me, and it'll be nice to have dinner and not worry about the stress of the tournament for a little bit. I'm sure Dean will have tons of questions for her as well.

I pat Dean on the back. "Alright, let's get out of here and get some rest."

CHAPTER TWENTY

The day passes quickly as Dean and I spend the morning and early afternoon training with Talia and Chadwick. We work on formations, pacing, and not losing one another when something goes awry. By staying together and coordinating our attacks, our average finishing position continues to improve. We even finish in the top ten a handful of times.

After we log out, Dean and I prep dinner as we wait for Aleesia to show up. Normally, I buy food from the cafeteria or have it delivered by drone, but tonight, Dean and I will be cooking. I bought a meal kit that comes with everything we need to make herb-crusted chicken with potatoes and green beans.

I tease Dean as he chops the small red potatoes into quarters. "Be careful with the knife. I don't want you chopping off your fingers before the tournament is over."

"Hey, I know you want to impress your girlfriend, but I've never cooked before. I can't be held responsible if you find a finger in your potatoes." He grins as the knife clacks against the cutting board with each slice. "I bet it was weird for you when you first moved here."

It's a statement, but I can tell by the way he continues to stare that it's really more of a question.

"Yeah, it took some getting used to. Even compared to Civic City, this was a major change. I went from having everything I knew in one small room to having the freedom to go and do as I pleased."

Dean sets the knife down, and his face goes serious. "Is this what things used to be like before?"

Before. It's hard for me to think about what things might have been like back then. Back before the whole world went belly up and the unfortunate ones were locked away in boxes. "I don't know. I feel like we're a long way from how things used to be."

I remember the special world created for the Pangea Developers. The one where my dad hid my present for my nineteenth birthday. It was full of houses so close together with front yards and sidewalks that were meant to be used. He said it was modeled after the way towns used to be built. When families were a part of a community.

Here, even now, there's no real sense of community. We say hi to one another, but people still interact within Pangea. Sure, I hang out and have dinner with Buzz and Grayson, but when we spend quality time together, it's almost always in a digital world. Part of me feels like that wasn't always the case. The world, the real world, doesn't seem to have all that much to offer anymore.

A knock at the door breaks us away from our existentialism.

When I open the door, Aleesia wraps her arms around me. She squeezes tight. "I've missed you. It feels like it's been forever since I've seen your cute face." She kisses me on the cheek.

"I've missed you too." I pull her in tighter, burying myself in her black hair and enjoying the scent of her lavender shampoo. "It's been a busy time for both of us, that's for sure."

She looks longingly into my eyes before releasing me and turning to Dean. "And you must be Dean. It's nice to meet you face to face. How are you liking it at head-quarters?"

Dean blushes. This may be the first time he's been face to face with a beautiful female. "It's nice. Way different than what I'm used to."

"Oh, I bet. What are you making?"

She and Dean engage in small talk while I finish up with the chicken. After his initial nerves wear off, I notice him visibly relax as Aleesia talks to him about her schooling and the internship.

"Are you serious?" His eyes go wide. "You're just an intern and they are letting you work on full-immersion? That's insane! You are living the dream."

She laughs. "It's a lot of work—I mean, a lot—but I really do love it. It's like real-life magic to be able to feel and truly experience another world."

Once the food is prepped and in the oven, we sit around the table with a deck of cards playing Go-Fish and chatting. The cards are old with frayed edges. Benjamin gave them to me when I first moved in. He said that the developers used to play cards when trying to work through new ideas back in the day. It's possible that at some point in the past, my dad held these very same cards in his hands.

"So do you know what is coming in the next stages?"

Dean hands Aleesia a seven of hearts.

She places four sevens on the table, and then asks me for a three, but I don't have one.

"Go fish." I smirk as she scrunches her nose.

She draws from the deck. "I know what's happening in the final stage, but your guess is as good as mine for stage two. It's not my department."

"Well?" Dean leans forward, desperate for information.

"Nice try." I laugh. "But if she's not telling me, then I doubt you're getting any info out of her. Now, Dean, do you have a queen?"

He grumbles as he hands me two queens. They complete my set and I place all four on the table.

"Nice, now, Aleesia, do you have a three?" I wink.

"You son of a—" She slides me the card across the table and my alarm system beeps, alerting me that a package has been delivered.

"That's weird. I'm not expecting anything." I place my cards face down and go to the door.

Outside, there are two black plastic boxes stacked on top of one another. They look almost identical to The Boxes we opened inside the maintenance shaft at the beginning of stage one. Sleek with two latches on each side. A packing slip is attached to each box, one labeled for me and the other for Dean.

I bring the packages inside. Both boxes have a digital lock on the outside preventing them from being opened, so I check the packing slip and find a note inside.

Esil Allen,

Congratulations once again on advancing to stage two of the tournament! The package before you has been shipped preemp-

tively to all contestants for use during stage three. The lock will be opened upon completion of stage two. If for whatever reason you do not advance, the lock will remain in effect and a drone will be sent to retrieve the package.

-Pangea Online Developers

Dean glances from the paper in his hand to the package and then back to me. "What do you think this is?"

I shrug. "I'm not sure, but I'd be willing to bet that it has something to do with Aleesia's mysterious project."

She pulls her thumb and index finger across her mouth as if zipping it shut. "You're not getting anything out of me."

Before long, dinner is ready. Dean inhales his food like he's never eaten before, not all that different from Buzz.

"This is so good," he manages to get out between bites. "I didn't even know food like this existed. It's so much better than the packaged meals we get in The Boxes."

Aleesia smiles. "And you guys made it all by yourselves. If this meal is any indication of your teamwork, then you're gonna go far in this tournament."

"You're in an awfully chipper mood," I tease.

She rolls her eyes. "Oh, stop. It's just nice to actually have some time to myself."

"Well, you know we would love to spend the evening with you, but I promised Talia we would run some more trial runs after dinner."

She stabs a piece of chicken with a fork. "I understand. You do what you have to do to win. I have a nice, hot bubble bath calling my name at home."

Dean's mouth drops open, displaying bits of unswallowed food. "Wait, you have a bathtub? With bubbles? All we have are cold showers at the orphanage."

"Ah, I remember those. They build character." I laugh at the memory of the frigid cold water. "No need to fear, at least we have hot water here."

Aleesia looks at us with a shocked expression. "Are you serious? You don't have hot water?"

I shrug. "You get used to it."

"That's..." She searches for the words. "...not right."

Dean scrapes the last bits of food off his plate. "I'd say that's about the least of our problems."

Aleesia's cheerful disposition instantly sours. She has a good heart and hates to see others suffering. But the truth of it is she'll never really understand. Cold water is par for the course. The real injustice is that the system is designed to keep everyone stuck there. I've helped those I can, but it will never be enough until they are treated as more than just people from The Boxes.

But this is nothing new. We've had this talk in a million different ways. For now, it's best to focus on the tournament, on helping the one person I know I truly can.

After cleaning the table, I pull Aleesia into my bedroom to talk privately. "I know you're upset, but this has been my and Dean's life for as long as we can remember. I don't want to dwell on how bad things are for him back there, but show him how good things can be when he gets out. We just need to get through the tournament."

She leans into my chest. "I just wish there was more we could do. I know I told you to focus on those that you can help, but meeting him, knowing that there are so many more just like him... I guess it never really hit me before. The world is a mess."

I take her face in my hands and look into her glistening eyes. "All we can do is try to make it a little better each day. Now, get out of here and enjoy your bubble bath."

I kiss her gently on the nose and she wipes away the tears that threaten to overflow.

Aleesia hugs Dean on the way out, thanking him for dinner. She may be going to rest, but for us, we're just getting started.

CHAPTER TWENTY-ONE

Over the next two days, we train like our lives depend on it. With each race, as we continue to gel with Talia and Chadwick, I become increasingly aware that this alliance will not last forever. There can only be one winner in the end, and I'll do everything within my power to make sure it's me and Dean.

At some point, our goals will not align with Talia and her brother. I just hope that moment comes in stage three and not sooner.

The night before stage two is set to begin, I receive a message from the developers with the time and location for the race. Tomorrow morning, 10am, Raceworld. Only competitors will be allowed in Raceworld until the tournament begins.

Dean and I remove our haptic suits and hang out in the living room before bed. We've done all we can to prepare. Now, it all comes down to execution.

"How are you feeling?" I want to give him the opportunity to get whatever he is feeling off his chest.

He brushes his shaggy hair from his eyes. "Ready as I'll

ever be. As long as we are able to stay near Talia, I think we've got a shot."

"I agree. The good thing about this tournament is that we're all on the same page. Everyone else has had the same amount of time to prepare." I stand up and stretch. "We should try to get some sleep. I need you to be as focused as possible tomorrow."

Advice is always easier to give than adhere to. Once in bed, I find myself wide awake, staring at the ceiling and playing through scenarios in my head. I know that there will be something tomorrow that we haven't prepared for, but it doesn't keep me from running through scenes that are likely to never happen. When sleep does come, my dreams are haunted by even more farfetched scenarios.

Scenes where Ryken pulls me from my car and tosses me off a bridge, forfeiting our position in the race. Or where every other competitor turns on us, using focused fire so that we never move out of last place.

I wake up in a cold sweat five minutes before the alarm is set to go off. Instead of waiting in bed, I go into the living room.

Dean sleeps peacefully on the couch, his fists balled together beneath his chin as he pulls the sheets in close. He's been through a lot. Even though he's so close to being a man, I'm reminded that he's still a kid. His life is only beginning, and winning this tournament could change his entire future.

The alarm goes off. A gentle beeping that slowly grows louder until Dean stirs beneath the covers. He sits up and wipes his eyes.

The look of confusion transforms into a smile. "Today's the day!"

After a quick shower and breakfast, we log into

Pangea. Once the time comes, we depart from my home portal to Raceworld, where competitors continue to materialize around us. Many stand in groups of four to six. Apparently, more and more people decided it would be a good idea to have an ally in a race this big.

"Ready?" A firm hand grabs me on the shoulder.

I turn to see Talia, her dreadlocks pulled into a ponytail.

"We're ready," Dean answers for me as he fist-bumps Talia and Chadwick in turn.

There's a flap of wings as Nancy takes to the sky on her pegasus. A moment later, her amplified voice carries over the crowd.

"Greetings, adventurers, and welcome to stage two of the Pro-Am Tournament! You once again find yourselves competing against the best of the best. Portal Pass may be a familiar track, but let me assure you, there are plenty of unexpected changes in store. Your positions have been randomly generated, so without further ado, let's get started."

She snaps her fingers, and everything goes black. The next thing I know, I'm sitting in a hovercar on the streets of a towering city. Neon lights flash all around us, reflecting off the wet streets. Holograms dance in the sky among the towering buildings. We're in some sort of shopping district in a futuristic cyberpunk world. I can't read any of the signs on the buildings. They're in a foreign language but the images of ramen, clothing, robots, and more cast some light on what each shop contains.

Revving engines fill the air. We're surrounded by other cars, each hovering about a foot off the ground. I search the area, but I can't see Talia anywhere.

I tap the floorboard with my foot as I search for the

gas pedal, but it's empty. When I tilt the steering wheel, the massive turret overhead changes direction.

"We need to switch," Dean yells over my shoulder.

He and I climb out of the vehicle. As soon as my feet touch the ground, a red timer appears in my vision counting down from thirty.

Warning! *Return to your vehicle immediately or you will be disqualified.*

That's good to know.

I climb into the front seat and the notification disappears. The dashboard in front of me has displays for speed, shield health, elemental charges, and equipped items. In the top right corner of my vision, there are displays for our position and current stage.

Position: *80/163*

Stage: *1/10*

The shield is currently at zero, so I assume it will activate once the race starts.

"Have you seen Talia?" I ask as I scour the competitors around us, looking for her dreadlocks.

To our right, there are two elves in jewel-toned cloaks. Straight ahead, there's a blue-haired beastman and a post-apocalyptic human. Next to them, two men with fairy wings protruding from their shoulder blades. A few rows up, I spot Ryken's massive frame. Dawn scowls at me as she points the turret gun in our direction. How has he managed to turn her against us too?

"They got lucky. Look all the way to the front." Dean fiddles with something behind me.

Sure enough, all the way in first place I see Chadwick in the gunner spot. He waves at me as our eyes briefly make contact. Talia sits ahead of him in the driver's seat.

There are over seventy cars between us and them.

Sticking to our plan is going to be a tall order, and I won't blame her one bit for not waiting around for us.

All around us, the other teams are getting into position, switching seats, and locating their allies for the race. One thing I notice is that we all have the same style of hovercar.

They are all matte gray, with one seat facing forward and the other facing the rear. Thrusters glow beneath each vehicle, changing from a dull gray to a bright yellow as drivers tap the acceleration.

One major change I spot is the way the turrets are mounted. Instead of having one blaster attached to the front and rear, a turret is mounted in between the driver and the gunner a foot overhead so that it allows the gunner to shoot in three-hundred-sixty degrees.

Nancy flies down the center of the street on her pegasus. Her shimmering mail reflects the neon lights, giving a cyberpunk glow to her Norse armor. Her mouth moves, but I can't hear her over the revving engines and constant chatter.

She taps her neck twice and the scream of feedback silences the noise around us.

"That's better." She smiles. "I can understand your excitement, but I have a couple of announcements before we get this race going. First off, I'm sure you've noticed our upgraded turrets. This allows the drivers to focus on driving and the gunners to focus on shooting. In addition to the new turret, Portal Pass also has new portal options and a few new items, but I don't want to spoil the surprise. And finally, you all received packages in the mail. Each one has a time-delayed lock that will open for those who finish in the top one hundred. For those of you who finish outside of the top one hundred, a drone will come to recover the package."

She hovers in the air at the front of the line. "Now that we have that out of the way, everyone take your positions. The race will begin in sixty seconds. Good luck and godspeed! I'll see you on the other side."

A timer appears in the center of my vision. I scout ahead, looking for any of the items or elemental charges on the track. From my position, I can't see anything beyond the first row of cars. We'll need to catch up with Talia, but there are over seventy cars between us.

The timer hits zero and whining engines surround me. The two elves smash into us from the right at the same time as the beastman reverses into us. Our shield cracks as more cars ram into us from behind.

Dozens of cars bypass us to the left and right.

I try to maneuver away, but we're pinched between the pileup. There's no one to our left, but we're so jammed that I can't break free. Our shield continues to decrease as more and more cars pile up around us.

Our shield hits zero and the acceleration gauge plummets. I press the gas, but nothing happens. That's when I notice that we have dematerialized into a ghost version of ourselves. Our car floats higher into the air, and the pileup of cars fills in our empty spot below.

"What's going on, Esil? Get us out of here." Dean yells.

"I can't do anything. Our shield is down."

Panic begins to set in. Are we already out of the race this soon? We didn't even make it past the starting line.

Several other cars begin to drift into the air, including the beastman in front of us. Our shield springs back to life and we're jostled as our car drops on top of the pileup. After a couple of seconds, the other cars regain their form and are dropped on the track. Once we touch down, I'm able to accelerate again. I press the pedal to the floor and we slide off the pileup, crashing down on the street below before our car resumes hovering. The fall damages our shield, but we're able to break free and finally start the race.

More cars crunch against one another, but the pileup eventually begins to disperse as more and more cars respawn on the track. I keep a wide berth from any of the other cars as we exit the first stretch and head into an underground tunnel.

Around the first turn, an elemental charge and item spawn sit in the center of the track. I pass over each one in turn, unlocking a fire charge and two shield cells.

"Now we're talking!" Dean immediately opens fire with his elemental charges.

Flaming balls of fire bounce across the street, and cars behind us swerve as they try to avoid them.

While I'm glancing behind us, an errant ice beam hits the front bumper as I crest the hill from the tunnel, dropping our shield by a quarter and slowing our speed. The icy effect makes it incredibly hard to steer, and the hovercar drifts to the right, almost colliding with the wall before the effect wears off.

"You okay up there?" asks Dean.

"Yeah, I'm good, just getting the hang of things." I activate one of the shield cells and it repairs our shield immediately.

For the moment, we're caught in no man's land between those that were able to escape the beginning chaos and everyone who got caught in the pileup.

"Up ahead!" I shout. "There's a car just getting up to speed, see if you can hit them."

Two dwarves sit in a car as their shield reforms and ghost mode fades. The thrusters glow yellow as they accelerate, but we're catching up quickly. The turret shifts overhead, and a stream of fireballs hits the dwarves' car, sending splinters cracking through their shield.

They point their gun at us, but their water beams turn to steam as Dean counters them with fire.

I wave to the dwarves as we speed past.

"We're almost out of fire." Dean alerts me.

I check the elemental gauge, and the fire emblem is nearly empty. "Nice job back there. I'll keep an eye out for more charges."

A glowing lightning bolt hovers in the air near the edge of the track. I swerve to hit it, filling a second gauge with electricity. I also unlock a speed boost that shows up as a picture of winged shoes.

As we hit the next stretch of flat track, there are three cars within striking distance. Beyond them, the first portal awaits. Only instead of one portal, there are three. Each one is circular, their center filled with purplish-black energy and their edges covered in glowing runes.

So it looks like there is more than one way to finish this race.

One of the cars disappears into the portal on the left. Another appears to be on track for the right portal.

"Hold on tight!" I activate the speed boost and the front of the car tilts up as we're thrust forward. "Trouble at two o' clock."

Dean points the gun in their direction, and I recognize a familiar face as Lyle, the vampire, showcases his predatory incisors while he fires on us. A gale of wind erupts from his turret toward us.

Dean hits the gale with a bolt of electricity and the

two elements converge in a thunderous explosion. A dark cloud forms and tiny bolts of lightning arc out from it for several feet. I swerve around the thunderstorm just as Lyle's apprentice Aliyah hits the far-right portal.

"Someone's catching up," Dean warns.

I glance over my shoulder just as an unlucky minotaur drives too close to the thunderstorm. A bolt of lightning hits the car, stunning them in place as we pass through the center portal.

For a moment, we travel through space and time before the portal dumps us into a desert wasteland at full speed. The track is nothing more than a dried-out riverbed. We hit the ground at top speed, and it takes a second for my eyes to adjust to the scorching sun.

For the first time since starting the race, I check our positioning.

Position: 113/163

Stage: 2/10

We're thirteen spots out of advancement currently, and way behind where we started.

As we speed through the winding riverbed, it's hard to gauge who might be in front of us. The river-bank and twisting track obscures my view of anything other than what is right in front of us. Our plan of staying by Talia has gone completely to hell. I hope that every other alliance faced the same problem we did.

The sun blazes overhead. Everything around us is a shade of brown or yellow. I hit an elemental charge for poison, and then one for earth. Since we can only keep three at a time, Dean is forced to choose which elements to keep, and discards the nearly-depleted fire charges. I also manage to snag a couple more shield cells, a second speed boost, and temporary invisibility—one of the new items.

The track is so windy that it demands all my attention to keep from crashing into the riverbank.

I turn another corner and slam on the brakes as a car sits stalled in the middle of the track. In the front seat, a knight in silver armor raises his hands into the air. I focus on the knight and his name appears in the air above his head.

Paul Campbell.

I remember him from the highlights Grayson showed us.

"Don't shoot!" He lifts his hands higher.

In the back seat, a purple fairy with green wings has her arms raised as well.

Dean aims the turret at them but holds his fire.

"What do you want?" I ask, hesitant of a trap.

It won't be long before someone shows up behind us, so we need to deal with this quick.

"We need to hurry, just hear me out. We lost our allies, and we're never going to catch up at this rate if we stay solo. Can we team up until we are in better positioning, then you can go your own way?"

I don't know that I want to let my guard down around someone I don't know, but I defer to Dean. "What do you think?"

"I don't like it, but he's got a point. Our entire plan is ruined, so it's worth a shot."

I nod. "Alright, we need to get moving before someone catches us. What charges are you running?"

"Right now, we have fire, wind, and water. You?"

"That'll work. We have poison, electricity, and earth. If we can coordinate our shots, then we should have some good effects. Water and poison make acid, fire and earth make lava, wind and poison make toxic gas, and the wind and electricity create a thunderstorm."

"Someone's coming!" Dean warns. He points to the fairy gunner. "Switch to wind. I'll hit them with electricity."

A hovercar turns the corner, and the eyes of the half-dragon driving goes wide when he sees us. A gale of wind and bolt of electricity hit the car at the same time, engulfing it in a thunderstorm and stunning it in place.

"Nice! Now let's go." I punch the gas, and we take off down the riverbed.

Paul follows behind closely, his silver armor looking almost yellow as it reflects the landscape. The turret swivels back and forth as his apprentice scopes the area for threats.

When we arrive at the next portal, a car sits in front debating which one to take. We hit them with a thunderstorm and zoom through the right. The portal spits us out going full speed in the jungle.

We speed down the dirt track when something crashes into us from the side, knocking us off course. I search for our assailant, but all I see is a log hanging by two ropes just as we fall into a ravine.

We lose five seconds to ghost mode before we respawn on the track. Not far up ahead, Paul respawns from a similar fate. Row after row of swinging logs sway back and forth like a pendulum.

I slowly inch us forward, waiting for the log to pass before accelerating through. "We need to take this one slow or we'll lose even more time."

We've managed to gain five spots, but we're still out of placement.

The drive through the jungle is slow-going. It seems like there's a new trap every few seconds, from spiked pits to rope bridges, and more swinging logs. They definitely made this stage much harder than the one we trained on.

We pass another handful of teams as we take our time. A team of robots curses us to seven hells as we hit them with a toxic cloud the moment they respawn on the track.

Position: *105/163*

Stage: *3/10*

With careful effort, we slowly gain on our competitors. After the jungle, we go through a tunnel track that winds all the way down a volcano. Ramps force us to jump over molten lava, and random geysers send us soaring through the sky between tunnels.

After the volcano, the race is less stressful as we pass through a medieval town and countryside. By the end of that stage, we are running fire, ice, and poison charges. Ice has the effect of slowing whoever we hit, fire leaves lingering burn damage, and poison does damage over time. By hitting our opponents with the ice beam first, it allows us to spam the other elements. Even if they manage to get away, the burn and poison damage keeps them hurting and a few times, we force a respawn even after they've escaped.

At the end of the medieval stage, we enter ninety-ninth place right as the portal spits us out onto a rainbow bridge. There are still six stages left, but things are finally looking up. Teaming up with Paul turned out to be a good idea after all. For as far as I can see, there's nothing but brightly-colored empty track that arches through the sky. Currently, we have two shield cells, three speed boosts, and one invisibility burst that makes us invisible for five seconds.

"I'm gonna use the speed boosts now," I tell Paul. "There's nothing but straight track ahead."

His eyes cut at me through his visor and he smashes into us from the side. The car swerves, nearly falling off the edge.

"What the hell!" I shout as he attempts to hit us again. "Dean, hit him."

"It's nothing personal." He scowls.

I hit the brakes and Paul swerves past, nearly falling off the edge himself. His fairy apprentice opens fire on us with a giant boulder from the earth elemental. Dean blasts it with fire and molten lava coats our shield, ticking down its health by the second.

Paul is beginning to pull away when Dean lands an ice beam. He must know he can't escape while slowed, because he shifts into reverse and tries to ram us again. I activate speed boost and hit reverse at the same time, blasting us out of the way. Dean hits him with another slow as I shift back to forward and use a second speed boost. Our shield continues to crack as we're hit with more and more boulders, but our increased speed rockets us around Paul before he can run us off the road.

"What an ass!" Dean yells at Paul as we pass.

Karma strikes hard when a cluster of cars emerge from the portal on top of Paul. I use the final speed boost to put as much distance between us as possible.

As we exit the rainbow bridge, we're in ninety-seventh position.

A blood-caked body smashes against the front of the car, and I fight back the urge to scream. We find ourselves in a desolate city, fires raging all around. Overturned vehicles are scattered across the road. The entire scene is gray and haunting. Dark figures shamble across the street, forcing me to slow to avoid them.

There's something very familiar about this level. As we pass an overturned semi-truck, I realize what it is. This track is based off of Apocalyptica, the first stage of the Developer's Tournament.

"Hey, Dean, I need you focused up front. We've got zombies."

He shoots a fire blast at the nearest zombie and it turns to ash. "Try to get me another fire charge, we're running low. These guys should burn like tinder."

I hit several item spawns, but the elemental spawns are nowhere to be found. A shield cell replaces the damage from the first two zombies I hit. The more noise we make, the more zombies turn in our direction.

I slow down slightly in an attempt to mitigate the sound from the thrusters. "Dean, hold off. We're drawing more to us."

He stops firing, but the undead are already shambling in our direction. Up ahead, a swarm of them have at least five cars pinned in place and unable to move. Each time they respawn, the zombies swarm them again.

"Help us!" someone shouts when they see us.

It's the two gnomes who made it through stage one without fighting.

"Help us and we will owe you one," the second gnome pleads.

"Should we help?" I ask Dean.

Every second we wait, more zombies enclose around us.

Dean grimaces as he thinks it over. "Do it. We might need help getting through this."

I look over our elemental charges again. We have fire, poison, and ice.

The first zombie reaches us and starts beating against our shield. One zombie isn't enough to break it, but more approach by the moment.

I call out to the gnomes. "Do any of you have a wind charge?"

The gnomes shake their head, but one of the other cars, the two pink-skinned cyberpunk girls, Annabelle and Kristen, I believe, say that they do.

"Alright, next time you respawn, shoot a gale in our direction. We'll handle the rest."

"Here we go," Annabelle shouts.

Their car and bodies dematerialize and hover in the air. A moment later, they're dropped to the ground and nearby zombies swarm them again.

"Shoot them with poison," I order.

A stream of green liquid fires across the street. It's feet from hitting the cars when Kristen fires a wind charge. The two elements converge in midair, forming a green blob of gas that hovers around them. The zombies charge at the cars again, but the toxic gas eats through their bodies like acid, leaving nothing but a pile of bones.

With the threat neutralized, we pass by the other cars as they wait for the zombies to fully decompose. I zone in on the track, avoiding broken-down vehicles and more zombies.

Dean discovers that shooting them with ice freezes the zombies in place, so that if we hit them with the car, they shatter like glass.

We travel a lot faster once we start smashing the zombies instead of trying to avoid them.

All of a sudden, our speed is cut in half. Ice crystals cover our shield.

Annabelle smirks at us as they creep closer. "Thanks for the help back there, but we didn't make any promises."

"Yeah, but we did." The gnomes hit Annabelle and Kristen with an ice beam of their own. "Hit them with wind if you have it."

Dean fires a gale of wind at the same time as the gnomes shoot a stream of water. The two elements combine as they hit the slowed car and a hurricane engulfs them, twisting them through the air and tossing them back a hundred yards.

The ice melts from our shield and we regain speed.

"We're even now." The gnomes nod to us as they use a speed boost and zoom by.

Soon, we hit another portal and emerge in a world of mushrooms. Shrooms of all shapes, sizes, and colors stretch for as far as the eye can see. Some are as tall as trees, other not much bigger than shrubs. Wooden fence posts separate the track from world beyond.

We pass too close to a mushroom that hangs over the railing, and it releases a toxic cloud that obscures my vision and damages our shield. Unable to see, I crash into the fence post and spin out.

As the smoke fades, a car comes passing by. It glows a bright pulsing yellow, and when Dean fires upon it with an ice blast, the beam has no effect.

"Suck it, loser!" The car swerves in our direction.

It crashes into us, knocking us into the railing again, but their vehicle takes no damage. They speed off like they hit nothing at all. Another mushroom explodes, cracking our shield and forcing a respawn.

"What the hell was that?" I hit the steering wheel as I wait for us to drop.

"No idea. Looked like invulnerability of some sort.

Dammit!" Anger coats Dean's voice. "We're out of placing again."

We drop in the middle of the track and I do my best to stay far away from the fences. We're currently in position one hundred two. So close to placing, but there are still two stages left.

There's a loud *doink* and suddenly we're flying through the air. I look behind and see a mushroom that just sprouted on the track.

Our hovercar lands without losing much speed and I notice a dark spot on the track. A moment later, another mushroom sprouts up.

This is it! If I can hit the mushrooms as they sprout, then they'll speed us through the stage.

I hit the next two I see, and we're in ninety-ninth position.

We soar over a pileup of four cars caught in a toxic cloud. Dean hits the cloud with a fireball, setting off an explosion and forcing all four cars to respawn.

"Nice one!" I pound my fist in the air.

Something intense must be happening on one of the other tracks, because by the time we reach the portal, we've moved up another forty places.

My neck whips forward when we exit the portal and slam into a wall of gray.

"Geez, what was that?" Dean grimaces.

The wall slides across in front of us and morphs into a tail fin. It's not a wall at all, but some giant fish.

When the fish is gone, a sandy track stretches before us. Coral reef and anemones grow on both sides and hundreds of tropical fish swim about. Sparks flutter from the tentacles of a nearby jellyfish and I stomp the gas before it catches us.

We're in an underwater track and our shield functions as a bubble dome to keep the water out.

If not for the fact that we were fighting for position, I could probably sit here and watch the fish swim by for hours. Even in the coral and anemones, there are hundreds of tiny colorful fish darting between them.

For a moment, I follow a yellow fish as it swims through the coral. It disappears into the depths of the tentacles, and two red eyes peer out from the darkness.

Sparks ignite around a long snake-like creature before something smashes into our car from the other side and I lose all steering. The car drifts across the track until we crash into the anemone's tentacles. The stinging tentacles damage our shield by half before I'm able to pull away.

"Dude, eel!" Dean yells, and I see his arm waving out of the corner of my vision.

A long eel hovers across the track, electricity coursing down its body into the depths of the coral.

I activate a shield cell and curse myself for the distraction. That was a rookie mistake. I need to keep my focus on the track and save the sightseeing for when this is over.

The eel bares its teeth before recoiling back into the coral to wait for its next victim.

I speed down the track. Dean scares off a very dangerous-looking hammerhead shark, and I weave between a group of jellyfish.

Not far ahead, there's a gap in the coral where the water appears to be moving differently. A stray fish swims into it and then disappears in an instant.

Jackpot!

"Hold on tight. I think I found a shortcut."

I aim for the gap, and the swift-moving current whisks us away. Everything blurs as the current rockets us across the track. We gain four more positions, putting us in fifty-first.

The current spits us out back on the track and I slam on the brakes. Fifty yards ahead, a half-dozen cars wait for a group of jellyfish to cross the road. The jellies are moving at a snail's pace, but they're packed so tight that they leave no other option. I wait back, not ready to reveal our position.

Deep within the group, sparks zap out. A car respawns above them only to be immediately trapped inside again.

We're too far away to tell who it is, so I creep up as quietly as I can. As we get closer, I notice laughter. Several drivers gesture at the car as it respawns over and over again.

"Hey, that's Talia and Chadwick." Dean points over my shoulder. "We need to do something."

I focus on the vehicle and even though it's far away, I can make out Talia's dreadlocks and Chadwick's afro. "What can we do? There's at least six of them against us. If we try to help, they may all turn on us."

"We have to do something." He pleads. "You know they would do the same for us."

He's right. Talia would do the same for us. But this is Dean's future on the line. Is it worth risking that for someone we'll have to fight against in the end anyways? I've never been one to stab someone in the back, but Dean is my priority here.

A crack forms in the wall of jellyfish, and the group begins passing through one at a time. I could easily activate invisibility to pass through behind them. Talia would be none the wiser.

"Get closer. I have an idea," Dean orders.

I push my thoughts of subterfuge aside and do as he says. This is Dean's show, for better or worse.

Once we are close enough, he shoots an ice beam at one of the jellyfish. It freezes in place, and even the tiny sparks of electricity turn to ice.

He blasts the entire row in front of us. "Now go through. I'll hit the other side."

I pass through the crack in their wall, only inches away from the frozen tentacles. Talia and Chadwick respawn overhead, and Dean freezes the jellyfish just before they land.

"Thank the gods for you two!" Talia beams. "I thought we were going to be stuck here forever."

They hit the frozen jellyfish and bounce off before landing in the sand next to us.

"No ally left behind. Now, let's get moving." Dean taps me on the shoulder.

We lost four positions during our rescue attempt, but we still have plenty of breathing room.

"I agree. Only one more stage after this one." I get straight to business. "What item and charges are you working with?"

We go over everything we have, and luckily, we have a couple of charges that synergize together. Talia has been holding on to an invisibility item as well, so there's a good chance we can coordinate them if an opportunity presents itself.

The group that snuck through before us is long gone. For the rest of the stage, we fight through sharks, jellyfish, and the occasional eel before we hit the portal for the final stage.

Position: *55/163*
Stage: *10/10*

This is it. As long as we don't screw things up, we'll be into the final round.

We pass through the portal and emerge into another medieval town. My jaw drops to the floor and I slam on the brakes. Talia crashes into our rear and a crack forms in our shield.

"Esil, what's going on? Why did you stop?" Dean's voice sounds distant over my shoulder.

Talia says something, but I ignore her.

To my left, smoke emerges from inside the city walls of the town. A drawbridge hangs open and two guards stand sentry outside. Above the walls, a massive pine tree towers over everything, white flowers dancing on the end of its branches.

Florian.

My pulse races. We're in Carolton, but how could that be? This isn't full-immersion. That's not coming until next round. Or did I completely misread everything? Is this what the Broken Lands have become, a sideshow track in Raceworld?

And what about the NPCs?

Carter steps into the archway of the drawbridge, and I instinctively jump out of the car. The red timer flashes across my vision, counting down from thirty.

"What are you doing?" Dean calls after me.

"Just give me thirty seconds!" I take off sprinting. "Carter! Carter, over here!" I wave my hands until I get his attention.

Carter doesn't acknowledge me. His face is contorted as he looks on in confusion.

"I'm sorry, do I know you?"

"Carter, it's me, Esil." I grab his shoulder and he recoils, pointing his trident in my direction.

"I'm sorry, adventurer, but I don't believe we have met. You must have me confused with someone else. Good luck with your race."

The timer hits fifteen seconds. I don't know what has happened to Carter, but it'll have to wait. I sprint back to the car, climbing inside right as the timer hits two seconds.

"What the hell was that? We're in a race, and you almost got us disqualified." Dean scowls at me. "We lost two positions while you were gone."

"You're right. I'll explain everything later."

I'm flooded by memories as we follow the dirt road that leads away from Carolton. We pass the farmhouse where I first spawned in the Broken Lands. The scarecrow I robbed of its clothing still stands perched above the cornfield.

A group of bandits block the roadway up ahead, but a toxic cloud allows us to bypass them with minimal damage.

In the distance, the black leaves of the forest loom ominously. Some dark challenge will certainly be waiting with the depths of the Cursed Oaks.

Soon, we cross the border into the forest. Broad-antlered deer roam across the road, forcing us to slow down. I dodge what we can, and attack what we cannot. A particularly tough buck runs along beside us, ramming its antlers against our car before Dean is able to take it out.

I turn a sharp corner and slam on the brakes once again. A wall of vines blocks our path. A high-pitched laugh echoes from the other side, sending a chill down my spine.

The laughter fades, and a green-skinned woman appears on top of the vine wall.

The dryad.

Vines wrap down her arms and several branches protrude from her shoulders and back. Moss covers her chest and drapes down her legs like a dress. Her long emerald hair is dotted with crimson flowers and the black leaves of the cursed oak.

I remember battling her with Carter and Kindra. Carter's fire magic set her ablaze like dry kindling.

"Hit her with fire! That's her weakness."

Dean doesn't hesitate, unleashing a maelstrom of fireballs at the dryad and her vine wall. Chadwick follows suit. The dryad bursts into flames, her screams echoing across the forest as the wall crumbles to ash.

"How did you know that would work?" Dean sounds astonished. "We never practiced this track."

"I'll explain everything later. For now, just do what I say and we'll get through this."

We zoom through the ash, leaving a smoky trail in our wake. The forest fades, and we find ourselves in front of sweeping wildflower-covered plains. My haptic suit does its best to mimic the aroma, but it doesn't compare to what I remember.

We grab new charges and a speed boost as they appear. Talia has a speed boost as well, so we activate them on the stretch of open road.

In the distance, there's a multi-car pile-up. Something darts through the air around the downed cars.

Fairies.

If it's anything like the Broken Lands, then the drivers have all been put to sleep with fairy dust.

At the front of the pileup, a hulking black figure abruptly turns a pulsing yellow before leaving the others.

I point in his direction. "It's Ryken. He must have used one of those invulnerability items."

"What's going on up there?" asks Talia.

I slow down so that we are side by side. "Fairies. They have a sleep debuff."

Some of the other cars begin moving again, so the effect must be wearing off.

"Still have that invisibility item?" I ask.

She nods.

"Good. I think it's time to use it. We can bypass the others and avoid the fairies. Once we are in front, Chadwick and Dean can coordinate an attack and slow the other cars down further."

Once we are close enough that the fairies become visible, I activate invisibility. A countdown appears, telling me I have ten seconds before it quits working.

The fairies dart through the sky. Several dozen of the small, winged humanoid creatures with pale blue skin fly through the air, sprinkling glittery dust beneath them. The creatures aren't bigger than the size of a kitten, but they fly with great speed.

We pass around them, avoiding the fairy dust. The other drivers begin to regain their composure, but right as we become visible again, Chadwick and Dean unleash their attack. Wind and earth charges combine, forming a tornado. The tornado rips across the road, melding with the fairy dust and knocking the drivers out again.

"Nicely done!" I congratulate them. "Now, let's finish this."

Up ahead, I can barely see Ryken's car. He disappears behind a copse of trees and once we pass through, he's barely a speck in the distance.

"He must have a speed boost," Talia yells from behind us.

We come upon another forest. The track leads through

it, but I can barely make out Ryken's vehicle on a path that goes around it. The path is nearly twice as long by going around, but there must be a reason he's going that way. He must have seen something.

"Take the road to the left," I tell Talia.

"What, why?"

"That's where Ryken went." I glance in her direction and our eyes meet.

"Are you sure? It could be a trap." She sounds hesitant.

We're already in a placing position, so I understand her concern, but I also know Ryken. The only thing trustworthy about him is that he will always look out for his own interests. "He would never risk his position this late in the race. If he's taking a side-route, it's because he sees something we don't."

I swerve from the main track and take the narrow path around the forest's edge. I stay vigilant, in case I was wrong, but there's no trap, at least not yet.

Several roars come from within the forest and trees shake in its depths. A moment later, we gain three spots, then two more.

When the path reconvenes with the main track, we've gained seven spots total. Only a flat stretch of road stands between us and the final portal.

I press the pedal to the floor, and the sound of snapping trees echoes behind us.

"Faster!" Urgency coats Dean's voice.

I look over my shoulder just as a massive green dragon emerges from the trees. Its wings flap like sails, whipping against the air. It soars higher, and I let out the breath I've been holding.

Then it barrels in our direction.

We're less than a hundred yards from the finish line

with an angry dragon on our tail. Our car hits top speed, but without a speed boost, the dragon is gaining on us fast. It could pick us up and carry us back to the forest for all I know.

I sure wish I had an extra invisibility right now.

Dean shoots at the dragon, but none of the elements work against the dragon's impenetrable scales, not even the combo effects.

Talia and I are neck-and-neck on the final stretch. Her face is set in stone as she focuses on the portal.

The dragon reaches for us, and I swerve to the right, nearly losing control but leaving the dragon grasping at air. A shrill shriek cuts through the air. A moment later, something jostles us, and I lose all ability to steer. Talia zooms past us and into the portal.

Two large claws rip into our car, cracking the shield and lifting us into the air.

My instincts take over. "Jump!" I say it without thinking. "Jump through the portal."

Dean doesn't question the order and stands on his seat. I grab his hand to steady him as he balances on the edge of the car. He pushes off and leaps toward the portal.

As the car lifts higher into the air, I climb onto the hood and jump with all my might, aiming straight for the portal. The dragon screeches again. I hit the swirling galaxy of the portal, and everything fades to black.

CHAPTER TWENTY-TWO

We portal back into The Vacuum, where over forty people are already celebrating making it through to the final round. Epic instrumental music blares from every direction, confetti falls from the sky, and Nancy soars through it all riding her pegasus.

"We did it!" Dean embraces me sporting a wide grin.

I return his embrace, but my mind is elsewhere. I can't get over the distant look in Carter's eyes when he saw me. He didn't recognize me at all.

"Man, I thought you guys were goners." Chadwick wraps his arm around Dean.

Talia extends a hand to me. "Yeah, the last thing I saw y'all were being pulled into the air by the dragon. How'd you manage to get away?"

"We didn't." Dean smirks. "We jumped from the car into the portal."

Talia tilts her head back and laughs. "Classic!" She stops laughing and frowns as her eyes bore into me. "Esil, what's up with you? You look like you've seen a ghost."

In a way, I have. I know I need to find answers, or I'm just going to bring everybody down.

"I need to head out. There's something I have to take care of. Keep an eye on Dean for me." I pat him on the back. "You did a damn good job today. I'll see you back at the apartment."

He looks at me with a shocked expression, but I don't wait for him to respond before returning to my home portal.

This is a big moment for him. He should be proud, and I will celebrate once I find out what the hell is going on. But I can't just pretend like this doesn't bother me. I spent over a year in the Broken Lands, and the NPCs like Carter were indistinguishable from anyone I've met in real life. If they changed their programming or erased their memories...

I have to know what happened to them.

I log out of Pangea and change into my sweatpants in record time, nearly knocking the lamp off the table as I scramble through the apartment. I take one last glance at Dean as he sits peacefully in his haptic suit before I bolt out the door.

I sprint down the sidewalk, across the courtyard, and into Pangea Headquarters.

Benjamin is stepping out of his office just as I arrive. He smiles, but his demeanor quickly changes. "Everything okay, Esil? I was just about to log in and give a speech to everyone who made it to the final round."

I hold up my hand while I catch my breath. "What did you do to them?"

"To who?" He gives me a confused look.

"The NPCs from the Broken Lands. What did you do to them? I saw Carter, but he didn't recognize me."

His smile returns and for the briefest instance, I have the urge to hit him.

"Here, step into my office." He scans his hand on the reader, opening the door, and gestures for me to step inside. When the door closes behind him, he finally speaks. "You have nothing to worry about. They—"

I cut him off. "I looked him in the eye, and he didn't know it was me. Did you erase all of their memories?"

He lifts his hands in defense. "Listen to me, Esil. They are all fine." He sighs. "I shouldn't even be telling you this, but that was nothing more than a mirror of the Broken Lands. We copied the code and tweaked it to run in Race-world. All the characters you saw run off of a script. We are going to use the footage from the race as a teaser to announce the last stage of the tournament."

"What?" I'm suddenly aware of how tense my body is. "So everyone is fine? They still know me."

He smiles again. "Everyone is fine. All of their memories are intact. I'm sure it was a shock to you, but we didn't think it was fair to let you in on the secret. You already know more than any of the other competitors about what's coming."

I take in a deep breath and my shoulders relax, though my hands still jitter from how worked up I was. I fix my gaze at the floor. I know I must seem insane to have made such a fuss.

"I'm sorry—"

"Don't worry about it. Your heart's in the right place. You were in full-immersion for a long time, so of course, they are real to you. I mean, they act of their own accord. Who's to say they aren't real?" He stands up. "I hate to cut and run, but I've got a few million people waiting for my appearance."

Benjamin escorts me out of his office. With a squeeze on the shoulder, he disappears down the hallway. I lean back against the pristine white wall lost in my own thoughts.

After today, I'm not sure if the world is ready for full-immersion. Look what just happened to me. I ruined what should have been an amazing triumph all because of my attachment to lines of code.

What happens when the entire world becomes that invested in all of Pangea?

I take a deep breath. Maybe I'm overreacting. Pangea is already more real to most people than their lives outside the game, so what is another layer of immersion? Most people have more outfits and items in-game than outside of it. Before I experienced full-immersion, I had already bonded with Fenrir and Merlin so much that I experienced real grief when I lost my pet owl.

But even then, I knew he wasn't real. What happens when the line between game and reality continues to blur?

I meander down the hallway, through the double-doors to the laboratory where I used to test full-immersion. For the first time I can remember, it's empty. There aren't even any scientists or technicians in the control room.

There are other labs at headquarters, even an overflow lab from when we expanded the beta testers for the Broken Lands. Maybe that's where Aleesia is. Either way, it appears that whatever they have planned for the final stage is ready to go.

Now that I have answers, I make my way back to the apartment. I open the door to find Dean sitting on the couch, the official Pangea Online stream running on the far wall.

He stares at me as I walk in. I'm not even sure how to begin explaining what happened, so I just stand there.

"Sorry about that," I finally say.

"What happened? You weren't yourself back there."

"Yeah, I kind of freaked out for a minute."

I go on to tell him about my experiences in full-immersion. How the final stage of the track was a replica of the Broken Lands, only I didn't know it at the time, and how I panicked when Carter didn't recognize me.

He gives me a sympathetic smile. "I don't blame you. I just wish I had known. It would have helped me make sense of the situation." His smile broadens, and I can tell there's real mirth behind it. "But hey, we made it. We're in the final round."

My self-pity fades, and I'm able to smile genuinely. "That we did."

"And you think the final stage is going to be full-immersion. Like the real deal?" His eyes are wide with excitement.

"I don't know anything for cert—"

Benjamin appears on the feed, and I let my words fade away. I turn the volume up, and Dean and I watch in silence.

"What a stage, am I right?" Benjamin winks at the camera, clapping his hands and showcasing his natural charisma. "We saw it all. Action, adventure, friendship, betrayal, heartache. Even a last-ditch heroic effort to abandon the hovercar and leap into the final portal. This truly was a race for the ages."

The camera pans out, showing Benjamin in between footage of all ten stages of the race.

"While most of the stages were classics with a twist, we brought two new tracks to the tournament. The first was modeled off of Apocalyptica, an homage to one of our great tournaments of the past." All ten feeds switch to footage of Apocalyptica, showing different teams as they took on the course. "We added zombies as obstacles, and the challengers didn't disappoint. There's more than one way to skin a cat, as they say, and our challengers proved it. They used ice, fire, acid, and much more to put an end to those pesky walking dead."

One of the panels shows Dean and I rescuing the gnomes, and the subsequent betrayal by the cyberpunk ladies. In another, Dawn freezes the undead and Ryken plows into them, shattering their frozen bodies like glass.

"But the real gem was right in front of your eyes the entire time. The forums have been hot with discussion about the track no one recognized." The panels switch to the Broken Lands track, panning above Carolton, the dryad, the faeries, and a devastating dragon attack in the forest. "This was your first glimpse into a new world, the Broken Lands, and a teaser for the final stage. A stage never before seen in Pangea, one that will change virtual reality forever, and the crowning achievement of Pangea's future."

Benjamin takes a long pause as he stares intensely at the camera.

"After this tournament, Pangea will never be the same. For the first time ever, we will be bringing full-immersion to Pangea Online—starting with a battle royale in our first full-immersion world, The Broken Lands. The final one hundred teams will compete for glory until only one team remains, winning a sizable donation to charity and an exclusive Pangea Online scholarship. Stay tuned for an introduction to Pangea's newest development."

The screen goes black, and a medieval style map

appears. The camera zooms in on a castle, then pans across to map past Carolton, the Cursed Forest, and Thunder Mountain. We see goblin society on the mountain as they toil among the rain and lightning, elves peer out from the edge of the forest with uncertainty plastered on their faces, and then a display of fireworks from Carter's nightly show. "Adventure Awaits" flashes across the screen.

"But first…a champion must be crowned. After millennia, magic has returned to the Broken Lands. Fountains have sprouted across the continent, granting magical powers to those who are worthy. Adventurers have come from worlds over for a chance at glory, and the fates have answered. A tournament of heroes awaits, and as the playing field grows smaller, only one victor will remain."

The screen shifts to an action montage, where I see several of the beta testers wearing leather armor or colorful robes as they battle one another inside of a translucent dome. They cast magic from their palms, some throwing fireballs, others bolts of energy. One hovers in the air and launches an icicle like a javelin. A woman shoots a gust of wind to block a barrage of arrows. Two more battle with swords, using magic with their off-hands. The camera continues to switch from one hero to the next as the number of fighters is whittled down. In the final scene, we follow behind a figure wearing a blue tunic as he summits a hill and lifts his sword into the air.

The clip ends and the stream focuses on the analysts as they speculate on the final stage. A new message from the developers draws my attention away.

Greetings Esil,

Congratulations on advancing to the final stage of the tournament! The package you received is now able to be opened. Inside, you will find the next wave of VR technology. The helmet inside provides neurological feedback that allows full-immersion without cumbersome machines. There's no need for haptic suits or gloves, as the deep dive experience melds flawlessly with your nervous system. The technology has been rigorously tested, and the full details can be found in the terms and conditions.

We have set up training grounds for each team so that contestants can acclimate to full-immersion before the final stage. You will find an access token in the home portal of each former champion.

Good luck, and as always, never stop leveling!

-Pangea Online Developers

I set my tablet aside and stare at the two black boxes stacked neatly in the corner. It's crazy how much full-immersion has changed in such a short time. From massive capsules and pods, now it's all compartmentalized in something so small.

"Ready to do this?" I ask Dean.

"I was born ready." He moves the two black boxes, sliding mine in front of me and then sitting on the floor in front of his own.

I press my finger to the locking mechanism, and it scans my fingerprint. The scanner flashes green, there's an audible click, and the lock opens. I lift the lid and find the helmet inside.

It's polished black with a mirrored purple facemask that covers the entire face. It looks more like something out of a sci-fi shooter than a gaming headset. Next to the helmet, there's a pamphlet marked "Instructions."

Place helmet over head and lie down in a neutral position. Once you are ready, lower the visor to begin setup.

"This is badass!" Dean stares at his reflection in the visor. "Can we try them on?"

"No, I was thinking we would just stare at them all day." I laugh. "Kidding. Let's do it."

I pick up my immersion helmet and head into the bedroom. Once the helmet is on, it feels incredibly light and snug, almost like it was molded just for me. I lay down on the bed and flip the visor.

The tutorial is simple enough. Lines of text scroll down the inside of the visor, telling me that it only works in full-immersion worlds, and that in order to gain feedback in the rest of Pangea, I will need to use the haptic suit connector. I'll be able to use the helmet to get to my home portal, I just won't experience true immersion until I'm in the Broken Lands or Training Grounds.

There's also a note that the helmet shuts off after six-hours of uninterrupted gameplay.

Inside my home portal, a gold coin hovers in the middle of the room, spinning slowly. Dean arrives a few seconds later, and I let him in.

When I focus on the coin, a message appears.

Broken Lands Training Grounds Token

Activate? Y/N

I focus on yes. The coin vanishes and a portal takes its place.

I step to the side and gesture. toward the portal. "After you."

CHAPTER TWENTY-THREE

The transition from visual-only to full-immersion is a bit jarring. For a moment, I'm disoriented as the world spins around me, but when I feel a cool breeze against my skin, everything stills. I close my eyes and take a deep breath. Fresh air fills my lungs and the scent of the outdoors washes over me.

I've missed this.

I'm standing in a stone courtyard. Pillars and weathered steps of some ancient ruins surround me to the right. Further away to the left, a rocky hillside descends to the edge of a forest. On the other side, there are rolling hills speckled with towering oaks. Several streams cut through the landscape.

If memory serves, this is the wilderness between Carolton and the Endless Forest. The terrain is great for a battle royale, offering plenty of places to hide items and provide cover. Multiple ruins are scattered through the area.

"Whoa!" Dean crouches next to the grass at the edge

of the courtyard, running his fingers over the blades. "This is crazy. I can feel every blade."

"You'd rather play with grass than this?" I point to a veritable treasure trove in the center of the ruins.

A variety of weapons lay scattered on the ground. Swords, axes, spears, bows, and much more. Behind them, rows of vials filled with colored liquids hover several inches off the ground.

I pick up a blue vial that's cool to the touch.

Ice potion. Drink to be instilled with elemental ice magic.

I uncork the vial and drink the blue liquid. A chill runs through my core, and ice crystals form along my left hand.

You have activated ice magic. Available spells:

Freeze: *Fire a beam of ice that slows upon impact. Cost: 10 mana*

Ice Dagger: *Fire a piercing ice projectile that deals double damage. Cost: 20 mana*

Ice Path (passive): *Freeze the ground for ten meters, allowing for faster travel. No cost.*

I test out the abilities, shooting snowballs and ice projectiles at one of the pillars. The magic flows out effortlessly, responding to my thoughts in perfect sync. When I use Ice Path, it freezes the ground, allowing me to skate along it.

Dean picks up a red vial and chugs it. "Ooh." He opens his mouth and breathes rapidly. "That's spicy!"

The next thing I know, he conjures a fireball and holds it in his palm like a miniature sun. He tosses it to the ground, leaving scorch marks on the ancient stone.

I take a moment to look over the user interface. It's changed a great deal since my first days in full-immersion. In the top right of my vision, there's a map. It displays a large square section. Within that is a circle that forms the boundary of the battle royale. Once the actual tournament starts, that circle will shrink between each round. As it shrinks, players stuck outside the circle will take damage until they get back inside. This forces players to fight one another as the circle gets smaller until there is only one team left.

If this is an accurate depiction of where the battle royal will take place, it keeps the NPCs from getting involved. All the towns are several miles from our current location. Not that anyone else would care, but it will be one less distraction for me.

To the left of my vision, beneath my name, there's a health bar, a mana bar, and a shield bar. The health and mana bars are both one hundred, but the shield is empty. Maybe that is for the different colored bracers lying on the ground behind the vials.

White, blue, and red bracers sit in neat lines. I equip the white one and my shield changes to fifty. Blue grants seventy-five, and red grants one hundred.

An envelope pulses in the corner of my vision next to the map. I focus on it and a sheet of translucent parchment unfolds in front of me.

Welcome to the training grounds for the Broken Lands Battle Royale. This is where you will find information to help you prepare for your upcoming battle.

The premise is simple. In the bowels of a long-forgotten underground dungeon, an ancient script has been activated, forming an ethereal dome in the countryside that is powered by the underground ley lines. To the citizens of the Broken Lands, you are mighty adventurers from distant worlds sent to test your skills. Once a sufficient number of competitors are inside, the dome will begin shrinking in various stages, until only the victor remains. The area outside of the circle is known as the storm. Those caught outside of the dome's boundaries will take constant damage until they return inside.

Each challenger will have the same amount of health and mana. All challengers start with no weapons, shields, or magical abilities. Vials contain liquids that grant magical abilities once ingested. Only one type of magic may be active at a time. Drinking a second vial will remove the effects of the first. Each branch of magic has three spells, two active and one passive. Active spells require a mana cost and include cooldowns. When attacks are combined, special reactions may be activated. Along with vials, weapons and shield bracers will be scattered at random around the map. Weapons deal flat damage, and shield bracers may be replaced or looted from eliminated challengers.

Players are eliminated when their health bars reach zero. Eliminated players will leave behind bags of loot consisting of any items they had equipped. If one player from a team is eliminated, the other may continue. When there is only one team remaining, the battle royale will end.

Pain sensitivity in the battle royale will be set to twenty-five percent.

It all seems simple enough. Gather weapons, shields, and abilities, then kick ass. All the items will be randomly generated, so luck plays a major part, but so does adaptability.

Dean tries out different vials as I go over everything I'm reading with him. He downs a light blue vial and then turns to me. "Check this out."

He runs to the nearby stream and steps in, except his boots don't sink. He stands on the water like it is dry land.

For a moment, I wonder if it is a glitch. I carefully lower my foot to the water, but when it touches the surface, my boot sinks.

"How?"

He smirks. "Passive ability from the water vial. Pretty cool, huh?"

"Very cool. Time to test them all out. Let's see what we're working with, and then we can pair back up."

I return to the courtyard and grab one of each vial. After we take one, another spawns a few seconds later.

First, I drink the fire vial and it burns like cinnamon.

You have activated fire magic. Available spells:

Fireball: *Summon a fireball that deals burn damage. Cost: 10 mana.*

Firewall: *Summon a wall of flame that deals burn damage. Cost: 20 mana.*

Burn (passive): *Fire attacks deal an additional 1 burn damage per second for five seconds, stacking up to five times.*

Not bad. An additional five bonus damage per second can really rip through one hundred health. Fire magic will be great for an aggressive playstyle.

I test out each ability and then down a silvery liquid for wind magic.

You have activated wind magic. Available spells:

Gale: *Fire a blast of air. Can also be used to move objects or deflect other elemental attacks. Cost: 10 mana.*

Updraft: *Summon a gust of wind, lifting you high into the sky for increased range. Cost 10 mana.*

Fleetfoot (Passive): *Increased movement speed and take no damage when falling.*

There are a lot of benefits to wind magic. As I move around, I feel lighter. Like I can run faster and jump higher. The increased movement speed allows for quicker retreat, and Updraft can be used to attack or scout. This one is great for mobility.

Out of curiosity, I pick up a dagger from the weapon pile and cast Updraft. There's a sudden surge of pressure as wind lifts me off the ground and carries me twenty feet into the air. The constant pressure of wind makes it surprisingly stable to stand on. I toss the dagger into the sky and aim Gale at it. The burst of wind catches the dagger and launches it fifty feet until it thunks against a tree trunk.

Wow. Now, that is deadly.

Updraft ends and I fall to the ground. Thanks to Fleet-foot, I land softly.

Next, I down the light blue water vial. I can't explain the feeling that accompanies it, but it's almost like I feel healthier and more refreshed, like my body and mind have been purified.

You have activated water magic. Available spells:
Stream: *Fire a steady burst of water. Cost: 10 mana.*
Cleanse: *Cleanses the body of any negative effects. Can be used while stunned or otherwise affected. Cost: 50 mana.*
Blessed (Passive): *Ability to walk on water.*

While water magic doesn't have the same firepower of some of the others, it still blasts like a firehose, and Cleanse is invaluable. The ability to clear burns, stuns, or other debuffs is a great advantage even if it uses half of the mana bar each time.

A bright yellow vial looks reminiscent of urine, but the taste is sweet like an energy drink. As soon as I down the vial, my arm hair stands on in, and a thin layer of static coats my body.

You have activated electrical magic. Available spells:

Bolt: *Fires a bolt of electricity. Cost: 10 mana.*

Chain Reaction: *Fires three bolts simultaneously, or double the damage of a single bolt, allowing it to jump up to three times. Cost: 20 mana.*

Stun (passive): *3 consecutive attacks within 2 seconds of one another stuns a target for 5 seconds.*

Electric magic has the benefit of crowd control. The ability to hit more than one target with a single attack is a great bonus as well.

I cast Bolt, and it zigs and zags before hitting the boulder with thunderous violence. While I can aim at the final target, the path the lightning takes to get there will always vary.

The vial for earth magic is a deep brown, almost like chocolate milk. When I drink it, it tastes exactly what I imagine dirt to taste like. My muscles tense as I down the vial, and my skin takes on an increased firmness.

You have activated earth magic. Available spells:

Boulder: *Launches a boulder. Cost: 10 mana.*

Rockslide: *A barrage of earth and rocks fall from the sky, covering a wide area.*

Thick Skin (passive): *10% damage reduction.*

Definitely the tankiest of all the options. Ten percent damage reduction on full health and a red shield pretty much grants an extra twenty health. In a fight to the death, it could make all the difference.

The final vial is neon green. The contents are so sour that I pucker my mouth after each sip.

You have activated poison magic. Available spells:

Acid: *Shoots a spray of acid in a cone that does 1 damage per second for 5 seconds. Cost: 10 mana.*

Gas Cloud: *Covers an area in toxic gas that deals 5 damage* *per second. Enemies trapped in the gas lose visibility. Cost: 20 mana.*

Immunity (passive): *Poison mages take no damage from enemy gas clouds and only take flat damage from acid.*

I like the ability to bombard an area with gas and then hide inside. This could be both offensive and defensive if done correctly.

All in all, each class has its perks, not to mention how they all might interact with one another. The elements are similar to what we used in Raceworld, and I'm sure it's no coincidence. If I had to guess, I bet some of them synergize in a similar way, too.

With the vials and bracers tested, I move onto the weapons. There are plenty to choose from, each with advantages and disadvantages. Spears, swords, daggers, battle-axes, warhammers, halberds, maces, bows, arrows, crossbows, and flails lay scattered on the stone.

With so many options, it's hard to choose which one to start with. The battle-axe is a natural fit. I equip it and take a few swings when a boulder crashes against the stone in front of me. Shards explode in all directions, damaging the shield from my bracers.

I duck and turn around. "What the hell was that?" I ask, more shocked than anything.

Dean wears a mischievous grin as he walks over. "Check this out."

He downs a vial of earth magic and fires a boulder into the air. It goes about ten feet up before gravity takes hold. Dean then chugs a vial of air magic and shoots a gale at the boulder. The gust of wind carries the boulder another twenty feet before it sinks into the stream.

"Nice!" I didn't even think about using it in that way.

He shrugs. "It's not the most economical use of our

items. We're pretty much wasting a full vial of the first magic, and it goes through mana twice as fast, but it does open up some interesting possibilities depending on how common the loot pool is."

"True, but if we had a good stockpile, we could get some really good synergy going. Any of them you're particularly fond of?"

His eyes light up. "Fire. I know it's pretty basic, but it's all attack-focused and the burn damage is too good to pass up. What about you?"

"I'm not sure yet. I see a lot of possibility with poison, but if other people are using it too then it won't be as effective. The mobility of wind is great, but it doesn't really have the firepower on its own. I like ice and electrical because of their crowd control abilities."

"So, everything." He laughs. "You really are a jack of all trades."

I shrug. "And master of none. Have you looked at the weapons yet?"

He narrows his eyes. "Who needs weapons when you can cast magic?"

"Considering how small our mana pool is, you might want to rethink that strategy."

He smirks. "I'm kidding. I like the bow and arrow for range, but I'm also digging the spear. The halberd is cool, but I don't think it has as many uses."

I nod. "Those are good choices. I was thinking along the same lines. Pick a weapon that can be useful in the most situations. I'm going to try and keep it simple and use a sword whenever I can. Not knowing what awaits, I want to have some practice with everything, though."

Over the next couple of hours, we scout the landscape, locating ruins and areas where we can make our best stand.

Not knowing which way the map will shrink means we need to have multiple options available so that we can find them quickly.

Once we have a handful of places marked, it's time to test out combat.

I down an ice potion and let the cold course through my body. "Ready to get your first taste of full-immersion?"

Dean cocks his head. "What do you mean? We're already in—"

I shoot him with Freeze and then Ice Dagger. The combo is enough damage to crack his shield. I follow it up with Freeze, and he loses a chunk of health from the attack. He yelps when the ice blast hits him.

"Ouch! Okay, I get it!" He lifts his hands up. "It hurts."

I fight to hold back my amusement. "Better you experience it now for the first time instead of when we're in the actual match. Now do me."

"You're insane, you know that?" He pulls out several vials attached around his waist. "Which one do you want me to hit you with?"

I turn my back to him. This is going to suck, but I might as well embrace it. "Surprise me."

After a moment of silence, a massive object hits me in the back, knocking my breath out and sending me sprawling to the ground. Half of my shield vanishes as I suck for air. The pain is manageable at twenty-five percent, but it still feels like someone punched me in the kidneys.

Dean rushes over and kneels next to me. "Are you okay? I didn't think it would hit that hard."

"What...did...you use?" I manage to get out between breaths.

"Boulder." He grimaces. "At least we know it hits like a truck."

Dean extends a hand and helps me to my feet.

I dust myself off and my breathing finally returns to normal. "Alright, on to the next one."

Dean groans. "Do we really have to test them all out?"

I grab him by the shoulder and look him in the eye. "If we want a chance at winning, then we need to be prepared for everything. We need to know how every ability feels and affects us so that we can plan how to react to it. Understanding how much ice slows us or poison obscures our vision will mean we know how to respond when they hit us. Offensive tactics are important, but defense is what will keep us alive. We can only attack a small number of people at a time, but there will be ninety-nine other teams who have marked us as the enemy."

"Ninety-eight." Dean shakes his head. "Talia and Chadwick are on our side."

"They are our friends, yes, but they want to win just as much as we do. When it comes down to it, nobody else is on our side because there can only be one winner." I pull out another vial. "Now get ready."

Dean nods. I think he might finally understand that for this stage, we're all we've got.

I down a poison potion, and my mouth puckers from how sour it is. Dean looks at me like a puppy dog as I prepare to attack him. This is going to be a long day.

CHAPTER TWENTY-FOUR

By the end of the day, Dean and I have probably killed one another at least a hundred times. Thank goodness for only experiencing pain at twenty-five percent, otherwise we might both be permanently scarred.

One thing we've learned is that even though weapons and abilities deal flat damage, this doesn't affect critical strikes. The bracer shields function as a thin energy barrier that surrounds the entire body. Decapitation and other fatal blows can kill instantly once the bracer shields have been broken. So getting an early jump on someone who hasn't yet picked up shield bracers could prove beneficial.

My vision flashes red and a notification pops up for the second time today.

Warning! *You are approaching the time limit for full-immersion play. Log out within the next thirty minutes or the machine will automatically shut down.*

Every six hours, users must log out for at least one hour. That's the biggest difference between these helmets and the pods originally used. While the nanites in the full-immersion tanks and pods are capable of keeping the body in stasis and preventing users from experiencing muscle and brain fatigue, the helmets have no such effect.

Dean and I use the mandatory breaks to eat and walk around the headquarters.

For our evening walk, we stop by Buzz's apartment.

He opens the door with a grin. "Well, if it isn't the gruesome twosome. How's training going?"

"I think Esil is getting some kind of twisted enjoyment from all the pain he is inflicting on me." Dean points at me.

"I wouldn't put it past him." Buzz winks.

We step inside. Grayson and Maria are playing cards at the dinner table.

"I'm surprised you aren't glued to a tablet." I squeeze Grayson on the shoulder and take a seat next to him.

He lays a card into the center pile before turning his gaze to me. "My work here is done. I helped you as much as I could in the first two stages, but you're on your own for this one. Besides, no one can stream their full-immersion training so there's not much for me to look at. Pangea has it all blocked out."

"We believe in you." Maria offers us a warm smile. "I have leftovers if you boys are hungry."

"Thanks, but we already ate. Dean and I are on our mandatory logout time, so we thought we would see a few friendly faces." I turn to Buzz. "I can't believe you were able to keep your mouth shut about the battle royale."

He grins. "I'm a man of many talents. Honorable deception is one of them."

I roll my eyes. "Right. So what happens to the rest of the Broken Lands during all of this? Is the battle royale going to stay or is just for the tournament?"

He shrugs. "Can't say for sure. That's a bit above my paygrade. From what I've heard, the rest of the Broken

Lands isn't changing, and this is some kind of regional event for the NPCs that will play into the story going forward."

Grayson nods. "Time will tell."

We sit and talk with them for half an hour. It's nice to talk about things other than the tournament for a bit. I think it's good for Dean to experience what it's like to have the kind of relationship that I have with Buzz and the others. That even if he doesn't have a family in the traditional sense, he can still make his own.

We say our good-byes, so that we can get in one more round of training for the night.

Grayson pulls me aside before we leave. "Remember what I said. Dean is a great asset. I've watched the replays, and he has natural instincts, probably better than any other apprentice in the tournament. Don't be afraid to rely on him when you need to. Treat him like a partner."

"I know. We'll give it our best shot." I clear my throat, realizing that my mouth is suddenly dry. "I just hope it's enough."

We head back to my place and log back in. Now that we've dealt with the pain of testing out all the abilities and weapons, we can finally move on to tactics.

For the next two days, we're going to grind like our future depends on it, because for Dean, it does.

"Time flies like an arrow." Dean smirks as he attempts to hold in his laughter. "Fruit flies like bananas."

I shake my head. "I don't care how many times you say it, it's still not funny. Now get ready, the tournament starts in an hour."

He rolls his eyes as he picks up his immersion helmet. "Oh, come on, it is funny. Show a little excitement. This is what we've been working towards this entire time. Everything up to this moment doesn't matter, and we have as good of a shot as anyone at winning it all."

I force a smile. Honestly, I'm not sure how he is the calm one when it's his future on the line. But if he can enjoy the moment, I need to do my best to do the same. I take a deep breath and grab my full-immersion helmet.

We've spent the past two days training nonstop, aside from the scheduled interviews we've had to do for the Pangea stream. If the forums are any indication, Dean has grown quite a following even without us being able to stream full-immersion. So much so that he might be able to get a streaming contract when this is all over.

The days passed quicker than I would have liked, but we're as ready as we're ever gonna be. We know the items. We know the terrain. The only part we're not prepared for is what the other challengers will do.

I'm pacing around my home portal waiting for The Vacuum to open when I receive a message. Notifications are muted for everyone except a few special people, so I pull it up.

Hey, mind if I stop by for a minute?
  -Aleesia

I quickly respond, telling her to come to my home portal. Seeing her will keep me from stressing during the time between now and the start of the tournament. Honestly, I would have been better sleeping in and getting ready at the last second, but of course I set five alarms to make sure we didn't oversleep.

Aleesia arrives wearing a black robe with flames embroidered down the sleeves. The outfit brings out her red eyes, setting them ablaze against the charcoal skin of her dark elf.

She wraps her arms around me. Without the haptic suit, I can't feel the embrace, but memory does a good job of filling in the details.

I can immediately tell something is wrong by the look in her eyes. "What's going on?"

"I thought you would have already seen it." She sighs. "It's Ryken. He put up a video this morning. He called out my father in front of everyone. Then he attacked me, and of course he had to throw in a few jabs at you."

Ryken always has been a first-class jerk. "It doesn't surprise me. What did he say?"

"It's probably just better if you watch the video."

I find the video and pull it up on the far wall.

Ryken sits on the obsidian throne in his home portal. His eyes are a menacing orange behind his hellish helm. When he speaks, his voice sounds distorted and demonic.

"Today, I will claim what is rightfully mine and prove once and for all that I am the greatest competitor Pangea has ever seen. Before I go in, I have a few things to say. First, to my father. You thought kicking me out would teach me a lesson. In a way, I guess it did. It taught me that I had the strength not only to survive without you, but to thrive. Your constant lectures and lessons did nothing but hold me back. Once I no longer had you to keep me on a leash, well, we see how well I've done. And to my stupid sister and her cheating boyfriend, you robbed a tournament from me once by cheating. It won't happen again. You better hope that someone finds you before I do, Esil Allen. My sister can't save you this time. And neither can your dead daddy."

"What a piece of trash!" Dean is on his feet, face contorted in anger. "I don't care if we win. I'm going to hunt down that jerk and make him pay."

I push my own anger aside to focus on keeping Dean calm. "Don't worry about it. He's just trying to get under our skin. He knows we have a shot at winning this thing and wants to throw us off our game. We stick to the plan and deal with Ryken only if we have to."

Dean clenches his fist. "I hope we run into him."

Aleesia puts her head in her hands. "I'm sorry. I was certain you would have seen it, or I wouldn't have brought it up. The video has been circulating all over since he posted it."

"Hey." I pull her hands away and look her in the eyes. "Don't worry about it. It'll take a lot more than a spoiled brat with daddy issues to get under my skin." I point to the portal that just appeared in the middle of the room. "Looks like we can finally go to The Vacuum now. We'll see you later. You should go watch the tournament with Buzz and Grayson."

She wipes away a tear from one eye before kissing me on the cheek. "Okay, I will. Go give them hell."

When we arrive at The Vacuum, it's much quieter than before stage two. Everyone stands further apart, and very few teams are talking to one another. Ryken towers over most of the people around him. The two gnomes nod at us, more of an acknowledgement than an invitation.

Talia materializes next to them and looks around. I wave to gather her attention.

Her eyes light up when she sees me, and she runs over, Chadwick following close behind.

"Well, this is ominous." She frowns.

People stare at us since we're one of the few teams talking to one another.

I grasp Talia and Chadwick around the forearm in turn. "I agree. I think we're all just wondering what to expect."

"You guys have a plan?" asks Chadwick.

Dean nods. "Yep. You?"

"Yep."

Even though we're friends, there's still tension in the air. We all know what's coming.

We stare at one another awkwardly and I have never been so relieved to hear Nancy's voice booming from above.

She soars in on her pegasus and hovers in the air wearing her Valkyrie armor. "Greetings, adventures, and welcome to the final stage of the Pro-Am Tournament! This is the match you've all been waiting for. One hundred champions. One hundred apprentices. All fighting for glory in front of Pangea.

"Over the past three days, we've introduced the world to the Broken Lands, Pangea's revolutionary new game world where users can finally experience deep-dive full-immersion. A world where you can taste the meat pie at the local tavern, feel the heat from the fireball before you incinerate your foes, and experience pain and pleasure at your desired comfort level. This is just the tip of the iceberg, but believe me when I say that the whole world is watching. More people are tuning into the Pangea stream than ever before. Before we get started, here's a message from Benjamin, President of Pangea Online Entertainment."

Benjamin's face appears in the sky like some god peering down from the heavens. Everything about him is perfectly manicured, and his eyes radiate with energy.

He smiles and his teeth sparkle. "First, I want to say thank you to each and every one of you. To the champions who continue to inspire countless others through your streams and competitions, you show the world the heights they can rise to if they choose to apply themselves. I hope you have enjoyed being a part of the first public showing of our full-immersion technology. And to the many apprentices, you are the future of Pangea. Your desire and drive to put in the grueling hours required for a shot at this internship are inspiring. It's proof that no matter one's background, they can still reach great heights across our many game worlds. For without the people, Pangea would be nothing. Good luck out there. I'll be waiting to crown our victor. Nancy, back to you."

His head disappears from the sky and Nancy swoops in his place. "Alright, adventurers..."

"Barf!" Dean places his finger in his mouth and fakes vomiting.

"What?" I laugh. "Are you not inspired to reach great heights?"

He rolls his eyes. "Come on, you know it's pandering. Pangea is not set up to give everyone a fair shot. I'm only here because of you. The beta testers are only there because of you. And you were only able to do any of this because you got lucky. When you had the lucky break, you used it, but there's a reason why you're the only famous person from The Boxes."

I place my arm around him. "Young grasshopper, aren't you a little too young to be so cynical?"

He laughs. "You know I'm right."

I do. But right now, we have bigger things to focus on. "We can get philosophical later. Right now is your chance to make the most of your lucky break."

"...and the ring will continue to shrink until the final circle. If multiple teams are still alive, the ring will collapse, damaging all parties until only one remains. So get ready, your chance at glory awaits!"

She snaps her fingers, and everything goes black.

CHAPTER TWENTY-FIVE

Cool wind blasts against my face. To my right, just like in any other battle royale mode, Dean is connected to me by an invisible tether as we fall toward the earth. The tether will disappear once we touch ground or one of us chooses to release it. All around us, one hundred and ninety-eight other players dive like falcons toward the Broken Lands.

From this high up, I can see the edge of the circle that marks the boundary of the battle royale. Beyond that, open fields and forests expand in every direction. Florian towers above Carolton in the distance, and lightning rages atop Thunder Mountain.

I focus on the circle below us, searching for a safe landing space. Our opponents begin to spread out, diving toward all edges of the map.

Ryken and Dawn dive straight down. My guess is they want bracers, weapons, and vials above all else. Ryken doesn't shy away from combat. For us, we want to play it smart, fight as few people as possible, and survive until the final round. While some champions will want to put on a show, I'll be happier fighting only one battle at the end rather than defeating a hundred enemies to get there. A win is a win, and there are no bonus points for showmanship.

Dean points at the far-left edge of the circle. "Let's hit those ruins. It doesn't look like anyone is going there."

I lean to the left and we shift course, diving faster toward the ruins of an old keep at the edge of the map.

I land in a superhero pose, knee bent and hand pressed to the earth as dirt and debris flare up around me. Luckily for us, the initial dive does no fall damage as we touch down.

We're scouring the area for items when someone lands nearby. I can't see them, but they are close enough that I heard them land.

My head turns on a swivel as I search for enemies among the trees and ruins. "I thought you said we were alone."

"I thought we were. They must have been in my blind spot." Dean disappears behind a rock. "Here, I found a battle-axe and a halberd."

He holds up a one-handed battle-axe with ax-heads on both sides and tosses it to me. It's heavy, but I catch it by the pommel. It's pretty basic with no fancy runes or engravings, but it doesn't have to look good to get the job done.

"There they are!" someone shouts.

A bright pink face snarls as she shoots an electric bolt at me. I dive to the right, and the bolt explodes against the earth.

Annabelle's black hair flutters around her as static coats her body. With her tight jeans, leather jacket, and combat boots, she looks like she belongs on the cover to some heavy metal album from the distant past.

Her apprentice, Kirsten, emerges from behind a cluster of bushes carrying a spear. She's dressed similarly to Annabelle, with a chain that runs from the piercing on her nose to her ear. "They don't have bracers or magic, only weapons. Let's push."

I take a step back and ready for their attack. "Dean, I need you over here."

He rushes to my side, halberd pointed forward. "This place was a crapshoot. We need to get moving."

I point out our two opponents as they approach. "First, we need to deal with these two."

Annabelle unleashes another bolt. I dodge again, but the bolt hits so close that my hair stands on end.

I take cover behind an ancient pillar with Dean. "One has electric magic. The other has a spear. I don't see any bracers, so we need to end this quickly. Aim for vital spots. You take the one with the spear; I'll deal with the other."

A branch snaps on the other side of the pillar.

"Come on out, and we'll make this quick. We know you don't have any magic. You put up a good run, but it's over."

Dean grips the shaft of his halberd. "Split on three?"

"One," I whisper.

"Two," he echoes.

"Three."

We attempt a technique we've practiced many times over the past few days. In the event that we get pinned down, Dean rushes out to the right and I do the same to the left in an attempt to divide their attention.

I jump out from behind the pillar and charge. Annabelle yells like a barbarian as she casts Chain Reaction, and three bolts of electricity hit me in the chest. Pain flares through my body but my mouth clenches shut, making it impossible to scream. I can't move, stunned in place by the three simultaneous hits.

Metal clashes nearby as Dean fights Kirsten, but I can't turn my head to look.

Annabelle steps in front of me, her lips curled up in a devious smile. She draws her finger down my cheek. "Like taking candy from a baby."

She reaches to take the battle-axe from me, but the stun has it lodged in my hand. She frowns, jerking again, but it still doesn't come free.

The stun fades. I push her back and kick her in the chest before she has time to attack again. Annabelle falls to her back, grimacing as she points her open palm at me. I duck and the bolt soars over my head. Before she has a chance to cast again, I bring my battle-axe down on her head.

My whole body feels jittery after the electrical attack.

Behind me, Dean and Kirsten are engaged in a fierce battle. Kirsten parries a swing of the halberd, letting the blade scrape down the length of her spear. She follows up with a jab of her spear, but Dean is ready, deflecting the blow to the side.

She's so focused on Dean that she doesn't even notice me before I bury my axe in the back of her skull.

Dean sets his weapon on the ground and shakes out his hands. "Man, I didn't expect my adrenaline to get going like that. This was intense. Look at my hands."

He holds them out and they vibrate with excitement.

We survived the first trial, but I doubt this is the last of the excitement. I give him a reassuring squeeze on the shoulder. "This is the real thing. Now, let's get moving. We need bracers and magic ASAP."

He drops the halberd to take the spear off Kirsten's body, and we head toward our next objective.

In the top right corner next to the map, there's a counter for the number of teams and players still remaining.

Teams: *89*

Players: *147*

Forty-three players eliminated already, and we've been in the ring less than five minutes. Judging by the numbers, there are quite a few solo players running around. They'll be less aggressive, so we'll need to keep our eyes peeled.

A gong reverberates across the battlefield, and the location of the next circle appears on the map. There's a ten-minute timer underneath the map icon, letting us know how much time we have before the ring begins to shrink. Once the ring closes in on the next circle, we'll receive another timer before the ring shrinks again. So on and so forth until a champion is crowned.

We're close enough to the next circle that we can take our time and make sure we find a suitable position to hunker down. We make our way toward the next set of ruins, careful to keep as low of a profile as possible.

"Sweet!" Dean kneels next to a boulder and picks up a brown vial. Earth magic.

He offers it to me, but I push his hand away. This is his show, so I want him as stacked as possible.

"You take it. I'll get the next one."

There's a sound like a sudden gust of wind just before I spot an elf hovering in the air holding a bow. Her back is turned away from us as she scouts the area.

"Quick, take cover under that tree." I point toward a towering oak that should keep us hidden if we hurry.

We run toward the tree and take shelter beneath its dense foliage.

"Close one." Dean peeks around the edge of the trunk. "Looks like she was heading toward the next circle."

"Good. We'll hang back for a minute and try to rotate farther east. We don't have the range to handle them at the moment."

At the next set of ruins, we find two pairs of white bracers and a vial of wind magic. There's also a mace and a second halberd, which we leave behind.

I down the silvery liquid from the wind vial, and we continue to creep around the edge of the map.

Something hits me lightly in the back, and I turn to see Dean about to toss a rock at me. I hold up my hand in apology. With the added movement speed, I have to remind myself to slow down for him.

The circle starts to shrink, and an energy field filled with silvery veins moves inward. We spent enough time in the training grounds that we know what's coming. The outermost circle is impenetrable while the match is going, but as the boundary shrinks, the space between the outer boundary and the inner circle becomes a constant storm. Players can stay in the storm but they take constant damage while doing so. Each time the circle shrinks, the damage from the storm grows. By the time the final circle comes, the storm can drain full health in only a few seconds. We stay a safe distance in front of the collapsing circle, but if things look daunting, we can always retreat into it to regroup.

Dean grabs me by the tunic and kneels behind a boulder, pointing to a bush at the top of a hill. "Looks like a solo."

Sure enough, a rainbow-colored clown crouches behind

the bush. His rainbow striped afro sways like a technicolor bush in the breeze. We observe him for a few minutes, but no one else shows up. I remember his apprentice as a pink unicorn centaur. He must not have been so lucky.

"It's an easy kill. Want to hit him with a little meteor shower?" Dean smirks.

We came up with code names for some of the magic combos so that we could easily call them out in battle.

We crouch as we move closer to get in range. Once in position, Dean shoots a boulder straight up overhead. I ready Gale, and once the boulder drops, I fire off a gust of wind. It launches the boulder like a cannonball, hitting the unsuspecting clown in the back. There's an audible crunch like glass shattering as his shield breaks and he loses half his health.

The clown crawls from the bush and uses gas cloud, covering the area in a thick cloud of poisonous gas. We lose visual as he hides in the gas. Unfortunately, for the clown, our current combo counters his gas pretty well.

Dean casts Rockslide, and a barrage of rocks falls in front of us. He doesn't have the range to hit the clown from our current position, but another gale launches the smaller rocks like a shotgun blast, ripping through the gas cloud. The player counter drops by one, and I know that we got our man.

When the gas dissipates, the clown's body lays hunched on the ground.

"Nicely done!" I extend my arm and fist-bump Dean.

We loot the body, finding a dagger, white shield bracers, and two minor health potions that restore twenty-five percent health. I give one to Dean and keep one for myself.

As the circle continues to shrink, we hang back,

staying a few yards ahead of it. When the gong sounds, signaling the start of the next round, over half the playable area is now outside of the storm. We've also lost over half of the challengers as well.

Teams: *63*

Players: *96*

We head toward the next ruins on the map, an old mill down by a rather large creek. The ancient water mill no longer works, but the stone walls and staircases offer great positioning during a fight.

I grip the battle-axe tightly in my hand as we walk. "We still need better gear. These bracers aren't going to cut it if we get caught in a big fight. And these aren't our best magic combos either."

There's an explosion to our right, so we change our trajectory slightly to the left. We've fought when we had to and when an opportunity presented itself but we're not ready to rush into battle.

"At least we're two for two on fights so far." Dean smiles.

When we arrive at the old mill, the ground is torn apart and close to a dozen bodies lay in the vicinity.

Dean kneels over one of the bodies to loot it. "Man, this must have been a heck of a fight."

I find a pair of blue bracers on a fallen dwarf. "No kidding. I'm glad we chose to stay further away."

I swap out my battle-axe for a sword I pick up off a werewolf. The werewolf's fur is singed in places, revealing blistered skin.

Dean calls to me from the bottom of the stairs. "Nice! I found a fire vial. This guy must have been going for it when he died."

A dead lizardfolk lies face down with an outstretched hand towards the small red vial.

I use Updraft to launch me into the air to the top of the dilapidated tower on the water's edge. No one else must have had the foresight to look this high up, because I find an electric vial, a crossbow, and a pair of red bracers.

"Here!" I toss the top-tier bracers to Dean. I'll upgrade mine again when we find more. "Any chance you want a crossbow?"

He shakes his head. "No, I'm happy with my spear. With the fire magic and these bracers, I'm pretty much set."

The gong sounds again, and the circle begins to shrink. The biggest ruins still remain within the circle, a location I aimed to avoid at all cost simply because of how populated it was certain to be.

There's likely to be good items, but if the water mill is any indication, then it was undoubtedly a bloodbath.

With nearly a hundred players still left, we'll be forced to fight again soon. We can't hide forever, and sooner or later, we'll run into opponents.

We wade through the cool water to cross the creek. On the other side, my boots slosh with each step and I find myself envious of anyone with water magic right now.

A long stretch of rolling hills stands between our current location and the next ruins. The terrain obscures our visibility, so we're extra careful.

The clank of a crossbow firing is followed by a cry of anguish not far ahead. As we sneak up the hill, a stream of ice shoots out in front of us. A moment later, a blood-covered Talia and Chadwick skate by on the ice path they've created. They alternate shooting ice at the ground, allowing for continuous travel. Talia fires an ice dagger over her shoulder, but there's no telling if she hit her target.

Both of their health bars are extremely low, around twenty-five percent, and their backs are ravaged with wounds. Chadwick pulls a crossbow bolt from his shoulder and tosses it aside. It wouldn't take much to take them out and lower the playing field even more, but that's not my style.

"Talia!" I call out. "What's going on?"

She turns around wide-eyed as she slides to a halt. They were traveling so fast on the ice that she's already at least fifty yards away. "We're being chased. Run!"

At that exact moment, her pursuers crest the hill, using the ice path to their advantage. A burly pig-man in studded armor and a cat lady wearing fine linens skate by without noticing us.

We could easily let this play out without helping, but I can see in Dean's eyes that he wants to help.

"When we catch up to them, melt the ice," I order.

We take off in pursuit on foot. Talia's ice path is winding, so we are able to cut the distance in half, meeting them as they crest another hill.

I hold up my hands. "Get off the ice. We've got a plan."

It will only be a few seconds before their pursuers crest the hill and see us.

Talia and Chadwick get off the ice path without questioning. Dean uses fireballs to melt the ice and form a large puddle. The pig-man and cat-lady skate over the hill and fall face-first when their feet hit the puddle at full speed.

I shoot the puddle with a lightning bolt, damaging half their shields. I follow it up with Chain Reaction, and the three simultaneous bolts are enough to stun them in place and crack their blue bracer shields entirely.

Dean summons a fire wall on top of them, but the stun prevents them from crying out in pain as their health dwindles. A few well-placed spear jabs finish the job.

I rush over to Talia. "You guys look like hell. What happened?"

Talia looks around panicked. "Can we move somewhere safer?" She downs a minor health potion and her cuts begin to heal.

"Yeah, let's loot the bodies first."

Dean is already sorting through their belongings and has them stacked neatly beside the corpses. He hands a set of blue bracers to both Talia and Chadwick. When a player dies, their shield bracers are automatically restored to full strength for whoever loots the body.

There's also a crossbow, a flail, and a major health potion.

I pick up the health potion and give it to Chadwick. "You look like you could use this."

He chugs it and hands the minor health potion he was about to drink to Talia. "Thank you."

Chadwick takes the flail, and Talia takes the crossbow even though it has no bolts. We retreat toward the stream and find an alcove to hide in while Talia fills us in on what happened. Her cuts have healed but her skin and clothing are still caked in blood.

She crouches against a tree as she tells her story. "We've been running for our lives since we touched down. I don't know how it happened, but we landed with Ryken. That apprentice of his almost took my head off with an axe, but I was lucky that I found bracers before anything else. Chadwick got hit with Rockslide, and had two other teams not shown up to try and take out Ryken, he would have died then and there. We didn't have any weapons, so we watched as Ryken and Dawn destroyed both teams. Then we ran as far as we could. But the next site was no better. We found two ice vials and barely survived a fight with two paladins. Right as we were trying to heal, these two came along." She points at the dead bodies. "They've been chasing us for about a mile, slowly picking us apart with her crossbow. Eventually, the cat lady ran out of bolts and we were far enough ahead that their magic did minimal damage, but it was only a matter of time before they caught us. We owe you big time."

As the circle approaches, we can hear the dull roar of the storm on the other side. We're not that far from the next circle, but we need to get moving.

I extend a hand and help Talia to her feet. "We've had our struggles, but we've definitely fared better than you two. Should we team up? At least until Ryken is dealt with?"

She scrapes away a flake of blood on her nose. "That's smart. It'll increase both our odds of making it to the final circle."

"Good." I shake her hand, cementing our temporary alliance. "Now, let's get you some weapons you can actually use."

We follow our same tactics, creeping in along the edge of the circle as is shrinks. It moves a lot faster the smaller it gets so we practically run to keep from falling into the storm. We loot a few bolts for Talia off a downed samurai and find a bow for Chadwick. While we're teamed up, they will be our range.

Chadwick finds a water vial underneath a tree. When

he drinks it, all the blood is cleansed from his skin, and the tears in his clothing instantly mend.

He holds out his arms and inspects himself. "Good as new."

"Look what I found!" Talia walks over carrying a pair of red bracers and hands them to Chadwick. "You take these."

He grins as he removes the blue bracers and tosses them aside.

There's a slight thunk as an arrow pierces his neck. He gasps for air, and the red bracers fall from his hands. Blood pours from the wound, staining his freshly-cleaned clothing.

Talia grabs him by the tunic, but the life has already left his eyes. Whoever did this waited until the precise moment when he removed his shield.

A chill runs down my spine. How long have they been watching us?

While Talia screams, head pressed against Chadwick's chest, Dean and I search for the culprit.

I spot the elven archer hovering in the air just as a second arrow hits Talia in the back. Her bracer shield drops by half.

I grab her by the arm, but she jerks away. "We have to go. He's gone, but you can still keep fighting. He's not out of the running unless you quit."

She wipes tears from her eyes, but there is no sadness. Only rage. "Who did this?" she demands.

"I saw an elven archer just over the hill."

She picks up the red bracers off the ground and marches in the direction of the archer.

"Talia, don't be crazy," I call after her, but she doesn't turn around.

Dean looks at me expectantly.

My eyes follow Talia as she disappears. "She can make her own decisions, but we're not looking for fights, remember?"

"I know." He sighs.

Talia is normally so level-headed. I'm surprised she would do something so reckless. Then again, I didn't just watch my brother die in front of me. Even though we all know this isn't real, she just got a glimpse of what it would be like to actually lose him.

Hopefully, she can take a few enemies down on her path to revenge.

The gong sounds once again as the circle stops. I check the players remaining.

Teams: *31*

Players: *53*

A large portion of those fifty-three players have to be solos. Probably hiding out around the map, waiting for someone to make a mistake.

I check the map to see what locations still remain inside the circle. The largest set of ruins left are from what used to be a castle. The moat surrounding it has long been empty and is now nothing more than a gorge. A fallen tree functions as a makeshift bridge across the moat.

With its nooks and crannies, the moat functions well for hiding but attempting to climb out while someone has the high ground could prove challenging.

The exterior walls of the castle are mostly crumbled, with the occasional section of wall standing by itself. All but one of the battlements has been destroyed, and the one remaining has gaping holes along the sides, offering little protection for the spiral staircase. The keep towers above it all, though without a roof and with one missing wall, it is easy to get in and out.

While the ruins would offer little benefit to an actual army, it provides enough shelter and hiding places to make it a formidable setting for a battle royale.

There's also an old farmhouse, a thick copse of trees, and an assortment of stones that are hard to decipher what they used to be. I'd put my money on most people flocking to the castle.

From our position at the edge of the circle, we can see the castle. Several times, we spot movement as solos or teams move into position. A wall of flame erupts inside the battlements. Occasionally, someone uses their wind magic to hover in the air to scout. We watch as someone is shot while in the air and tumbles to their death.

Somewhere out there, Talia battles alone. Or maybe she's already been eliminated.

One by one, players continue to drop. By the time the circle starts to shrink again, we're down to thirty players. The location of the final circle appears on the map: the castle ruins.

Dean takes a deep breath. "We're so close and there are still way too many players left to feel comfortable."

I feel the same way, but I need to keep him calm. "Don't think about that. Focus on what is right in front of you. Take everything one moment at a time."

He nods, then crouches, slowly walking forward with his spear pointed ahead of him. I lower myself and keep my sword at the ready. We didn't spot anyone clinging to the storm like us, so most of the remaining players have likely already established their positions.

As we approach the castle, a gnome head peeks above the moat. Luckily, he's not looking in our direction.

Dean spots him too and immediately raises his hand for an attack.

I grab him by the wrist. "Wait. These are the gnomes that helped us in stage two. They aren't stupid. This has to be some kind of trap."

A second gnome peers over the edge nearest the castle. He climbs out and runs across the tree functioning as a drawbridge. He looks panicked as he zigs and zags through the empty courtyard.

I'm certain he is up to something, because no one is that stupid.

Then all hell breaks loose. Ice beams, fireballs, electric bolts, and a myriad of other offensive magic and weapons shoot out from every edge of the castle. The gnome downs a silvery vial and begins moving faster, using the bonus movement speed from wind magic to evade the attacks.

My skin is suddenly on fire as the storm crackles past us. Dean groans and runs ahead. While we were watching the scene unfold, neither one of us kept an eye on the circle. It bypasses our armor, depleting our health directly. We hurry back into the circle and sprint toward the moat while all eyes are on the gnome.

We run a safe distance from the gnomes and slide down the embankment into the depths of the empty moat. I down the only minor health potion I have. As I look around, the gnomes' plan suddenly makes sense. Further down, the moat is covered in a sea of green gas. So much gas that they must have been planning this for a while. The second gnome drinks a green vial as he jumps down and disappears inside.

Magical explosions carry from up above. His little charade revealed a lot of people's positions and forced their hands.

Two human rogues, one male and one female, peer down into the gas-filled gorge. They both pull a green vial from their pockets and chug them. Then they equip their daggers and leap into the pit.

So much for luring someone into a gas trap.

Dean and I are scaling the moat in order to sneak into the castle when a green updraft launches one of the gnomes out of the moat. A second later, the other gnome follows, a red vial in his hand. He downs the liquid and shoots a single fireball into the gas.

The explosion is deafening. The ground shakes and rubble comes tumbling down on top of us, knocking us back to the bottom of the moat. My ears ring, and I cough as I inhale dust into my lungs.

The gong sounds as the circle comes to a halt, its boundary humming with energy in the center of the moat. The roar of the storm makes it hard to hear the fighting going on above.

The location of the final circle appears on the map, directly in the center of the keep. In ten minutes, everything is going to come to a head.

"You okay?" Dean extends a hand to help me up.

I brush dirt off my shoulders and arms. "Yeah, I'm just glad they didn't see us. That was a hell of an explosion."

"Yeah, usually the gas clouds dissipate after a few minutes, but I guess the gas had nowhere to go down here. Brilliant plan."

Grayson was right for us to worry about those two.

We scale the moat for a second time and make it out. We take cover outside of the perimeter wall. If we keep a low profile, we can creep along the outer wall and enter the keep from behind.

We stay low to the ground, the echoes of battle

carrying from the other side. The clashing of metal, crack-ling of fire, crunching of ice, and crashing of boulders mixes with barbaric yells and painful screams as the death count rises.

A halfling mage crouches against the wall up ahead watching the madness unfold. He peeks through a hole in the ancient wall. Everything is so loud that he doesn't hear us approaching.

Dean and I attack at the same time, hitting him with fire and electricity. We follow up with melee attacks, and he dies almost instantly.

I let his body fall into the moat and take his position. The hole in the wall is big enough to see the front side of the keep. On the far wall, Ryken battles with a mace against a shirtless orc. He uses wind magic to jump between higher and lower levels with ease, making him hard to hit for someone so bulky.

Dawn hits the orc with electricity, stunning him, and Ryken finishes him with a kick into a gas cloud below. The remaining players continue to tick down. Twenty. Fifteen. Ten.

We're so close.

There's a loud whoosh as someone casts Updraft nearby. I look up to see the elven archer who killed Chad-wick shooting arrows at those fighting below. She nocks her arrows with great speed, letting them fly with abandon.

A dark figure emerges from the shadows of the stair-well and sprints toward the archer. They step into the light and I realize it's Talia.

She charges like a lioness, crossbow draped over her shoulder and hand outstretched. Red energy flares in her palm as she casts fireball.

"Burn, you bitch!" She launches the fireball, and it mixes with Updraft, creating a cone of flame that burns the archer from beneath. The archer screams as she tries to take aim at Talia, but the constant burning must have her aim off.

Talia drops to one knee, aiming her crossbow as she slides, and pulls the trigger. The archer's shield cracks from the fire damage, and the bolt hits her in the neck. The same spot where Chadwick was shot. She clutches her throat, and a moment later falls to the earth with a thud.

"Talia, behind you!" Dean yells.

And then I see it. Ryken is a good thirty yards away, but his ember eyes are focused on Talia. He casts Updraft and uses the force to launch him forward. Just as he is about to hit the ground, he points his palm down and uses Gale. The air pressure extends his fall for a few feet and he lands in front of Talia.

She turns around but not quickly enough. He hits Talia with the mace, knocking her to the ground and nearly cracking her shield.

Before I know what's happening, Dean is climbing over the wall. I call for him, but he doesn't hear me. He shoots a fireball at Ryken, but the death knight uses Gale to deflect it.

While lying on her back, Talia summons a flame wall in front of Ryken, but Dawn extinguishes it with a water blast. Considering Dean and Talia are both using fire, this is not a good matchup.

Ryken swings his mace again, but Talia rolls to the side and his weapon smashes into the earth.

I climb the wall and follow Dean into battle. Ryken notices me, and his glowing eyes flare from within his helm.

The momentary lapse gives Talia a moment to escape, and she leaps through a hole in the wall. Ryken curses and casts Updraft, rejoining Dawn up along the wall.

"I should have known you would be here. Did you have to cheat to get this far too?" Ryken's voice carries over the sudden silence.

I ignore his jab and deliver one of my own. "At least I'm not doing all of this because I have daddy issues."

Ryken laughs. "Right, because you don't have a father, do you?"

His comments don't bother me. Maybe if I remembered my father they would, but all I see before me is a spoiled brat looking for attention any way he can get it.

Dean hurls another fireball, which Ryken nonchalantly deflects with Gale.

"Let's kill this jerk." Dean's lips curl up in anger.

I hold my hand out in front of his chest. "Easy. Patience is what got us here. He has height at the moment so we can't push. We need to wait for him to make a mistake."

For the moment, we're in a standoff, neither one making the first move.

A beam of ice hits Dawn in the back, and ice crystals erupt across her body. Her movement slows for a moment before she uses Cleanse and the ice melts away.

A gnome soars through the air like he was launched off a ramp and lands in front of Dawn brandishing a dagger. He stabs at her, but she uses the end of her bow to parry the blow. The dagger cuts through the bowstring, making her weapon useless.

Ryken pushes Dawn aside and lifts his mace. The gnome takes a step back and shoots ice at Ryken's feet, coating the wall in a slick layer. Ryken and Dawn both steady themselves to keep from falling.

"This is our chance," I whisper.

I run for the stairs. As I'm climbing them, Dean breaks off and heads straight for the wall. He jumps across two broken pillars, using his spear to vault himself into the air, and casts Flame Wall underneath Ryken and Dawn.

Flames melt through the ice and eat at their shields before Dawn extinguishes them with her water blast.

I use Chain Reaction at the puddle underneath their feet, shocking Ryken, Dawn, and the gnome all in one hit.

Dean tries to tackle Ryken as he falls, but the death knight uses Updraft, launching himself into the air and sending Dean rolling off the wall and grabbing at air.

A fireball shoots up from the ground below, setting Updraft ablaze. Talia emerges from inside the keep. I toss a bolt at Ryken, but he abandons Updraft and falls to the ground with a thud.

The gnome presses on a weaponless Dawn, and Dean is nowhere to be found. Right now, I need to trust that he can handle himself.

I look to Talia. "Help me with Ryken."

She nods.

Ryken stands between me and Talia, but I finally have the high ground.

The familiar sound of shattering glass rings like an alarm to my left as shields crack while Dawn and the gnome trade blows.

It's the perfect time to push them, but I can't leave Talia alone with Ryken.

She throws a fireball, and I use Bolt at the same time. Ryken casts Updraft to launch himself into the air. As he's rising, he jumps off and lands behind Talia.

The fireball and electricity are engulfed by the updraft, creating an electrical inferno. Before Talia can turn around, Ryken bludgeons her in the back with his mace, and her shield cracks. He kicks her forward and she flails into the inferno. She screams as she's scorched and electrocuted simultaneously. Her health depletes by ninety percent before the spell fades away.

She turns her back to me and raises a dagger at Ryken, but it's no match for his mace.

To my left, Dawn has somehow managed to defeat the gnome. She sways as she walks, like she can barely stand. Dean is still nowhere to be found, and I have no idea if he is dead or alive. As far as I know, all his hopes and dreams are resting on me.

Dawn jumps down from the ledge. "I did it, Ryken. Let's finish him, and we win."

She stumbles over next to Ryken.

"Silly girl. Like I need your help. The only reason you are here is because of me. Now go home and watch me take care of business with the rest of the world."

Before Dawn can comprehend what is happening, Ryken smashes her in the head with his mace.

He laughs coldly. "I guess it was always going to be me and you. Only this time, my sister isn't here to protect you. Time to fight your own battles."

A red vial soars through the air over Ryken's head, and I catch it with one hand.

"Wrong!" Dean climbs on top of a stone arch and summons a gas cloud where Ryken is standing.

I down the fire vial like my life depends on it, letting the spicy cinnamon liquid warm my insides. As soon as it takes effect, I throw a fireball at the gas cloud and brace for what comes next. It explodes like a bomb, sending out a shockwave and cracking Ryken's shield as he disappears within gas and smoke.

The cloud fades, and Ryken kneels on the ground. His armor groans, and he uses his mace as a crutch to climb to his feet.

Dean pulls a flail from his waistband and jumps. He whips the spiked head of the flail in a circle as he falls, and the ball rings out like a gong when it connects with Ryken's helm.

The death knight stumbles forward, dazed. He attempts to lift his mace, but it falls from his hands. Dean delivers the final blow and trumpets sound all around us.

"Jerk." Dean tosses the flail to the ground.

I turn around, ready for our next opponent, when I finally process what the trumpets mean.

We won.

Dean runs toward me as the trumpets blare. I pull him into a bear hug and squeeze tight. I can't believe we actually won.

"We did it! We actually freaking did it!" Dean buries his head against my chest, and sobs ripple through his body.

I close my eyes, fighting back tears of my own. Applause radiates all around me, and when I open my eyes, we're on stage surrounded by thousands of people.

CHAPTER TWENTY-SIX

The applause is deafening. Confetti rains down around us as Benjamin grabs Dean's hand and lifts it in the air. Benjamin is dressed for the red carpet, wearing a navy-blue tuxedo that shimmers under the bright lights. This is the same coliseum where I was crowned victor after the Developer's Tournament.

Kind of fitting that I'm back here again.

Lights flash all around us, and giant video boards replay highlights from the battle royale. The crowd is full of thousands of people of all races and classes. Ordin gives me a thumbs-up from the front row.

"Talk about a photo finish!" Benjamin pumps Dean's hand overhead.

Every video replays the moment where Dean hit Ryken with the flail. The death knight stumbles forward in slow motion, and Dean delivers the winning blow. The crowd goes wild again.

"Of all the storylines throughout the tournament, this one was one of the most fun to watch. Like an onion, it was full of so many layers. Two competitors from The

Boxes. A reluctant former champion pulled back into the public eye. A new kid searching for his place in the world. Old rivals meeting once again at the final moment." Benjamin flashes a pearly-white smile. "We couldn't have written a better story!" He wraps his arm around Dean and holds the microphone in front of him. "What's going through your mind right now?"

"Uh." Dean stands silently for a moment. "I'm just really happy that Esil took a chance on me. I never thought I would have an opportunity like this. I dreamt about it, and I prayed for it, but I never thought it could really happen."

Benjamin takes a step back and gestures toward the crowd in a sweeping motion. "Well, you're not dreaming now. You've just won one of the most coveted scholarships on the planet. An opportunity to learn and work alongside some of the most brilliant minds Pangea Online has to offer." He steps between Dean and I, focusing his attention on me. "And here we have Esil, Dean's guiding light, his mentor, and his co-champion." He winks at me. "I know you're not one for speeches, so let's just get right to it. What charity will you be donating the tournament winnings toward?"

I take a deep breath. "This is actually something I have been putting together for a while now. I didn't want to make anything public because I didn't want to get anyone's hopes up, but I guess it's time to let the cat out of the bag. I've set up a scholarship for orphans from The Boxes. It's designed to help them with equipment they might not normally have access to, and each year, a handful of students with excellent grades will receive a full scholarship to the Pangea school of their choosing."

Benjamin nods in approval. "Excellent. A worthy cause

if I ever heard of one. I'm sure you two want to celebrate and enjoy the moment. We'll certainly be hounding you for interviews in the coming days, but for now, enjoy the victory. Here's Nancy with a recap of the tournament."

Thunder cracks overhead, and Nancy emerges from a cloud on her pegasus. She soars across the crowd before landing on the stage. Her voice booms as Benjamin leads us away.

Once we're out of view, Benjamin pulls me aside. "Congrats again. I always knew you had it in you. Go catch up with your friends, but whenever you get a minute, stop by my office later. There are some things I want to discuss with you."

I nod. "Will do." But I can't help wondering what could be so important that he needs me to stop by today?

Benjamin and I shake hands, and then he returns to the stage.

I turn and pat Dean on the back. "Ready to get out of here?"

He hasn't stopped smiling since we left the stage. "Yeah, but I just want to say thanks again." He pinches himself. "Are you sure I'm not dreaming?"

I can't help but laugh. "You're definitely not dreaming. Now, let's get out of here. There's something I want to talk to you about."

He scrunches his eyes, but I don't elaborate any further. I want to see the look on his face, his real face, when I tell him the news.

When we log out, I'm surprised to find there's a crowd of people in my living room. Buzz, Grayson, Maria, and

Aleesia erupt into applause when Dean and I enter the room.

"How'd you guys get in here?" I ask.

Aleesia comes over and kisses me on the cheek. "You gave me access to your apartment, remember?"

I kiss her back. "Oh, right. That was forever ago. You've been so busy that I guess I forgot."

Grayson stands up, his mustache curling with the smile underneath. "I knew you had it in you." He points to Dean. "Way to put that bully in his place."

"Yeah," Buzz nods in agreement. "You were a little too passive for my tastes most of the match, but that final battle was *epic*!"

Maria hugs both me and Dean in turn. "Good job, boys. I just feel terrible for that Talia, though. She looked like she lost it there at the end."

She did lose it. And there's no way we would have won without her. I need to make sure to check in on her once things calm down a bit.

"So, what now?" asks Aleesia.

"Well, I was hoping to talk with Dean in private, but you're all family, so I guess this is as good of a time as any."

Dean stares at me intently. I'm sure he's wondering what the heck is going on.

"First and foremost, this decision is yours. You don't need to feel any pressure one way or another, but I wanted to offer. After spending these past few months with you, I've gotten to know what kind of person you are. You're smart, driven, and a little mischievous at times, but above all, you're a good kid. I know what it's like growing up in an orphanage. For so long, you haven't caught a break, but I want to change that. You've got a little over a year before you turn eighteen, so I understand if you want to stay there and finish things out. I also realize I'm only a few years older than you, but if you'd like, I'd be happy to get the papers in order so that I could adopt you and you could move in and live here with me. Mr. Green says he can put me in touch with the right people."

The rest of the room watches in silent anticipation. The color drains from Dean's face, and he stares blankly.

"No, I wouldn't like that."

Those words hit me like a punch in the gut. But it's his decision. "It's okay. I under—"

"I'd love it!" He laughs as he wraps his arms around me. "But I'm not calling you daddy."

Everyone bursts into laughter.

We spend the next couple of hours celebrating with cake and ice cream as Dean recounts the final stage for everyone. Honestly, sitting here, surrounded by all these people I care about, this is one of the best days I've had in a long time.

I squeeze Aleesia on the knee. "I've got to head out for a bit. I promised Benjamin I would stop by his office. Don't have too much fun without me."

I knock on the door to Benjamin's office. A few seconds later, it opens with a hiss. Benjamin sits behind the polished mahogany desk grinning.

"You're something else, you know that?"

I take a seat in front of his desk. "Why's that?"

He leans forward, pressing the tips of his fingers together. "Do you know how hard it is to win one of Pangea's official tournaments? It's pretty damn hard. And yet here you are, a kid who had never set foot in a game world until you turned eighteen, and you've won the two biggest tournaments of the past five years. Not only that, you've won the only two tournaments you've ever entered. I'll eat my shoe if they don't write a book about you someday."

It feels weird being complimented, so I do my best to deflect it. "It was nothing but luck and determination. I wouldn't worry about keeping that shoe too clean if I were you. With full-immersion coming to all of Pangea, who's going to have time to read anymore?"

Benjamin laughs. "As humble as always. But you do touch on why I wanted you here. Full-immersion is going to change things drastically. With all of the former champions promoting it to their followers, the hype is going to be through the roof. I want to make sure that when we finally start rolling it out for real that we get it right. There's no room for hiccups on this."

I sit up straight in the chair, uncertain of what he's getting at. "What does this have to do with me?"

"We're going to need beta testers. And a lot of them. Pangea is composed of thousands of game worlds, and each one is going to need to go through testing. I think it is high time we do something about The Boxes, and I wanted you on board before I take my motion to the Board of Directors."

I lean forward. He definitely has my attention now. "What exactly do you want to have me on board with?"

"I want to ship immersion helmets to everyone in The Boxes and hire them as beta testers. You've been right all along that the conditions they live in are inhumane. It doesn't matter if we spend ninety percent of our lives in Pangea, we still need a place that feels like home when we log out. What I'm proposing is the construction of new housing units across from the Pangea Headquarters Campus. It'll take some time to get it all up and running, but I think it is the right thing to do. They are people too, regardless of the situation they were born into. You and Dean have shown us that a person's beginnings do not define where they will end. I'm sorry that it took me so long to realize this."

My mouth hangs open, and I don't know what to say. All I've ever wanted to do was to help those in The Boxes, to show the world that we had something to offer. It looks like that is finally happening.

My throat is suddenly tight, and I have to clear it before I can speak. "Thank you. You have no idea the impact this will have on their lives."

Benjamin looks down at his desk, lost in thought for a moment. "I wish that I did. I'm sure you want to get back to your friends, though, so I won't keep you. I just wanted to run it by you beforehand."

As I'm walking out the door, a thought crosses my mind. I stop in the doorway and turn around. "What happened to all of the immersion tanks and pods?"

He smiles. It's a genuine smile that reaches his eyes. "We sent them over to the medical testing lab. The preliminary trials have been so positive that we're bringing in more volunteers. After so many years of focusing on profits, it feels nice to know that I'm finally using my power for good."

"I'm glad to hear it. I think in the end, our most lasting legacy is not the fame and the glory, but the mark we make on other people."

Aleesia's words come back to me. "You can't help everyone. Focus on the ones you can." If we all did that, then this world might not be such a bad place.

EPILOGUE

*O*ne year later.

Saltwater spray kisses my nose from the bubbling pool. I take off my boots and dip my feet into the warm water. A fish nibbles at my toes, startling me. The torchlight along the cave walls and gentle bubbling in the water offers a peaceful ambience.

Everyone has been so busy the past few months that this is the first time we've been able to meetup as a group inside Pangea.

"What is this place?" Dean crouches next to me. A year later, and he still wears the same red tunic that mirrors my own.

"Just wait." Grayson takes a seat next to me, and his many necklaces jingle across his tattooed chest. "They'll be here shortly."

Buzz rolls his eyes. "I still can't believe you never took me here. I mean, after everything we've been through."

"You're lucky I brought you this time," Grayson teases. "But even you deserve to experience Pirate Bay in full-immersion."

As of late, there seems to be a new full-immersion world opening in Pangea every week. The game worlds still work for those using haptic suits, but sooner or later, this will be the norm for everyone.

Grayson pulls a golden pocket-watch from his pants and flips it open. "Get ready."

There's movement in the water, and a moment later, a tan face breaks through the surface. Beautiful black hair drapes across her shoulders as she climbs up from the pool and sits along the edge. Her green eyes sparkle even in the dim light. Shimmering blue-and-green scales run along the lower half of the mermaid's body, and clam shells cover her chest.

Buzz's mouth hangs open as he watches her. Soon, four more mermaids join her along the pool's edge. They sing a song in a language I can't understand, but the words are beautiful. Their song bounces off the cave walls, engulfing us in their graceful harmony.

"Wow," Dean whispers. "How'd you find this place?"

"That is a story for another time." Grayson closes his eyes. "Just enjoy the moment."

I don't know if it's minutes or hours, but we sit and listen to the mermaids sing. For once, even Buzz sits in silence.

I lean in toward Dean. "I wanted to show you this place before you went off to college. To remind you that Pangea isn't all about leveling and tournaments. There's beauty here. There's peace. It's okay to take time for yourself when you need to. And no matter how bad things may seem outside, people come here to escape, to feel some-thing. Don't ever forget that."

He nods, and then lays back on the cool stone floor.

I lay back and close my eyes, losing myself in the song of mermaids.

The end.

ACKNOWLEDGMENTS

First and foremost, thank you for reading my book. I hope you loved it! If so, please leave a wonderful review. Reviews are as rare as Developer's Chests and the more positive reviews I have, the more likely it is that others will read my books as well.

This book has been a long time coming, and I hope you have enjoyed Esil and Dean's adventures across Pangea. I had originally planned for this to be an ongoing series as you can probably tell by the emphasis on the Broken Lands in book two. But after getting back to the adventure and wonder that made people love the first Pangea Online, I think this is the perfect ending for Esil's story. However, I have learned to never say never, so if the readers demand it, there is an option to continue Esil's story if book three ever surpasses 300 reviews. The fate of the series lies in your hands, dear reader.

There are many people who played a role in making this book a reality. Thank you, Cindy Koepp, for your valuable insight and feedback on my earliest drafts. Thank you to my beta readers: Joe Krug, Heather V. Little, and Brett Siegel. You helped affirm that I was on the right track with this story.

To all of my Patreon supporters, you're the real MVPs, supporting me even when I'm not releasing as fast as I would like.

Platinum Tier supporters: Tim Krason.

Gold Tier supporters: Eric Sprague, Michael Percell, and Robert Schaefer.

Silver Tier supporters: Steve Caldwell, Nicholas K, Justin Thomas James, and Heather Jarvis.

Bronze Tier supporters: Frank Pisauro, Rachael Osterhout, Elizabeth, Cindy Koepp, Roxanne Baechler-Gill, and Ricky Brookes.

To everyone who waited patiently as I put out multiple books in other series between Pangea 2 and 3, I hope the wait was worth it.

If this was your first foray into my worlds, I highly recommend you check out *Sentenced to Troll,* the story of an online gamer forced to play as a troll in a new form of behavior rehabilitation. It's full of humor, action, and adventure.

Stop by my Patreon for exclusive content, signed paperbacks, and much more.

If you're looking for more books similar to my own, check out LitRPG Books.

ALSO BY S.L. ROWLAND

Tales of Aedrea

Cursed Cocktails

Sword & Thistle

Pangea Online

Pangea Online: Death and Axes

Pangea Online 2: Magic and Mayhem

Pangea Online 3: Vials and Tribulations

Sentenced to Troll

Sentenced to Troll

Sentenced to Troll 2

Sentenced to Troll 3

Sentenced to Troll 4

Sentenced to Troll 5

Path to Villainy: An NPC Kobold's Tale

Collected Editions

Pangea Online: The Complete Trilogy

Sentenced to Troll Compendium: Books 1-3